3 Genres

- Greek Myth
- Science Fiction
- Horror

CHRISTIAN SHORT FICTION
BY
A. J. MITTENDORF

2020

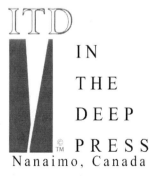

ITD

IN
THE
DEEP
PRESS
Nanaimo, Canada

ITD

IN

THE

DEEP

PRESS

Nanaimo, Canada

ABOUT THE AUTHOR, A. J. MITTENDORF

A. J. Mittendorf earned his bachelor's degree in English education with a music minor from the University of Minnesota, Moorhead, in 1992. He completed his master's degree from North Dakota State University in 1998 with concentrations in literature and composition.

He has taught English and related subjects to both high school and college students in both the US and in Canada. From 1999 to 2012, he taught at the College of New Caledonia in Prince George, B. C., Canada, until his move to the southern part of the Provence to be closer to his daughters and grandchildren.

He currently teaches English, History, Philosophy and other subjects in private lessons to home-school students and to those who require tutoring in those subjects. In his off-time, he writes poetry, articles, short fiction and longer works.

A. J. is an accomplished musician and an actor, presenting song and poetry on stage for a variety of purposes, including charity work.

OTHER BOOKS BY A. J. MITTENDORF

From Both Sides of Creation:
Poems of A. J. Mittendorf
2013

Carnival of the Animals
2015

Autoantonyms (173)
2017

Autoantonyms (204) 2nd Edition
2018

'Dear Stuart,' Writes A. J.
2018

Autoantonyms (254) 3rd Edition (The Dallas Edition)
2020

It Is Well With My Soul: Horatio Spafford's Story
2020

Q de Gras (A Star Trek novel)
Fan Fiction
2020

AS EDITOR
In Memoriam, A. H. H.
By Alfred, Lord Tennyson
2020

PENDING BOOKS BY A. J. MITTENDORF

Unnamed Collection of Poetry
(Illustrated)
2021

'Dear Stuart,' Writes A J:
revised and expanded edition
2021

Autoantonyms
revised 3rd edition
2021

DEDICATION

To my three
darling, delightful daughters:

April Louise,
Bella Elizabeth,
Erin Maybalee

My inspirations,
my joys,
my *raisons d'être*.

May they find their own
inspiration, joy and *raisons d'être*
in the bounty and blessing
of their own children.

TABLE OF CONTENTS

PART I: GREEK STORIES

TABLE OF CONTENTS

PART II: HORROR STORIES

TABLE OF CONTENTS

PART III: SCIENCE FICTION STORIES

PART 1:
GREEK STORIES

Introduction to Greek Stories

One of the first things I learned about the Greek epics when I was an undergraduate—a Freshman, even—at Minnesota State University, Moorhead, is that the epic is rendered in what we call "elevated" language, which means that the language of an epic is excessively formal, verbose and generally inaccessible. When many of those epics are translated into English, the translators all too often resort to using King James English ("with all the 'thee's' and 'thou's'"). They do this in a puerile attempt to imitate the "elevated" style of language the originals were written in. So Renaissance English became the English equivalent of elevated language, which, in my mind, removes a great deal of the fun of reading the Greek epics, which I so adored and in fact, on many levels, I still adore.

In one of my first university English courses at University (This was after I had already read some of the Greek plays and poems in other university courses and, of course, in high school.), I was required to read *The Iliad* translated by E. V. Rieu. Assuming that some readers don't know the name, allow me to explain. E. V. Rieu (1887-1972) was the English poet, classicist and translator who founded the famous publisher, Penguin Classics. He did so to publish his own translation of Homer's *The Odyssey* personally. Shortly thereafter, he published his translation of *The Iliad.* The great thing about these editions is that Rieu translated them into prose, not into poetry as so many translators are wont to do, and I believe that he was the first to do so. It helped a great many people to enjoy these tales, and that, in part, is what made Penguin Classics so successful. But Rieu also broke with tradition by avoiding Renaissance English, creating renditions of both epics that are also readable and enjoyable. I fell in love with Rieu's translation, and to this day, his translations remain my favourite of the several that I have read.

Now, I never had any ambitions of learning to speak Greek or Latin well enough to be able to translate Greek or Roman epic poetry, and yet, I had dire aspirations to contribute in some way to Greek lore, hoping to encourage other people to read and enjoy the great sagas of that distant culture as E. V. Rieu had done. In fact, in 1991, the *Star Trek: The Next Generation* episode, "Darmok," incorrectly summarized the Babylonian epic poem, *The Epic of Gilgamesh.* Even though the summary was inaccurate, students began taking classic literature courses because this episode had encouraged them to do so. I am a writer, and I decided to enjoy writing my versions of these tales for modern audiences. I wanted to create short fiction based on the highlights of the original epics, doing my best to employ all the Greek traditions, of which there are many. But like Rieu and largely because of him, I decided that, while I would still use the "elevated" English in my Greek stories, I would do so without resorting to archaic English, even though King James' English is considered to be "modern." Ha!

When I got my idea for the storyline of "Onessimus: Troy's Fall Denied," I was determined to incorporate myself into the milieu of great writers and translators of these marvellous tales, and I refused to settle with King James' English to accomplish my goal. I decided that I would follow in Rieu's footsteps by inventing styles and techniques for writing in elevated English, and yet, to do all I could to keep the language accessible to those who enjoy reading.

So, those who don't enjoy reading as much as others may not enjoy my Greek tales because of the formal language. While that is sad, I still feel that I have realized this general but proud goal with my five stories and Glossary of Greek Names, and I do believe that I have created some engaging stories.

I should add before closing that these ancient tales were harsh in their original versions. Brutality and carnage were integral components of the great epics, and I have not shied away from that where it is necessary for the story. None of it is gratuitous; if it needs to be there, it is there. *Cave lectorem.* But for your convenience, I have added to the beginning of each tale—just before each introduction—what I call a "Gore Score." It is a measurement of carnage in my Greek tales so that, if gore is something you prefer to steer away from, you can use my Gore Score as a guide. A gore score of 1 has no carnage while a gore score of 5 is simply the most gory of the stories in this volume.

Glossary of Greek Names and Places

GORE SCORE: 0

The entries in this glossary are chosen specifically to shed light on the names and places mentioned in the five short stories in this volume that are based on Greek mythology.

The pronunciations in this glossary are printed with the primary stressed syllables in all capital letters, secondary stressed syllables with only an initial capital letter, and unstressed syllables with all lower-case letters. Underlined words are defined alphabetically in the glossary. The names of geographic locations are followed by asterisks.

A

Achaean (uh KEE an): One of several alternate names for the <u>Greeks</u>. Other names include Arcadians, Argives, <u>Aegeans</u>, and Danaans.

14

Achilles (uh KILL eez): The son of the <u>nereid</u> <u>Thetis</u> and the mortal <u>Peleus</u>. According to the <u>Greek</u> myths, Achilles is the greatest <u>Greek</u> hero, largely responsible for the Greek victory against <u>Troy</u>. His skill in battle is superior to <u>Memnon</u>'s according to the original myths, and his only vulnerable spot is his heel where his mother held him as she bathed him in the River <u>Styx</u> in an attempt to wash away his mortality and render him divine.

Aegean (a GEE an): See <u>Achaean</u>.

Aeneas (a NEE oos): One <u>Trojan</u> leader. After the destruction of <u>Troy</u>, he, with his father, Anchises, and several hundred other Trojans survive the <u>Greek</u> invasion and escape certain death. He ultimately sails to <u>Hesperia</u> (Italy) where he founds a new city (which becomes Rome), thus fulfilling a prophecy of <u>Aphrodite</u> which says that Aeneas would be the ruler of the Trojans.

Aeolus (ay O loos): The god of the winds.

Aetolia* (ay TOL ya): A region of western <u>Greece</u> just north of the <u>Peloponnese</u> where <u>Calydon</u> is located.

Aetolians (ay TOL yanz): Those who live in <u>Aetolia</u>; they include the <u>Curetes</u> and the <u>Calydonians</u>.

Agamemnon (A ga Mem non): The commander of the <u>Greek</u> forces at <u>Troy</u>, <u>Menelaus</u>' brother.

Ajax (Ay jaks): One of the greatest soldiers among the <u>Greeks</u> at <u>Troy</u>. He is the son of <u>Telamon</u>. According to Homer, there are two Greeks named Ajax; the other Ajax is the son of Oileus, who is known for being short and stocky (whereas <u>Telamon</u>'s son is known for his great stature).

Alexander: See <u>Paris</u>.

Althaea (al THA ya): The queen of <u>Calydon</u>, the daughter of <u>Thestius</u> of the <u>Curetes</u>, and the mother of both <u>Meleager</u> and <u>Tydeus</u>. (In the original myths, these two have different mothers.)

Amalthea (am OL tha ya): She who nurses the infant Zeus, and, with the aid of the Curetes who make great noises by singing and banging their spears on their shields, hides Zeus from Kronos who would otherwise have eaten him, as he had all Zeus's siblings (See "Zeus.").

Amazons (AM uh zonz): Women warriors who actually remove their right breasts so that they can shoot their arrows unimpaired. They live near the south-east area of the Black Sea in what is now north-central Turkey.

Amphiaraus (AM fee Air oos): Better known in association with that of Tydeus and dealings with Thebes, in Calydon he is noted for his talents as a seer (soothsayer). It is he who interprets the omen of the eagles when Nestor finds Onessimus among the rubble of Calydon's wall.

Ancaeus (an Kah yoos) The helmsman for the Argonauts and one of the three men killed during the hunt for the Boar of Artemis' Anger at Calydon.

Antilochus (an TIL uh koos) Son of Nestor, adopted brother of Onessimus. Antilochus is eventually killed by Memnon.

Aphrodite (AF ro Di tee): The goddess of love and one of three goddesses who claims the title of "the fairest" found on the Fruit of Discord. She is also the one to whom Paris awards that honour, and she is the mother of Aeneas.

Apollo (uh PALL oh): The archer god of song and poetry, health and healing, and, according to Apollonius of Rhodes, who recorded the tale of the Argonauts, he was also the god of embarkation. He and Poseidon build the walls of Troy.

Apple of Discord: A golden apple with the inscribed title, "For the Fairest." Discord, a.k.a. Eris, deposits this apple during the feast of the wedding of Thetis, the soon-to-be mother of Achilles. Eris, of course, had not been invited, so this was her way of sewing discord where Discord had not been made welcome. Three Goddesses vie for the title on the apple: Hera, Aphrodite and Athena. This is one of four major events that together lead to the Trojan War.

Aratus (AR uh toos): One of the Curetes, the spokesman during Meleager's final battle. He is not part of the original myths.

16

Ares (AIR eez): The god of war, an abstraction for war, and war personified. He is a son of Zeus. One who talks about meeting Ares is discussing going to war.

Argo (AR go): The ship on which Jason and his crew, the Argonauts, sail to Colchis in search of the Golden Fleece.

Argolis* (AR go liss): A region of the Peloponnese south-east of the Greek Isthmus.

Argonauts (AR go nauts): The crew of the Argo under Jason's command. It is one of the finest groups of heroes ever assembled.

Artemis (AR t' miss): The archer goddess to whom Oeneus forgets to offer harvest sacrifices. So angered is she that she sends a wild boar, The Boar of Artemis' Anger, to make all of Calydon suffer. When the boar is not enough, she leads Calydon and the Curetes to war against each other. Artemis is the twin sister of Apollo and the daughter of Zeus.

Atalanta (AT uh Lan tah): An expert marksman with a bow and arrow, she is known as the virgin huntress and is, according to Ovid alone, counted among the Argonauts. All sources agree, however, that she is among the hunters of the Boar of Artemis' Anger.

Athena (uh THE nah): The goddess of wisdom and one of the goddesses who claims the title of "the fairest" from the Fruit of Discord.

Athens* (A thenz): The capital city of Attica, and named for Athena; it is located on the south-eastern corner of the Greek peninsula.

Atropos (ah TRO poos): The Fate who tells Althaea that her son, Meleager, will live only as long as a certain log is not fully burned. Atropus is the eldest, best, and shortest of the three fates, and she deals primarily with future events. She is often depicted with a pair of shears, for it is she who cuts the thread of a person's life on earth. Clotho was the one who spun the thread, while Lachesis measured its length.

Attica* (AT ti ca): The south-eastern part of the Greek Peninsula. See Athens.

B

Bellerophon (bell AIR o fon): In *The Iliad*, Book VI, the grandsons of Bellerophon and <u>Oeneus</u>, Glaucus and <u>Diomedes</u> respectively, agree to never fight each other despite the fact that Glaucus is fighting for the <u>Trojans</u>, and Diomedes for the <u>Greeks</u>. Their agreement is based on the friendship between Oeneus and Bellerophon as it is described in "The Calydoniad" and in *The Iliad*. Bellerophon is, perhaps, best known for killing Chimera, a mythological monster—a composite creature capable of breathing fire.

Boar of Artemis' Anger: Also known as the <u>Calydonian</u> Boar, the Wild Boar, or the Great Boar, it is the first wave of aggression against <u>Calydon</u> from <u>Artemis</u>. She is angered because <u>Oeneus</u> forgets to honour her during his harvest sacrifices.

C

Calliope (KALL yo pee): The <u>muse</u> of heroic poetry.

Calydon* (KALL y don): A city in <u>Aetolia</u>, on the south-western edge of the <u>Greek</u> peninsula. Its king is <u>Oeneus</u>, the father of <u>Meleager</u> and <u>Tydeus</u>.

Calydonian (Kall y Don yan): One who lives in the city of <u>Calydon</u>. Of or associated with Calydon.

Calypso (kall IP so): A beautiful goddess who lives on the island of Ogygia somewhere in the western Mediterranean, but its precise location has been "forgotten." When <u>Odysseus</u>' ship is destroyed by <u>Charybdis</u> while sailing for home from <u>Troy</u>, all his men are lost, and Odysseus alone makes it safely to Ogygia where Calypso nurses him back to health. She falls in love with him and promises him eternal life and youth in exchange for his love. He rejects her gift out of longing for his home, <u>Ithaca</u>, and his wife, Penelope. She keeps him in her home, though, and for seven years tries unsuccessfully to persuade him to lover her. He would have remained there until his death had <u>Athena</u>, his mother, not pleaded for him to <u>Zeus</u>.

Cassandra (kuh SAN drah): A daughter of <u>Priam</u>, and one who is made a prophetess by <u>Apollo</u>, but because she angered him, he made it so that no one would believe her prophecies.

Cephus (SEE foos): One of the <u>Argonauts</u> who participates in the <u>Calydonian</u> boar hunt. He is also the king of <u>Tagea</u>.

Charybdis (KAR ib dis): A sea monster who, twice daily, sucks in water of the Tyrrhenian Sea consuming all life in and on the water. She is associated with a giant whirlpool between the Italy and Sicily.

Cleopatra (KLEE o Pat ra): Not one of the seven queens of Egypt of the same name, this Cleopatra is the daughter if <u>Idas</u> and Marpessa, and is the wife of <u>Meleager</u>. Little else is known of her.

Clio (KLEE o): The <u>muse</u> of history.

Colchis* (KOL kiss): A city in Asia Minor (modern-day Turkey) east of the Black Sea.

Colossus of Rhodes: A 105-foot-tall statue of <u>Apollo</u> located on the island of Rhodes. It was one of the seven wonders of the ancient world.

Corinth* (KOR inth): A city located on the western shore of the isthmus between the <u>Peloponnese</u> and the mainland <u>Greek</u> peninsula.

Curetes (kyur EET eez): A people of the <u>Aetolian</u> region of <u>Greece</u>. They are a warrior race, and it is said of them that, to protect the infant <u>Zeus</u> from certain doom at the hands of his father, <u>Kronos</u>, the Curetes made an enormous din of song and ruckus of banging armor so that Kronos would be unable to hear Zeus crying.

Curetian (kyur EE shun): Associated with the <u>Curetes</u>.

19

D

Dardanus (DAR dun oos): The son-in-law of <u>Teucer</u> who is the founder of <u>Troy</u>. The region north of Troy is Called Dardania (the modern-day Dardanelles) in his honour, and <u>Trojans</u> are often called Dardanians because of him.

Dawn: The goddess of morning or morning personified.

Diomedes (di Oh muh deez): Leader of the <u>Aetolians</u> against <u>Troy</u> in the <u>Trojan War</u>. He is the son of <u>Tydeus</u>, and grandson of <u>Oeneus</u>, the king of <u>Calydon</u>.

Dioscuri (DI o Sku ree): The name given to the two sons of <u>Leda</u>, Castor and Pullox (or Polyduces). They are brothers of <u>Helen</u> and Clytaemnestra, and are said to be "twins by separate fathers" because after <u>Zeus</u>, in the form of a swan, rapes Leda, her husband, a mortal called Tyndareus, also has sexual relations with her. Leda later gives birth to quadruplets: Castor and Clytaemnestra, who are both mortal, are fathered by Tyndareus; Pullox and Helen, who are semi-divine, are fathered by Zeus.

Discord (DIS cord): a.k.a. Eris. The goddess of anger who, having been left uninvited to <u>Thetis</u>'s and <u>Peleus</u>'s wedding feast instigates a battle between <u>Hera</u>, <u>Aphrodite</u>, and <u>Athena</u>, by anonymously delivering to the assembly a golden apple, the <u>Fruit of Discord</u>, with a label on it that says, "For the Fairest."

E

Echion (ESH yon): One of the <u>Argonauts</u> who also hunts the <u>Boar or Artemis' Anger</u> at <u>Calydon</u>. He also shares his name with one of the <u>Curetes</u> and, presumably, fights against the Curetes for Calydon.

Echion / Coresus / Evenor / Tyllus / Udaeus / Trachius / Thaumas / Dolops: Those <u>Curetes</u> killed by <u>Meleager</u> in the first wave of the <u>Calydonian</u> battle. He kills others too, including his four uncles, but count is quickly lost.

Elis* (EL iss) Both a region and a city on the north-western area of the <u>Peloponnese</u>.

20

Eos (Ay oss): Another name for <u>Dawn</u>.

Eris (Air iss): Another name for <u>Discord</u>.

Eros (AIR oss): More commonly known as Cupid, he is the god of sexual love (hence, "erotic") and the son of <u>Aphrodite</u>. He makes both gods and humans fall in love by piercing them with arrows shot from his bow.

Eternal War: A reverent title for <u>Ares</u>.

Ethiopia* (E thee Oh pya): The area ruled by <u>Memnon</u>.

Eurypylus (ur IP uh loos) The third or fourth of <u>Althaea</u>'s brothers killed by <u>Meleager</u>. See also <u>Evippus</u>.

Eurytion (ur IH shun): One of three men killed during the hunt for <u>The Boar of Artemis' Anger</u>.

Evippus (EV IH poos): The third or fourth of <u>Althaea</u>'s brothers killed by <u>Meleager</u>. See also <u>Eurypylus</u>.

F

Fates: The fates are three sisters who decide human destiny (hence, "fate" in English): Clotho, who deals with things that were; Lachesis, who deals with things that are; and <u>Atropus</u>, who deals with things that will be. The fates are honored by all the gods because they distribute justly.

Fruit of Discord: When <u>Thetis</u> and <u>Peleus</u> are married they hold a feast on <u>Olympus</u>. All the gods are invited except <u>Discord</u>, the god of anger. In vengeance, she tosses a golden apple into the assembly. On the apple is inscribed, "For the Fairest." <u>Hera</u>, <u>Athena</u>, and <u>Aphrodite</u> all lay claim to the title. This event is one which eventually leads to <u>Troy</u>'s destruction in the <u>Trojan War</u>.

21

G

Golden Fleece: The pelt of a golden, winged, talking ram which is sacrificed to Zeus at its own request. The pelt is set in a grove near Colchis, there guarded by a dragon until Jason and his Argonauts, assisted by Medea, the daughter of Aeetes, the king of Colchis, steel it and take it to Alcaeus, in Greece.

Gorgon (GOR gon): Three sisters who have snakes rather than hair, tusks like those of boars, golden wings, and bronze hands. Their names are Medusa (who is mortal), Stheno, and Euryale (who are both immortal). People who look at a gorgon turn instantly to stone.

Greece*: A peninsula east of Italy and west of Turkey. It is bordered by the Aegean, Ionia, and Mediterranean seas.

Greek: Those who live in Greece. See "Achaean." Of or associated with Greece.

H

Hades (HA deez): Ruler of the Underworld which is also known as Hades. He is the brother of Zeus and Poseidon, and the husband of Persephone.

Hephaestus (ha FES toos): The god of fire; he is a master craftsman with many great works to his credit including the armor that Achilles wears when he fights Memnon.

Harpy (HAR pee): Hybrid monsters of uncertain or indeterminate origin. By name, they are Aello, Caelaeno, Ocypete, and Podarge. They have bodies of birds and faces of young girls. They are known to be swift thieves, especially of food, and they leave a foul stench in place of what they take; one cannot stand in a harpy's presence for long because of the odour.

Hector (HEK tor): The eldest son of Priam, King of Troy during the Trojan War. He is Troy's general during the Trojan War. He is known as the pillar of Troy until his death at which point Troy's future becomes uncertain, and it is ultimately overthrown. According to Homer, Hector is killed by Achilles in revenge for the death of Patroclus near the end of *The Iliad.*

Hecuba (HEC yu bah): The wife of <u>Priam</u>, the queen of <u>Troy</u>, and the mother of both <u>Paris</u> and <u>Hector</u>.

Helen [of Troy]: The daughter of <u>Zeus</u> and <u>Leda</u>; the wife of <u>Menelaus</u>, and she who is held captive in <u>Troy</u>, thereby causing the <u>Trojan War</u>.

Hellespont* (HELL 's pont): The strait that lies between the Sea of Marmara and the Aegean Sea, directly north of <u>Troy</u> in modern-day Turkey.

Hera (HAIR ah): One of three goddesses who attempts to claim the title of "the fairest" of the <u>Fruit of Discord</u>. She is the daughter of Rhea and <u>Kronos</u>, and thus, the blood sibling of her husband, <u>Zeus</u>. And as his wife, she is also the queen of Heaven (<u>Olympus</u>).

Heracles (HAIR uh Kleez): More commonly known as Hercules, he is regarded as <u>Greece</u>'s most famous hero and greatest warrior. The accounts of him in "Priam and Heracles" are accurate according to the original myths. <u>Apollo</u> and <u>Poseidon</u> build the walls of <u>Troy</u> for king Laomedon, <u>Priam</u>'s father, who refuses them the promised payment for this task. As a result, Poseidon sends a sea monster to Troy who snatches up the people living on Troy's plains. Laomedon learns that he can rid Troy of the monster if he offers his daughter, <u>Hesione</u>, as a sacrifice. When Heracles sees Hesione, he promises to save her in exchange for the horses that Zeus had given to Laomedon. Laomedon agrees and Hesoine is saved, but again Laomedon refuses payment, so Heracles kills Laomedon and his elder sons, leaving the throne of Troy to Priam, and he gives Hesione to <u>Telamon</u> who aided him.

Hermes (HER meez): The messenger god often depicted with winged ankles and a winged helmet.

Hesione (HESS ee Own ee): <u>Priam</u>'s sister, and a concubine of <u>Telamon</u> granted to him by <u>Heracles</u> as a reward for his assistance against <u>Troy</u>.

Hesperia* (hes PAR ya): Meaning "Evening Land" or "Western Land," Hesperia applies to Italy when discussed by the Greeks, and to Spain when discussed by the Romans.

Hestia (HESS tya): The goddess of the hearth.

Hippolytus (hip OL uh Toos): He is the son of Theseus and, as a worshiper of Artemis, the virgin goddess, he keeps himself chaste. When his step-mother, Phaedra, tries to seduce him, he refuses. So Phaedra tells Theseus that he had tried to seduce her. Then Theseus banishes him and prays to his own father, Poseidon, for Hippolytus to perish. His prayer is granted.

Hyleus (HI lyoos): One of three men killed during the hunt for The Boar of Artemis' Anger at Calydon.

I

Ida (Eye dah): There are two mountains named Ida. The first is in Turkey, about 80 kilometers south-east of Troy. The second is dead in the centre of the island of Crete. In the original myths, Paris is left to die on Mt. Ida near Troy, while Zeus is protected from his father while hidden on Mt. Ida in Crete. The two characters were not infants on the same mountain.

Idas (EYE dass): One of the Argonauts who also participates in the Calydonian boar hunt. He is also, apparently, the father of Cleopatra, Meleager's wife, and presumably fights for Calydon against the Curetes.

Iphiclus (IF ih Kloos): One of Meleager's uncles and a leader of the Curetes. He is the second of Althaea's brothers killed by Meleager, but since the first two are killed prior to the official opening of the war between the Calydonians and the Curetes, their deaths are seen as causes of the war. See also Plexippus.

Ithaca* (ITH ah kah): An island off the western coast of Greece. It is ruled by Odysseus.

J

Jason: The king-in-waiting of Iolchus in eastern Greece, and the leader of the Argonauts, the men of the expedition to Colchis to retrieve the Golden Fleece.

24

K

Kronos (KRO nos): The son of Üranos, and the second king of the Greek gods. With Rhea, Kronos becomes the father of Poseidon, Hades, and Hera, but he eats each of them as they are born so that they can not grow up to usurp his throne. Rhea hides baby Zeus, the youngest of Kronos's offspring, at Mountain Ida, where he is nursed by Amalthea and has the sound of his crying covered by the Curetes. Zeus survives and eventually rescues his siblings from Kronos' belly, confines Kronos to Tartarus, and begins his own Olympian regime.

L

Laconia* (La KOWN ya): A region on the south-eastern point of the Peloponnese.

Laelaps (LAY laps): The name of Priam's ship in "The Calydoniad." Priam's ship was named for a dog that was so swift, no prey could escape it.

Laius (LA oos): A king of Thebes and the famous father of Oedipus. It was prophesied when Oedipus was an infant that he would kill his father, so Laius leaves him for dead in a forest. He is saved, of course, and grows to manhood. When the two meet for the first time outside of Thebes, Laius challenges Oedipus who accepts and kills his father in fair combat, not knowing that he is fighting his father.

Laocoön (LAH oh koon): A son of Priam and Hecuba (see "Hector" & "Paris") and the seer who was among the few Trojans to suspect that the Trojan horse was a Greek trick. Laocoön is also the subject of a Hellenistic sculpture which depicts him with his two sons being consumed by snakes. Its expressive nature was a major influence on Michelangelo centuries later.

Leda (LEE dah): The mother of the Dioscuri and of Helen. She is impregnated by Zeus when he, in the form of a swan, rapes her. This event is considered the first in a series of events that begins the Trojan War.

M

Mountain Ida*: There are actually two such mountains. One is on the island of Crete, and this is where the infant <u>Zeus</u> is "really" hidden from <u>Kronos</u>. The other is south-east of <u>Troy</u>. For the sake of the story, "The Judgment of Paris: A Retelling," the Cretan Ida is disregarded.

Medusa (muh DOO sa): One of the three <u>Gorgons</u>, and the only one who is mortal.

Meleager (mel YEAH gr): The eldest son of <u>Oeneus</u> and <u>Althaea</u> of <u>Calydon</u>. As a hero, he is considered second only to Heracles, even though the less-than-flattering account of him in "The Calydoniad" is essentially accurate according to the myths. However, there are two distinct traditions about his death: 1) that he gets separated from the other <u>Calydonians</u> and is ambushed by the <u>Curetes</u>. 2) that his mother, in a rage, places a certain log (see <u>Atropus</u>) into the fire for it to be burned, at which point Meleager dies. According to "The Calydoniad," both accounts are true, occurring simultaneously.

Memnon (MEM non): The ruler of <u>Ethiopia</u> (not the one in Africa) during the <u>Trojan War</u>. He is also a nephew of <u>Priam</u> and a mighty warrior. As he makes his way to <u>Troy</u>, he conquers every nation, bringing them into submission to his own rule. According to the original myths, his skill in battle is perhaps greater than that of both <u>Ajax</u>, son of <u>Telamon</u>, and <u>Hector</u> (Homer suggests that these two are equal in skill), but not as great as <u>Achilles</u>'.

Menelaus (Men uh LA oos): The king of Sparta, husband of <u>Helen</u>, and the brother of <u>Agamemnon</u>. It is because of the <u>Oath of Tyndareus</u> that he and Agamemnon are able to raise such an enormous army against <u>Troy</u>.

Messenia* (mess EN ya): A region in <u>Greece</u> located on the south-western area of the <u>Peloponnese</u>. <u>Pylos</u>, the home of <u>Nestor</u>, is located there.

26

Muse: Sources differ on precisely how many Muses there are, but all agree that they are the demigods who inspire writings and/or art, each muse being responsible for a different form. 1)Aoede: song. 2)Calliope: philosophy, epic poetry. 3)Clio: history. 4)Erato: lyric poetry. 5)Euterpe: music. 6)Melete: practice. 7)Melpomene: tragedy. 8)Mneme: memory. 9)Polymnia: works of immortal fame. 10)Terpsichore: dance. 11)Thalia: comedy. 12)Urania: Astronomy. The narrators of Greek lore would pause in the telling of their stories so that they could invoke the aid and wisdom of the appropriate Muse.

Mygdon (MIG don): A ruler of an area of Phrygia near Troy. Priam and Mygdon are friends in the original myths and frequently come to each other's aid.

N

Nereid (NAE ree id): The fifty or so sea-dwelling demi-goddess-daughters of Nereus, the god of the Aegean sea and the son of Sea and Earth. In the hierarchy of the gods, Nereus would fall under Poseidon's rule. The Nereids, then, would fall under Nereus' authority. Thetis, Achilles' mother, is one of these Nereids. While they may be low on the totem pole, they are not to be trifled with. It is when Queen Cassiopea of Ethiopia boasts of being more lovely than they that the Nereids and Poseidon send the Kraken, an enormous sea monster, to destroy Ethiopia. This account takes place during the myth surrounding Perseus and Andromeda.

Nestor (NES tor): The king of Pylos and, in his old age, the chief advisor to Agamemnon during the TrojanWar. He is the father of Antilochus, and the adopted father of Onessimus. There is no account of him, in the original myths, being friends with Priam, nor is there any account of Priam at Calydon. It is interesting to note, however, that Nestor had wanted to be one of the Argonauts but was stayed by Pelias, the king who originally sends Jason after the Golden Fleece. Why Pelias would do so is uncertain.

O

Oath of Tyndareus: When <u>Helen</u> comes of age, her earthly father, Tyndareus, calls for suitors. Most of the kings of <u>Greece</u> respond. And since most of these suitors are also warriors, Tyndareus fears that if one wins Helen, the others will fight for her. <u>Odysseus</u>, in exchange for the hand of Penelope, Helen's cousin, offers a solution: Before Helen is given in marriage, all the suitors must swear that if she or her husband should come to grief as a result of the marriage, all the other suitors must come to their aid. The oath is successful in as much as none of the suitors wishes to battle what amounts to all the remaining city-states of Greece. However, when Helen is abducted by <u>Paris</u>, nearly all of Greece is constrained to go to war against <u>Troy</u>, Paris's home. Thus, the Oath of Tyndareus is also one of the primary causes of the <u>Trojan War</u>.

Odysseus (o DIS yoos): One of the more clever members of the <u>Greek</u> army at <u>Troy</u>. It is he who invents <u>The Oath of Tyndareus</u> and who suggests the building of the wooden horse at the close of the <u>Trojan War</u>.

Oedipus (ED ih poos): The king of <u>Thebes</u> who unwittingly kills his father, <u>Laius</u>, and marries his mother—an act which so disgusts the gods that they sentence him to a life of misery, a punishment which, in turn, falls to his two sons, Eteocles and Polynices, and to his famous daughter, Antigone.

Oeneus (Own yoos): the king of <u>Calydon</u>, <u>Meleager</u>'s father. <u>Artemis</u> punishes Oeneus with the <u>Boar of Artemis' Anger</u> after he forgets to honour her with his harvest sacrifice.

Olympus (oh LIM poos): It is the mountain home of the gods where the throne of Zeus stands.

Onessimus (oh NESS ee Moos): The child of unidentified parents who are killed under the breached wall of <u>Calydon</u>. He is adopted and raised by <u>Nestor</u>, king of <u>Pylos</u>. There is no character of this name in the original myths. The name means "useful."

Orion (oh RI on): A great hunter of antiquity. His constellation can be seen in the southern sky; the three stars of his belt are his most identifiable feature–his belt. South of the belt, his scabbard is composed of a line of stars, the brightest of which is really the Orion Nebula, an illuminated cloud of dust and gas.

P

Paris (a.k.a. Alexander) The son of Priam and Hecuba of Troy, Paris is left do die on Mountain Ida as an infant because prophesies say that he will cause Troy's destruction. The baby Paris is found and raised by shepherds who call him Alexander. When Paris is fully grown, three goddesses, Hera, Athena, and Aphrodite, seek his judgment on who among them is "the fairest" (see Fruit of Discord). He finds Aphrodite to be the fairest. She awards him Helen, the recently-made-wife of Menelaus of Sparta, and he sails there to abduct her.

Patroclus (Pa TRO kloos): The beloved friend and squire of Achilles. According to the myths, it is his death at the hands of Hector that brings Achilles back to battle against Troy.

Peleus (PEL yoos): The father of Achilles; one of the Argonauts and one of the hunters of The Boar of Artemis' Anger. He is also the husband of Thetis and the brother of Telamon.

Peloponnese* (PEL o pen Ess a): the large area of the Greek peninsula south of the Isthmus and Gulf of Corinth. It includes the regions of Achaeia, Elis, Arcadia, Argolis, Messenia, and Laconia. Some of the more important cities of the Peloponnese include Tagea, Pylos, Corinth, Mycenae, and Sparta.

Penthesilea (PEN thuh Sil ya): The daughter of Ares and Otrere, and the queen of the Amazons during the Trojan War. Despite the fact that Priam had been at war with the Amazons decades earlier, Penthesilea comes to war on Troy's side in order to teach Achilles some manners and humility; she brings with her a retinue of Amazons. (This takes place after Hector's death.) She is quickly defeated by Achilles who shoots her in her remaining breast, and falls in love with her just as she dies.

Persephone (per SEF oh nee): The wife of <u>Hades</u> and queen of the Underworld. She was abducted by Hades while she, as a little girl, was out picking flowers.

Philemon (FI luh mon): A <u>Greek</u>, and friend of <u>Onessimus</u>. While there is a Philemon in the original myths, the character of that name in "Onessimus: Troy's Fall Denied" is not the same.

Phoenix (FEE nicks): While <u>Peleus</u> is <u>Achilles'</u> father, Phoenix is primarily responsible for raising him. Phoenix and Peleus are both hunters in <u>Calydon</u>, though Phoenix is not counted among the <u>Argonauts</u>.

Phrygia* (FRIH gya): A large region of what is now called Turkey. It extends from the Sea of Marmara south to Smyrna (modern-day Izmir). The city of <u>Troy</u> is included in the northern part of Phrygia.

Plexippus (PLEX ih Poos): One of the <u>Curetes</u> and the first of <u>Meleager's</u> uncles to be killed by Meleager.

Poseidon (po SI don): The god of the sea, the brother of <u>Hera</u>, <u>Zeus</u>, and <u>Hades</u>, and the patron god of <u>Troy</u>. He and <u>Apollo</u> build Troy's walls.

Priam (PRI um): The final king of <u>Troy</u> and the father of some fifty sons including <u>Paris</u> and <u>Hector</u>. Most of these sons die in the <u>Trojan War</u>. There is no account in the original myths of Priam's friendship with <u>Nestor</u>, nor of his presence at <u>Calydon</u>.

Pylos* (PI lohs): The home city of <u>Nestor</u> located on the south-western tip of the <u>Peloponnese</u>.

R

River Thermodon: See <u>Thermodon</u>.

River Styx: See <u>Styx</u>.

S

Satyr (SAT ir): Deities of the woods and mountains. The upper portion of their bodies are essential human-like, but with the horns of a goat, while the lower portions are traditionally composed of goats' tails, flanks, and hooves. They are common companions of Dionysus, the god of wine, and are known for their dancing, drinking, playing of their pan flutes, and chasing nymphs. The latter characteristic gives them their common association with sexuality, but all of them identify them as personifications of lasciviousness.

Samothrace* (SAM o thrays) A small <u>Greek</u> island off the southern coast of Thrace and Macedonia in the Aegean Sea.

Sarpedon (sar PEE don): A mortal son of <u>Zeus</u> and the commander of the Lycian contingent that fights for <u>Troy</u> in the <u>Trojan War</u>. According to the original myths, Sarpedon is a major player in the attacks against the <u>Greeks</u> under <u>Hector</u>'s command. He is finally killed by <u>Patroclus</u> who fights in <u>Achilles</u>' stead, and there is a great battle fought for possession of his body.

Scaean Gate (SKA un): One of six gates in the walls of <u>Troy</u>.

Siren: Often associated with mermaids (the French word for mermaid is "Siren"), they are quite different in the <u>Greek</u> myths. They have girl's features from the hips up, but birds' form from the hips down; they also have birds' wings. With the use of songs that use deceitful lyrics, the sirens trick sailors into the rocky harbor of their island off the coast of Sicily causing the destruction of their ships and their deaths. The number of Sirens varies from source to source.

Strife: The consort of <u>Discord</u>.

31

Styx: A river which surrounds the realm of Hades altogether, in some traditions, corralling the souls of the dead into Hades with its nine spiraling circles around Hades. In other more common traditions, it is the river the souls must cross on the ferry of Charon to enter the realm of the dead where there is relative peace, albeit bleak. These souls can pay Charon for this service by the coins they receive when their bodies are buried, otherwise they remain in a state of limbo and eternal grief. In any event, the River Styx is not something to take lightly. The gods will swear by it and then fear breaking their oaths. It is in this river in which Thetis washes Achilles, holding him by the ankle only, in order to wash away his mortality. She is somewhat successful; his only vulnerable spot is his ankle where she held him.

Syrtis* (SEER tiss): The large bay on the northern coast of both Libya and Tunisia. According to Apollonius of Rhodes, the author of *The Voyage of Argo*, no ship can escape this bay because of a combination of several factors: extremely high and frequent flood tides, excessively long beaches, and dangerously rocky shallows at low tide.

T

Tagea* (tah GEE uh): Ruled by Cephus, Tagea is a city in the east-central region of the Peloponnese.

Tartarus (TAR tah roos): Roughly equivalent to Dante's innermost circle of Hell, Tartarus is a place beneath the Underworld at such a distance that the distance between Hades and the Underworld equals the distance between Heaven and Earth, and it, along with the River Styx, is actually revered, if not feared, even by the Olympians, some of whom are held captive there, including Kronos.

Teucer (Too ser): 1) The original founder of Troy. 2) A son of Telamon by Priam's kidnaped sister, Hesione. He fights against Troy in the Trojan War.

Telamon (TELL uh mon): The brother of Peleus, one of the Argonauts, and one of the hunters of the Boar of Artemis' Anger. He also, presumably, fights the Curetes for Calydon. Additionally, he and Heracles attack Troy when its former king, Laomedon (Priam's father), refuses them payment for saving Hesione and all of Troy from a sea monster (see Heracles). Heracles awards Hesione, to Telamon. Telamon and Hesione become the parents of Teucer(2) who joins in the Trojan War with the Greeks (see Ajax). In *The Iliad*, both Ajax and Teucer stand behind Ajax's shield while Ajax fends off the Trojans, and Teucer shoots them with his bow and arrows; thus, they fight as one.

Thebes* (THEEBZ): A city just north of the Isthmus of Corinth where Oedipus rules at about the time of the "The Caldyoniad" and where war is ever present. The two sons of Oedipus, Eteocles and Polynices, according to agreement, were later to each rule Thebes in successive years. When it becomes Polynices' first turn to rule, Eteocles refuses to step down. War ensues, and Tydeus, son of Oeneus, king of Calydon, for various reasons, fights Eteocles on the side of Polynices.

Themis (THEEM iss): The goddess of Law who prophecies that any son of Thetis will be greater than his father. This prophecy is fulfilled in Achilles, Thetis's son by Peleus.

Thermodon* (THUR mo Don): A river on the eastern end of the Black Sea, probably on the boarder between Turkey and Georgia.

Theseus (THESS yoos): The king of Athens and one of the hunters of The Boar of Artemis' Anger. He is one of the few to show hospitality to Oedipus after the latter had been blinded and had been sent away from virtually every other city in Greece. He is one of the eminent heroes of Greek mythology, many of whose exploits are shared with Heracles.

Thestius (THESS tee oos): The Commander-in-Chief of the Curetes and the father-in-law of Oeneus, king of Calydon, who is roughly the same age as Thestius.

Thetis (THEE tiss): She is a <u>Nereid</u>—a third-generation demigod, and the mother of <u>Achilles</u> by <u>Peleus</u>. It is at her wedding that <u>Discord</u>, who is snubbed by all the gods, rolls <u>The Fruit of Discord</u>, causing a din among three goddesses. Additionally, <u>Zeus</u> had had eyes for Thetis, but the prophecy of <u>Themis</u> dissuaded him from her lest he should one day be forced to abdicate his throne.

Titan (TI tan): Sons of <u>Üranos</u> who, because of their size and strength, dare an attempt at usurping <u>Olympus</u>. Their efforts are mostly frustrated, and they are imprisoned in <u>Tartarus</u>, the deepest part of <u>Hades</u>, but not before making a substantially well-known name for themselves.(<u>Kronos</u> is also considered a titan and is also imprisoned in Tartarus but for different reasons.)

Toxeus / Thyreus / Clymenus / Aegeleus / Periphas: The brothers of <u>Meleager</u> and <u>Tydeus</u> who are killed in the war of <u>Calydon</u> against the <u>Curetes</u>.

Trojan (TRO juhn): A citizen of <u>Troy</u> or something associated with Troy.

Trojan War: For the better part of ten years the <u>Greeks</u> fight the <u>Trojans</u> in order to return <u>Helen</u> to her husband, <u>Menelaus</u>. The actual causes of the war, aside from Helen herself, are <u>The Fruit of Discord</u>, and the <u>Oath of Tyndareus</u>.

Troy*: A city in <u>Phrygia</u> east of the Aegean Sea and directly south of the <u>Hellespont</u>, in modern north-western Turkey.

Tydeus (TI dyoos): The father of Diomedes and the son of <u>Oeneus</u>. He is the one son who survives the war in <u>Calydon</u>, only to be killed not much later in <u>Thebes</u>. According to the original myths, Tydeus is <u>Meleager</u>'s half-brother, having a different mother.

U

Urania (ur AYN ya): The <u>Muse</u> of astronomy.

Üranos (OOR un ohss): The first king of the gods whose throne was threatened by the Titans, of which, his son, <u>Kronos</u>, is one. Üranos was dethroned by Kronos who was subsequently dethroned by <u>Zeus</u> and confined to <u>Tartarus</u>.

W

War: See <u>Ares</u>.

Wild Boar: See <u>Boar of Artemis' Anger</u>.

Z

Zeus (ZOOS): The king of the gods throughout most of <u>Greek</u> mythology, Zeus is known as the cloud gatherer and the lightning bearer. He is the youngest offspring of <u>Kronos</u> and Rhea, and the only one to survive divine infancy without being ingested by Kronos who had eaten all of his previous offspring: <u>Hera</u>, <u>Poseidon</u>, and <u>Hades</u>. Rhea, however, hides the baby Zeus on <u>Mountain Ida</u> (on the island of Crete according to the original myths), has him nursed by the goat <u>Amalthea</u>, and has his crying hidden by the noise of the <u>Curetes</u> so that Kronos won't discover and devour him along with his siblings. When Zeus is grown, he defeats Kronos, saves his siblings from Kronos' belly, and confines him to <u>Tartarus</u>. Zeus is often symbolized by golden eagles whose presence often indicates his will. His character is considered to be happy (his Roman name, Jove, is the root of the English, "jovial"), and the Greek gods are frequently called "the happy gods."

Introduction to
"Onessimus: Troy's Fall Denied"

GORE SCORE: 1 2 3 **4** 5

Spoiler Alert

I was still a very young and inexperienced writer when I began writing my tale of Onessimus. Had I waited to write it until I had more writing experience, I would, first of all, not have employed my invented character of Onessimus, whom I lifted from the book of Philemon in the New Testament. (I changed the spelling of the name to differentiate him from his biblical counterpart.) Instead, I would have used Ajax (the greater) and his half-brother, Teucer. They would have been much better choices than Onessimus and his adopted brother, Antilochus. According to the Greek legends, King Priam is Teucer's uncle. Decades earlier, Heracles had given Teucer's mother—Priam's Sister—to Telemon as a concubine, then Telemon became the father of both Teucer and Ajax, but Teucer is the son of a slave woman who just happened to have been Trojan royalty in her youth, while Ajax is pure Greek noble blood. When you read "Priam and Heracles," you'll understand then if you don't already. But, had I used Teucer rather than Onessimus, I would have had a more realistic "in" regarding Teucer and Priam than I did with Onessimus and Priam. Still, I am content with the outcome.

When I fell in love with E. V. Rieu's translation of *The Iliad* during my first year of university in Moorhead, Minnesota, I realized that, were Helen to be killed somehow, the Trojan War would instantly stall, and that's how the story came to be. I had already wanted to incorporate Greek legends into my writing for some time when I finally began writing my Onessimus story. But that story alone kept me learning and growing for a long time while I figured out how to write in elevated English without alienating my readers, and to incorporate a large number of other traditions without boring them.

I wrote it first as a poem and submitted it to a Canadian literary magazine called "Tickled by Thunder" in 1997. It won an honourable mention in the magazine's annual contest for lengthy poems. Still, the story felt stilted in my mind. I was, as yet, only in the process of inventing techniques for using "elevated" language, and the poem format I was using, called "blank verse," only served to hinder the freedom of just telling the story. I needed to grow as a writer more, and yet, I had only this story to help me succeed at that time. "Onessimus: Troy's Fall Denied" is my earliest story in this volume.

But, as a novice writer then, I also needed assistance when writing certain scenes. One of my favourite movies was *Conan the Barbarian*, and loving that movie as much as I did—indeed, as much as I still do—gave me the references and visions I needed to complete "Onessimus," my first real story. If you haven't seen *Conan the Barbarian* (and I do not mean the 2011 attempted reboot, apologies to Ron Pearlman—a brilliant actor, but his presence was not enough to save the film from the trash bin, in my mind. No, I mean the 1982 film with Arnold Schwarzenegger and James Earl Jones), it is something you should see if you enjoy tales of ancient warfare even a little less than I do.

The scene when Conan's mother is killed inspired the beheading scene in my story. The scene at the end of the movie when the followers of Doom drop their candles into the water fountain strongly influenced the scene in my story when the soldiers drop their armour on the field and disburse to their respective camps.

When I wrote the story, I would not have been able to finish it without *Conan the Barbarian's* influence. I lacked the ability to see those incidents, let alone write them. There are other scenes from the movie referenced in my story, but there are also scenes that are more directly inspired by Homer's tale, even though I scaled them back to lend brevity to a short story rather than needlessly stretching out the incidents out as Homer would have done.

So, if I had written my Onessimus story later in my life, the overall plot would have been pretty much the same, but important details would have been substantially altered from those in the story in this volume, which is almost identical to the story as I conceived it. In a revised version, I would have had different characters with other capabilities, and I would likely have envisioned on my own the scenes that, in this version, are inspired by a favourite movie.

I write all of that to say this: I have been tempted to rewrite the entire story for years, and was considering that prospect again when I began planning this volume of stories. I would have started from scratch with the right characters and less overt influence from a beloved movie. But I was finally able to set that craving aside. When I read the story now, I am happy with it. Not only do I still find it to be an engaging tale, but it also allows me to see me—like in an old photograph—as a writer decades ago who struggled with his vision and developing his voice. So it has historic and nostalgic importance for me. And it did help to bring about four other stories based on the Greek myths. I am content with it as it is, and I hope sincerely that you will enjoy reading it.

Onessimus: Troy's Fall Denied

Part One

My tenuous tongue serves you only poorly, my Muse.
Tell through me, then, the deeds of Onessimus,
for I have no voice to sing, no lips to make known, no understanding to impart
if you are not the singer, the speaker, the one to disclose.
Use me as one might use a harp to declare the true tale.

I sing of wars and rumours of wars. I sing of Achilles' exploits far on the windy plains of high-towered Troy, of his defeat over Hector, and of his mercy to Hector's father, Troy's king. I sing of Odysseus' cunning defeat over Troy by means of a hand-crafted horse and of his nine-year voyage back to his island home of Ithaca. I sing of Aeneas' narrow escape and of his odyssey to Hesperia, where he fought for Troy anew. I do not sing these tales themselves, I sing only of them, for they are mismatched threads in an ancient cord. They are lifeless islands in a windless sea. They are Calypso's charms that hold men captive. They are the Gorgons' glorious tresses, the Harpies' sweet perfume, Sirens' song. I was there. Not that I am anyone. I am a mere nail in one of more than a thousand ships—a simple gust of wind in a single sail—a lone oar among hundreds of thousands, but I know what happened. Long before Aeneas would have need to escape Troy's destruction, before Odysseus was able to use his craftiness, even before Achilles returned to the fray or Troy could tumble to shake the earth, Onessimus rose from the ranks of Greece, putting a stop to the battle for the golden apple—the conflict for the prize worth many lives: the godlike woman, Helen of Troy.

Achilles had too long been absent from the fight, and we were losing ground under Hector's triumphant tirade laying siege at our beaked ships. So Agamemnon, our Commander-in-Chief, sent three emissaries to Achilles—Odysseus of the nimble wits, grey-headed Phoenix, and the formidable Telamonian Ajax—entreating him to return to the fight. That night, having quenched our hunger and thirst, having buried our many dead, and having washed the gore from our bodies, we sat silently on the beach beside our fires, none caring to speak. When war hangs in the balance, anyone who speaks, whether for or against, opens the door for all to be lead back to battle; it is a favoured technique of the Fates into whose arms we were less than eager to run. So all those who were both wise and reluctant sat silently staring into our campfires as if Medusa herself, with snakes of wisps of flame, were providing warmth and light. Then Agamemnon, standing on the prow of his ship, called us to assembly on the beach, and when he had our ears, he began: "My faithful soldiers, attend to what I have to say. As I have already told you, not long ago Zeus sent a dream in the form of Nestor, telling me that we had approached the time to complete our goal here at Troy—to bring her to the ground, plunder her, and return Helen to Menelaus, her rightful spouse, saving her from those kidnapping thieves and sparing Menelaus more years of concern for his gentle bride. It is a noble goal, to be sure, but we have lost many lives, and Achilles has not returned with those I sent to him. I see now that Zeus tricked me into bringing Greece to ruin, and that we should instead return to our families and friends at home."

Each of us, nodding to his neighbour, conceded that this may be the wisest of all possible decisions, so we began to gather our armour. But Diomedes, the red-haired giant among us, marched toward Agamemnon through the assembly, once or twice forcing men's armour crashing to the ground. "My lord Agamemnon, who has bewitched you? You accused me of cowardice just yesterday. Even as I was saddling my horses in full armour, preparing to sally forth, you claimed that I was holding back from war. I swallowed my pride and said nothing, but went off to battle, even battling the gods themselves, and now you dare suggest to the men, in my presence, that we retreat? Now you listen to me: Victory walks among us, not unlike the way Achilles walks with Patroclus. We need only reach out our arms to embrace her, then she will carry us home with honour, with Troy's plunder—their gold and women—and the very prize we set out for: the wife of Menelaus. It is indeed a noble goal, and it is hours, maybe days away. We have been too near the mark for too long to quit so hastily like the child whose mother has called him home for supper." At this, he turned to all of us, and, with the voice of Ares himself, he declared bravely and clearly, "My sword will drink its fill of the finest Trojan wine. My ships will carry as much of the Trojan spoils as they can bear. My Calydonian cohorts will return to their wives as wealthy men. All of us must take like men what is ours, then return with our heads high to the wine-waters of home!"

We turned again to don our armour and prepare our hearts for war, acknowledging to one another the power of Diomedes' leadership, and vowing to fight well in honour of one so great as he. Then Onessimus stepped forward to share his thoughts with Agamemnon. He was only one of the men, not a general or a king, not even the firstborn of a king, but as a younger son of one of our wisest kings, the generals would often hear his thoughts and, on occasion, take his counsel. Nestor almost tried to stop him but thought better of it. He halted and let him speak, and Onessimus, having bowed low to Agamemnon, began: "Mighty Agamemnon, I am persuaded that you are correct. It is better for us to return home with all heads intact than only a few held high; perhaps I can sway the rest. May I address the men?"

Agamemnon offered his army's ears, and Onessimus called to them, "Fellow warriors, we have heard much wisdom of the elders, our generals and kings. Listening to them, following their commands, has done well to keep us fighting-strong these nine years of war. We have lost only half the men we came with, and only half of Troy remains! This war can last another nine years before numbers fallen from our ranks force us to return home. Will our families not rejoice in seeing us then? Our graying mothers will ask us, 'I sent a babe to Troy with Agamemnon; who are you?' Our wives, their eyes wide with surprise at seeing us so unexpectedly, will greet us in the doorway with great smiles, glancing eagerly over their shoulders toward their inner chambers. In another nine years, my friends, only the dogs who survive our absence will remember us when we return. Now, I tell you that there is no reason to continue this fight, not for another nine years, not for another nine days. The prize we came for will have long lost its value by now, and greater rewards await our 'rescuing' from Ocean, who now reaches shoreward to carry us out safely like a young woman with child who longs to coddle her young. Aeolus urges us to the ships, providing, even now, ample wind for our sails, and look! The rising fingers of Dawn wave us seaward, promising a smooth day of fair sailing. Let us go to sea. What wonders await us there, and what greetings will welcome us home?"

With those words, Onessimus struck such longing for home in each of us that we roared in unison and threw our fists high in the air, saluting our friend whose powerful words were to lead us all home to ageing parents, lonely wives, and growing children. But as our cheers subsided, Menelaus stepped forward to challenge Onessimus: "So you miss your mummy, do you? Fine, then, go on home. No one will stop you. A soldier who is unable to keep his eyes away from home is no good to any of his comrades. Go, but first, I want you to explain what you mean by the prize having lost its value. Helen is the prize; she is Zeus's daughter, a queen, and my wife. So, tell me what you mean, boy. Speak up; no one can hear you, but speak well also. You wouldn't want to go home to Mummy minus your head."

Blanching, Onessimus was in no hurry to respond, even though Menelaus waited with his hand on his blade. He considered his words carefully, praying for wisdom and realizing that he had overstepped his bounds. It is no small thing to stand at odds with a king. "I wish no dishonour upon you, Mighty Menelaus. Your deeds are great, befitting a king, but not even a king's wife is equal in value to nine years of this army's life, and I doubt an honest answer from any of the men would praise your queen's splendour." He paused as Menelaus angrily eyed the men around him; in turn, we all stepped back. He brought his eyes back to Onessimus, who swallowed and cautiously continued, "Smell this salty air, Menelaus, and feel the wind; even the loveliest face caught in nine years of this weather would turn quickly to leather. In sum, Peerless Menelaus, favoured of Ares, the face which launched a thousand ships nine years ago, would launch no more than ten today."

Onessimus closed, and Menelaus snapped his blade to his young opponent's throat. "I should slice you where you stand; your soul would be en route to Hades before your body fell to the dust. But you are young and the son of a king we all admire, and none more than I. You are speculating, and I would teach you to think better of Helen." Onessimus could do nothing but concede Menelaus's point, cautiously nodding in response. Menelaus smiled wryly and withdrew his blade. "Good answer!" he nearly cheered. "This would not be the first time for your speeches to cause trouble. Lucky for you, I was around this time. I know that you are no coward, but when we do not know for sure, we must assume the best." There was no response from Onessimus. "I do not want to enforce my point again; are we still in agreement?" Onessimus bowed reverently to the king and backed away. Menelaus turned his attention back to the men and stabbed his sword in the air. "Achaean men at arms, the battle is still ours!"

All of us took our own swords to cheer, thrusting them toward the stars, mimicking Menelaus, jabbing and brandishing them with delight of battle. Diomedes jeered at Agamemnon. Even Menelaus turned to him an evil eye, and Agamemnon sank away, flushed, not unlike a ship caught in the great whirlpool of Charybdis when she drinks in the sea, swallowing all afloat on it.

Menelaus sheathed his blade without expression when the cheering died. All warriors, following the call to battle, adorned themselves for war, but Menelaus stood by the ships, silently watching for a time. Nestor approached him from behind and clapped his back. "Well done, my friend. Until Achilles returns, we need only bide our time on the field, and you have secured the battle for us, perhaps even our victory. Look at the bold eagerness of our men now!"

"With little thanks to Onessimus." Menelaus began then shrank, dropping his eyes. "Forgive me, Nestor. But I do fear that, if we are to avoid disaster, we should have left him where he wishes most to be."

"That would not be so good a thing as you imagine, Menelaus. I brought him along with good reason in mind. He is Onessimus, and we must allow him to be Onessimus. Despite his continuous contrary advice, he has done his part in keeping us focused on the fight, just as he did today with your assistance. The soldiers' hearts had melted with dread and become like water running downhill, away from Troy, toward the sea—and home. You said yourself that a soldier's eyes must remain on the battle. Your words to Onessimus reached deep within all our men to pull out the spirited warriors that would have otherwise remained buried. Now they will fight! As one who has no ship, no place to retreat except to his sword, so each man shall fight. Without Onessimus, you would have had no voice, and we would be scattered sheep, but with Onessimus, we are a flock."

*   *   *

Part Two

Speak through me Clio, my muse who shares with all who care to know what is right.
Give to me the speeches of Onessimus and his brother.
What was it that transpired between them when they stood at odds on the battle field?
Speak through my feeble pen and ink so that all may learn.

Onessimus returned to the fray with the rest of us, but not to fight. He neither challenged the Trojans nor did he accept any challenges. Instead, through the entire morning, he stood on a small mound on the field of battle. He wore his armour, but was not armed; his sword lay in its scabbard, and his sturdy spear stood thrust in the ground beside him. He studied Troy—the well-built walls and the watchers of war upon them—but as sword collided with sword all around him, sending tiny stars dying to the ground, his good friend, Philemon, in the midst of fighting, called to him, "Onessimus! Come! Join the fight!" And having run his opponent through, Philemon stood straight, letting out a breath with a smile, and declared, "The kill is good!" just as another man's sword sliced with a vengeance to the bone of Philemon's neck, and his head lolled away to the side as his body fell dead to the dust.

Onessimus, struck to his heart by his friend's fall, was about to draw his own sword in vengeance when Antilochus called out to Onessimus, availing him to his senses. Antilochus' sword was drawn, and his shield raised as he made his way through the fray to Onessimus' side. "I know you all too well, Onessimus. Nearly born an orphan, your parents were killed after the wild boar hunt at Calydon, where my father fought the war-like Curetes for you in his prime. He searched the city's wreckage for spoils and found you almost dead yourself. He took you as his own and raised you as my brother. We played many a wargame together, you and I as boys, in order to learn to fight as one, like the sons of Telamon, but you were always too quick to show mercy to your fallen foe—a despicable gesture! Only a brute stirs up trouble for his friends by ending a match before the enemy is fully vanquished. Father tried to teach you to hide your mercy, to keep it locked away and to display it proudly only for a countryman or the love of a good woman. You had no shame, and I doubt that you have learned it even in all these years fighting Troy. I see the look in your eye and saw the same last night. What could you possibly do that would not cost us your life, Onessimus? As your brother, I ask you, do nothing brutish. Fight while the fight is in you; you may be dead tomorrow! Honour your father and mother; honour Nestor, who loves you as a

43

son. You are a strong soldier, an enormous asset; fight to kill and be glad for each life lost that is not your own—and do nothing brutish."

Onessimus smiled lightly, not meeting his brother's eyes. "I hear conflict in your words, Antilochus, but remember what our father sings, 'A sweet song is sweeter after sadness; fine wine is finer after tears.' Those who are brutish are the tension that sweetens the wine when the tears have dried."

Antilochus pointed at Onessimus accusingly with his sword, "You flatter yourself, Onessimus."

"No, Antilochus. I am not speaking of myself, but of Mercy. This war is wounded, and Helen—Helen is the sweet, sweet fruit of Discord, and we are spoiled goddesses demanding her for ourselves when she can neither be had nor divided." Here he turned to look at his brother. "Tell me, Antilochus, whose children will be the next to fight for an apple whose nature demands a fight but can never be won? Mercy is brutish, but not so much as Mercy's absence. Like a fine horse gone lame, this war must die. If we try to nurse a lame horse, it simply goes on hurting. Then when dies, we are saddened, of course, but not so much as by the memory of a horse whose life was consumed by pain—a horse who was once great, but which no one could any longer ride or work but only watch as it ate grass and walked the pastures being not dead. Then we would remember the glorious days when it was still strong and healthy—the horse we rode across the country on the hunt—and hate ourselves for not showing mercy."

"Does mortal man show mercy to Eternal War, Onessimus? Are you not mortal? No, you must be an Eternal, and so you can heal?" Antilochus fell to his knees in mock obeisance. "Regard Onessimus, stellified! Allow Ares to live according to your mercy, my brother; heal him, I beg you! Were you to be so very gracious, there is no doubt that he will bow before you in gratitude and vow his allegiance for all your days. Or is the Eternal Ares so badly wounded in the sight of one so great as Onessimus, that even he is unable to heal and must, with his mighty sword, in but a single blow, end the misery of War? Such judgments reside solely on the shoulders of Onessimus, for all the gods seek his power and wisdom—cowering before him, for he is greater and, without equal, mightier still than all-powerful Zeus who also pleads for the mercy of Onessimus on his warrior son's behalf!"

"Your antics are not without their merit, but you must remember, Antilochus, I am driven by what I am."

"What is it, then, that you have decided to do?"

Onessimus paused to consider the question. "I will find for certain if the prize we fight for is as glorious as we have painted her with our blood. If she is, then

I will fight as eagerly as any of our leaders to win her back. If she is not, however I am able, I will show mercy to these hobbling hostilities."

Antilochus scoffed and left his brother's presence, marching back to the mêlée. As Onessimus watched, the earthy cloud that the fighting men raised hid Antilochus from his view, and he was gone. Onessimus looked again on the walls and breathed deeply. Then, with spear in hand, he began his own march on Troy.

*　　*　　*

Part Three

Now whisper to me, my muse, that I may be plain.
Onessimus spoke face to face with Priam as a man speaks with the gods.
What, in heaven's name, was he able to say to such a man
to accomplish such a feat as he did?

Onessimus marched through the battlefield much as a comet moves against the sky—paying no heed to the tiny stars around it. And as a comet draws the eyes of people in wonder to itself, so Onessimus drew his comrades' eyes, and the eyes of Troy, to himself. In a great wave across the battlefield, pairs of men ceased their various fights to ponder together the meaning of Onessimus' actions. He marched through the armies and across the plains between them and Troy; his appearance became a point of light set against the base of the walls of Troy.

Nearly two hundred archers stood on those walls with their bows and arrows poised and aimed and ready to claim a part of Onessimus' heart. Priam also stood on the walls with a great company of distinctly amused spectators watching Onessimus; Laocoön was among those who gawked at the boy-soldier beneath them as Onessimus addressed the king: "Lord Priam, your great wisdom of war betrays you. Not so very long ago, your sword would sing its slaying as you would strike; perhaps your skill out-weighs even Nestor's with whom you fought the Curetes side-by-side at Calydon. But your great experience, like a council of elders, forbids you to fight anymore, for with experience comes age. I invite you, my lord, to defy your years and join the battle again; be a part of this war."

"Is that a challenge? What is it you want, boy? Speak quickly. I have better things to do that to be entertained by you."

Feeling the first pangs of indecision, Onessimus resigned himself to his task and, raising his palms, asked plainly, "I ask that you send out Helen."

Priam stood straight and looked around at his citizens, as though asking if they had heard the same thing he had. The stunned silence on Troy's walls seemed tangible as every Trojan recoiled in wide-eyed disbelief. Heads turned from one to another as if to make certain they had heard correctly. The archer's eyes, praised for their lack of expression, danced back and forth to the archers beside them as though Onessimus had made an off-colour joke at Priam's expense, and they were wondering how Priam would react, wanting to follow suit. But the tension grew too great for the bubble of silence, and it finally burst as the entire assembly fell into laughter together. Even the many archers found their aims aquiver while they snorted and teared, trying to hold their laughs.

46

Looking down on Onessimus from his walls, wiping tears from his eyes and gaining control over his laughter, Priam called again, "Allow me, as one oh so very wise in war, to explain this outburst to you, son. The very reason our two nations are at war is that Helen is within my walls and not within your own. For nine years, we have held her and fought with your army to keep her. I doubt that we will so lightly hand her over to you, even having asked as sweetly as you did. Now away with you! Fight your fight!"

Onessimus stood his ground. Before losing his audience behind the walls, he called back to Priam, "My lord, I am not so young as to be foolish enough to think that you would surrender Helen even if I were to ask with all the sweetness at my disposal. I am not asking that you turn her over to me, but that you simply allow me to see her."

Priam responded sharply, "You will see her if your army defeats mine. Otherwise, you will be dead. Why should I risk losing the cause of this great war to you? What reason can you possibly give?"

"I am one man with every available Trojan archer ready to kill me at the slightest sign of treachery. I am too near the walls for you to miss me, and too far from the battle line for my countrymen to come to my aid. My sword is sheathed, and I now lay my spear on the ground at your wall. I wish only to see if Helen is worthy of the blood I spill."

Priam looked to Laocoön, seeking his opinion, feeling uncertain in his own decision. Laocoön responded emphatically to Priam's unspoken question: "Surely you will not consider it, my king. Kill him!—now!—while his defences are down. I have no doubt that our enemy's leaders sent him to perform some twist of thought. We have yet to receive any reason to trust a Greek; I would not trust him even if he brought as a gift their largest and most powerful horse to offer as a token of peace. My advice is this: do not trust him."

"What danger do you see? This young man's arguments are strong: My men stand ready, his fellows are far off, only watching; not one has moved in toward us. His shield is down, as is his lance, and his sword is sheathed. If this is a trick, it is most unorthodox. I find myself almost wanting to proceed with it if only to see the outcome. But if you see a danger, tell me; I will take your advice if your reasoning is as sound as this young man's."

Laocoön's posture continued to show concern but became arrested, acknowledging that his argument is not as strong. "I have no idea what he has planned, my king; I only know that he must have planned something or there would be no such request, however unorthodox. Do not trust him."

47

Priam looked around at the rest of his advisors. They all, with urgent eyes, silently beseeched him to take Laocoön's advice and not allow the captivity of their great prize to be compromised. Cassandra also stood nearby and warned Priam, "My lord, do whatever best suits your purpose, but know this: If you grant the request of the young soldier at the gate, both sides will lose their prize." "Rubbish!" Priam declared, "How is that even possible?" But she did not respond. As she walked smugly away, she kept to herself the knowledge that there are far worse outcomes for this war than what her father would choose, and she was gratified to know that she had at least once been able to use her punishment to her homeland's advantage.

Priam watched Cassandra leave, confused and distracted by what she had said and more than a little frustrated that she had been on the walls in the first place if she wasn't going to make herself useful by giving sound advice rather than ridiculous riddles. Since Zeus's eagles offered no help, he was left to his own devices. He leaned again over the edge of his wall, "Boy, what are you called?"

"Onessimus, my lord, son of Nestor."

Priam's eyes widened in surprise and recognition. "You are Onessimus? Ha! I was with your father when he found you nearly dead among the rubble of Calydon. It was I who advised him to keep you—the finest booty of the city—a young warrior! Much to the chagrin of Meleager. You have grown well." Onessimus looked bashfully away from Priam, who shook his head in pleasant disbelief at the well-developed youth before him. "Very well, Onessimus, you shall have your request. Remember, though, that even though you are the son of my friend, you are also a son of my enemy. At the first sign of treachery, you will die. My men stand at the ready with me, yours are still at bay. Leave your spear, and keep your sword in its scabbard. Helen will be sent outside of the Scaean Gate there before you; you may see her for but a moment, then she will be brought back within my walls. If you act honestly, your safety is guaranteed until you again reach the battle line. If you do not, you will die."

Before Onessimus could respond, the Scaean Gate opened just enough to allow Helen to silently emerge. She was armed with studied defiance, and well-learned courage radiated from her like a crown. In her nine-year captivity, she had hoarded every piece of dignity that was allotted to her, so that when Onessimus met Helen, he met Strength as a child meets a great warrior of renown, and he was awed by her beauty, by her careful control of fear, by the sea of tears that she held back as if at low tide, by her stamina against unnumbered abusers. He stepped closer to her, her age impossible to guess. She seemed a child; she seemed an old woman.

48

When he moved toward her, every archer in unison moved with him, pulling harder on the strings of their bows and taking more careful aim. Onessimus regarded them for a moment before looking back at Helen, and he saw her pleading with him; he saw her mocking him; he felt her instructing him and saw her resigning herself to her own instructions. Onessimus nodded, understanding finally. Then he began his turn toward the ships, back to battle, away from Helen without immediately taking his eyes from her. As slowly as the stars move from the East, so Onessimus turned, and all of Troy began to breathe calmly, fanning themselves and smiling meekly, feeling secure now in the decision of their redoubtable king. Then, with the swift speed of a meteor, and the lithe grace of a discus thrower, Onessimus drew his sword, spun around and sliced through Helen's neck to watch her body fall limply to the ground.

The archers pulled their strings tighter in reflex but caught themselves. Stunned by the audacity of Onessimus, many simply lowered their bows as they had their jaws, allowing the strings to loosen gently. Others allowed their arrows to aimlessly escape their bows, striking the wall or ground without effect. Then, as though they had only a single mind to share among them, they all turned from the wall, disappearing behind it.

Out on the battlefield, the men who had all been watching the scene at Troy's Gate, stood now in dumb confusion—what to do now? One formerly fighting pair looked at each other and shrugged before they simply dropped their swords and shields where they stood. Nearby, other men did the same; near them, other men followed their lead, and soon the entire field once again, in a climactic finish to the fight, briefly echoed with the sound of clashing arms until every sword and spear and shield lay lifelessly on the ground. In peace then, every man silently retreated: the Greeks to their ships, the Trojans to Troy. The Scaean Gate opened again, welcoming Troy's warless warriors, each of them passing by Onessimus, who had slunk to the ground beside the body of the great prize of Greece and wept.

THE END

Introduction to
"How Meleager Meets His Maker"

GORE SCORE ı 2 3 4 <u>5</u>

This story of Meleager had been a much larger story that had, in a completed draft, severe pacing issues. It was called "The Calydoniad," which essentially means "the story about Calydon." Don't misunderstand: I loved the story myself, but when I tested in on my Literature classes at the College of New Caledonia, I could see that the story was overly drawn out. Alas. People lost interest in it or got too confused by all the details and the names of the many characters.

It was supposed to have been a prequel to my Onessimus story. In that tale, there is a scene in which we learn that King Priam of Troy and Nestor had once been friends, and that they had fought side-by-side at the Greek city of Calydon, of which Meleager was a prince. (Nestor is one of Homer's Greek characters in *The Iliad*, and I made him the adoptive father of Onessimus.)

So, when readers read "The Calydoniad," they would see Meleager start a war with Calydon's neighbour and ally, the Curetes. They'd see Meleager kill six of the Curetes' Nobility who are also his uncles, brothers of Meleager's mother, Althaea. They'd see Althaea enter the battlefield to curse Meleager for the deaths of her brothers. They'd see Meleager back out of the fight because of that curse, and they'd see the Calydon city walls destroyed enough to allow the battle to carry on within them. These incidents are all true according to both the original story and my version, but in my account, "The Calydoniad," readers would then see Nestor finding Onessimus lying under rubble, protected by the bodies of his deceased parents. Then they'd see Meleager, eager to raise a son as a warrior (even though his wife had just told him that she was pregnant), try to claim Onessimus for himself and his wife, Cleopatra. (No, not *that* Cleopatra.) Meleager does this because it was he who saved the city of Calydon from utter destruction, both according to the original myths and "The Calydoniad." However, since Meleager himself had both started the war and then abandoned that war effort at a critical point, his father, King Oeneus, decides that Meleager hasn't earned such a prize, if any at all, even though it was Meleager who ultimately saved Calydon from complete destruction. Oeneus further concludes that Nestor, who found the child, should be allowed to raise him, and Nestor names the child Onessimus, which means "useful." Thus is my story for Onessimus all nicely set up in "The Calydoniad," Nestor raises this child as a brother of his own son, Antilochus.

50

It's a fine story to that point, but it lacks a healthy theme, and it's hard for those not familiar with the story of Calydon to keep track of all that goes on. Plus, the story—MY story—isn't finished at that point, which leaves me with some readers who are already confused by the complexity of the tale, and some others of the less literary types who are bored. Plus, there are still five or so pages to go, and, to be entirely honest, the last five pages are also the most intriguing to read.

There has always been a question as to how Meleager's death came about. You see, just after he was born, the Fate Atropos came to his mother, Althaea, as she rocked the sleeping child. Atropos is one of three Fates; she decides *how* a person will die; she is often depicted with a large pair of shears for cutting the thread of a person's life. Clotho, her sister, was the Fate who spun the thread of a person's life, while Lachesis is the Fate who doled out the thread's length, indicating *when* a person would die. Atropos points to the freshest log on the fire of Althaea's private chamber and announces that Meleager will live as long as that particular log remains intact. Once it has entirely burned, Meleager would die. Needless to say, Althaea sets the baby down and reaches into the fire with her bare hands to save the log, thus saving Meleager. After dousing it with water, she hides the log, storing it where only she would know. As a result, Meleager becomes invincible in battle; the unburned log keeps him alive in all warfare.

The problem is that he did die, and there are two conflicting acccounts as to how that came about. In one account, the Curetes find Meleager alone in the woods and slay him in a final glorious battle of hundreds against one. In the other account, Althaea, in a fit of grief that Meleager slew her brothers—some before the war and others during it—places the log back on the fire, thus causing Meleager's demise. The goal of the last five pages of my original story (and all that's left of the story in this publication) is to reconcile both accounts. No more are they two separate stories; they are two parts of the same story.

So, because the last part is so much more entertaining than the long, laboured opening, I abandoned the first part of the story in favour of a prologue designed to summarize that part of the story. It is now left only with the one incident regarding Le Morte de Meleager. So, while there is still the point in my Onessimus story regarding how Nestor finds and raises the title character, the two tales stand now entirely independent of each other.

How Meleager Meets his Maker

Prologue

"Stop, friends! What are you saying!? I caution you against praising any man too highly, especially one you do not know. I heard you ask, as you raised your cups just now, for your sons to grow into Meleager's image; your toasts are surely misguided. How much have you had to drink?

"Yes, it is true that Meleager saved the city, Calydon. That he routed all the war-loving Curetes from its walls cannot be denied, and all alone as well, for he had been blessed with invincibility; this is how the story goes in every land as far as men may sail, which is just, for that is how all who fought for Calydon decided that it should be remembered, but not for Meleager's sake! For his father's, for Oeneus is a man of honour. I was among those who fought for Calydon with Priam. I am Mygdon, a king in Phrygia, and Priam's right-hand when we sailed to Calydon where the real hero is Oeneus, followed closely by king Priam. These men are heroes! Do not curse your sons with Meleager's deeds.

52

"Sit with me, and I will tell you the tale, all I saw with my own eyes; what I did not see, I learned from Priam, who heard from Oeneus, who learned, again, from witnesses and other worthy sources. Now, after every harvest, Oeneus was dutiful in his sacrifices to the Olympians, except, one year, after he had begun to grow old, he overlooked Artemis. She became so enraged that she cursed him with a giant, boar that would ravage Calydon. That boar caused much damage, but it was hunted and killed, and its hide became an envied prize—a parody of the Golden Fleece claimed by Jason and his doughty Argonauts. We Trojans missed the hunt, having arrived at Calydon too late, so you know as much of the boar as I. So I begin my tale in the middle of things. But let me first invoke the muses that I may accurately tell you all that happened with Meleager and Calydon.

"Bend low my muses, Clio and Calliope. Touch my tongue that I may sing the song of wrath—Meleager's wrath and war and the death he bore, for naught."

Now, Meleager had wanted the boar's hide to give to a woman, but the Curetes had drawn first blood upon the beast, so they rightly claimed it as their own. When Meleager, the child-man that he was, couldn't get his way, he killed the Nobility of the Curetes, two brave men who were also his uncles, his mother's brothers. So Meleager started the war with his own hands, as the Curetes swore vengeance upon Meleager. But during that war, brief though it was, Meleager killed yet two more of his own uncles, and when his mother, Althaea, heard of it, she marched out onto the battlefield and cursed Meleager to death.

Upon being cursed, Meleager hid himself away from the battle—hid in the arms of his wife, Cleopatra. King Onenus came to urge him to rejoin the fight as all of Meleager's younger brothers had been claimed by Curetes' swords. Diomedes, son of Tydeus, Meleager's own brother, came to embolden Meleager, but he would have none of it. Finally, Cleopatra herself conceived the idea of how to return the much-needed Meleager to battle: She knew that if the Curetes won the war, she would be slain, so she conceived in her mind a boy child. And that was enough to urge Meleager back to the fray, and not a moment too soon. With Meleager's help the Curetes were routed and the war was won, but because Meleager had caused the war and had abandoned it when he was most needed and had refused the counsel of both the king and prince Tydeus, Oeneus, King of Calydon, decreed that Meleager should win no rewards for his efforts in the war, and that Diomedes—son of Tydeus, Memeager's bother—not Meleager, should succeed Oeneus to the throne, even though it would have been lost without him. And so, Meleager, the shame of Oeneus and all of Calydon, cowered once more, this time, into the forest ...

Meleager's Demise

. . . "How like a child Meleager sulked away; in his hand he held his sword that he swung at shrubs while he kicked pebbles lying in his path and declared under his breath: 'I never get the things I want even when I deserve them.'" . . .

. . . And even as he mumbled on his way, Curetian soldiers, waiting, hiding among the trees, surrounded him, one by one, showing their faces. They had waited there in hopes of such an opportunity to seek revenge, but had not expected it to be so sweet. "And here we find Meleager, friends," one man spoke. "We never thought the prince himself would leave the safety of his city's walls, such as they are since our last visit. Defend yourself, Meleager; you have won the right to die in vengeance for your four uncles—our countrymen—whom you slew. I am Aratus, and I will avenge Plexippus."

Another spoke up, "And I avenge Iphiclus!"

"And I Evippus!"

"And here is a sword for Eurypylus!"

Cheer up, Meleager," Aratus said, "you may defeat us four, but there are many more still hiding in the trees, more Curetes whose lives you may take; will that not be great fun! I wonder how long you can last. You may be great in war, Meleager, but not even you can fight forever."

Meleager smiled broadly, "When the new-born baby cries because he no longer bathes in the warmth of his mother's womb, the parents hear the infant's anger, and they smile, charmed, not intimidated by his wrath. Bring out your men, bring on the fight, and we will see how long I can last. Long enough to outlive you, certainly."

"Poor Meleager, you do not see it, do you? You did not win the boar's hide, you usurped its power. Look at your city in tatters, Meleager. You have accomplished for Artemis what the boar did not, and now we Curetes hunt you. We may yet win the prize of a boar's hide, am I right men?"

In the greatest rage a man can wield, Meleager swung his sword at Aratus, beginning the offensive attack against the Curetes that would take every one of them to beat.

* * *

54

Within the remaining walls of Calydon, and deep within her home, Meleager's mother, Althaea, sat dismayed for what she knew she must do. She sat, dazed and distraught, holding a log of fir cradled in her arms as though it were her baby. As in a stupor, she could hear the baby's sleeping breath as she rocked it, singing gently and patting it softly. This was the log that she had rescued from the fire with her bare hands when Meleager was only days old. It was the very log that Atropos pointed to with gnarled, tendril-like fingers as she warned that Meleager would live only so long as the log remained. Were it to fall to ashes, Meleager would die. Althaea saved Meleager instantly, doused the log with water, and when it dried, she wrapped it in a cloth of silk, placed it in a box of bronze, and stored it in a chest of wood. But what is taken from Hestia must one day be returned, and this, the brand that Althaea held, she now sacrificed in the hearth—a burnt offering for the souls of her lost brothers and sons who had died—every one—in a battle that Meleager had instigated because of his arrogance and pride.

*   *   *

Meleager fought as though he were a child dancing to the joy and music of summer play. The first four men he dropped without a spot of his own blood released to the air, and he felt he knew the heated passion Úranos himself had known when all those mighty Titans fought him for his throne. As when a wolf is cornered by a man, he then will fight, making sure that he will be the victor. Thus Meleager fought, inflamed by his desire to beat these dogs into their places, returning then to home, to his beloved wife, Cleopatra, and to his unborn son.

*   *   *

For her part, Cleopatra sank in bed, her heart in pain of grief, for she and he may have had another time alone wrapped in passion's arms and love's embrace for one last, long encounter together as one. She had known that when the city's walls were broken, Meleager's days were done. It was her lie that sent him back to battle. Her lie doomed the name of Meleager to die as surely as he, too, must die on that very day. She had thought to save the name 'Meleager' from disgrace and had thought her feelings true and noble, but now she wondered: perhaps her pride had sent him; or was it simply her fear? Either way, she longed to have him back and safe and in her arms that they may make the child of her lie, but it was for nothing. Mere hours after Meleager left her side, Cleopatra died alone of grief.

*   *   *

55

Meleager fought and fought some more. His eager smile began to fade, but he continued fighting, killing more Curetes than all he had before. Their bodies, broken and bloody, lay where Meleager had tossed them once he had vanquished the life from them. Their bodies lay in heaps, and the many heaps of bodies formed a ring for the fight, a circle of gore all about him. Still more and more Curetes came; Meleager, growing weary, continued killing.

*   *   *

Althaea sat blinklessly watching the brand burn, but even as her tears welled, her heart remained as cold as the stone her husband had used to build the walls of Calydon.

*   *   *

And still more and more Curetes came; Meleager grew still more weary. He had been wounded here and there about his arms and breast—and back—but he fought on ... and on and on not losing the fight, but losing energy for it. But still more and more Curetes came—and died.

*   *   *

Althaea roused herself from her daze and, looking into the fire, she saw what she had done. The fire warmed her heart and with her tears repentance flowed. She fell to her knees to beg the gods to change things, but what the gods will, will be done. It occurred to her suddenly that somehow she, as yet, might save the log as she had before, but as her eyes gazed into the hearth and beheld the log that she herself had placed in Hestia's temple, she saw that there was none to save, none, at least, that could withstand the cooling wash of water, and so she wept. Utterly alone, with no more brothers, no more children and a body to old to make more, bitterly she wept.

*   *   *

And still more and more Curetes came; Meleager, breathing hard, saw his nearing end, but still he fought, bleeding fast from wounds inflicted by the Curetes, but still he fought and killed, until Artemis—she whose wrath had brought the boar and the war, and who had watched the war and all its deaths, disguised herself as Meleager's remaining brother, Tydeus, and stood beside him in the bloody circle of dead Curetes.

Encouraged by his brother's appearance, Meleager addressed the goddess, "Tydeus, you are just in time to help me rid our land of all Curetes. They sang

56

and banged their swords to shields to save the infant Zeus from crownéd Kronos' fury, but they will have no song to sing to save themselves from us. Together we will train these hounds to sit and speak at our commands. But let me rest for but a moment. You will fight alone just for now. In but a little time I will stand again to fight at your side, even as you said last night." And so Meleager sat to rest himself, and each Curetian stood in wonder seeing neither goddess nor brother, but just Meleager, hearing him speak to no one, and watching him sit to rest.

*   *   *

Althaea sat, still alone, in grief no less horrible than that which claimed Cleopatra. She hung a noose and stretched her neck with it as the log of her son's birth and death finally fell to the finest of fibers in the hearth.

*   *   *

Meleager looked again and realized that he had lost. He saw that he was sitting while the battle laboured on. He saw that he, surrounded by living and slain, was slain himself. Tydeus had vanished, and Meleager understood that he had seen a vision—not his brother but an Eternal's trick. And even as he stood to raise his sword, the Curetes fell upon him; he was dead.

*   *   *

The Curetes skinned Meleager from head to cloven hoof and hung the skin in a tree as though daring the Argonauts to set sail again. With that, Artemis was appeased and there was room in the hearts of the Curetes for peace again between them and Calydon, that all Aetolians should be united. In time and as allies once again, the Curetes would help Oeneus rebuild his walls, and they would build them stronger and grander.

When Meleager's remains were buried in a tomb of honour befitting his rank, Oeneus hosted a celebration of the heroic deeds in those days of war. Abundant food he served, and drinks—oh, how the wine poured and the women danced, but there was no celebration in the hearts of his guests. Each man sat silent, eyes to the floor—a sombre celebration at best for Oeneus and all the losses he sustained in the few days of warfare. But Oeneus mourned, instead, the loss of cheer, so he called for all his scribes, and to the whole assembly he said, "Dear friends, I thank you for your service in my home. I know that you are saddened now, and I am twice honoured, for your hearts are weighted for these many death, and you labour in sadness for my sake. Do not let your hearts be troubled, and do not think that I might be hurt by gaiety. My heart will carry grief enough when the time is right. This is a celebration! Think on all the glory we have seen during this war, as brief as it was. Let us together retell the tales, that they may be recorded for posterity. No tongue will be stilled today, my friends, no lyre will be silenced for my sake. Please, speak."

But no one spoke for many moments. All looked to the ground, only glancing up at those beside them to see if anyone else had words. Finally Nestor stood; he met the eyes of Oeneus and spoke bravely: "No other tale need be told, my lord, Oeneus, and let it be remembered for all time:" He raised his cup and claimed for all, "Meleager saved this city; let us remember the name Meleager and the honour he brought to Calydon for his lord and father." Thus he toasted Oeneus. Some of the men blanched at Nestor's words, but soon enough they understood. Then Priam stood to raise his cup, "Meleager saved this city by his might, Oeneus, for he alone stood invulnerable . . . To Meleager, the victorious dead!" Tydeus, too, stood to honour Oeneus: "Alone he routed every enemy from our sight, my lord. Indeed, Meleager saved this city! Any other tale is tale only. To Meleager!" Every soldier stood repeating, "To Meleager!" And so they toasted Oeneus together in their hearts, saving him from the continued shame that Meleager's deeds would have brought upon him and upon Calydon; and were she to have heard it, Cleopatra would have been ungrieved . . .

. . . *"Oeneus sat with honoured tears, glad that his name stood redeemed by men for all to follow; the tale of Meleager's shameful actions would never be revealed, or so we thought. Meleager, then, is remembered, to this day, as a hero to all who know of Calydon"* . . .

*   *   *

Epilogue

"By telling you all this, I betray those comrades from that time so long ago; I would have kept my peace, but for your sons you cursed in gleeful ignorance—for their sakes I spoke, and for you, for now I see the danger of our pledge to honour Meleager for his father's sake. It too can be a curse. We must all know Meleager's shame to save our sons pathetic fates brought on by people telling legends, myths, and lies. No longer does the image of Meleager stand, and I will do what I can to topple any remaining monuments.

"Now, friends, I must be on my way. Priam is expecting the return of his lost son, Paris, who, I am told, has a new bride; I must stand with Priam as they meet, but I leave you with this:

"You may say to yourselves, 'It was not Meleager himself, but the familiar image of him that we wished for our sons, for we were ignorant of his shame. The gods will honour prayers of honest intent,' Not so, I fear. For if we pray the gods for gifts in ignorance, they, in knowledge may respond, and so our prayers are spoken wrongly, and our offspring pay the price. Consider the curse that Oedipus called on the murderer of Laius not knowing that he, himself, was the murderer. Was the curse cancelled on account of ignorance? Not at all; his curse fell on his own head: banishment; blindness; horrible deaths for his two sons at each other's hands; himself rejected from every home, having to trudge out his remaining years in turmoil, day after agonizing day, all because he cursed in ignorance.

"And what of Theseus who cursed his son in his own father's name? Was it declared null and void because he cursed in ignorance or did the curses of exile and death fall to Hippolytus? They both fell to him, and in a single day! A curse, after all, is nothing different from a prayer, for who can grant a curse besides a god? Who can respond to a prayer more powerfully than a god? And what is it you wished upon your sons other than a curse? Consider this as you pray anew for your sons!

"I pray that all our sons may grow to be as Oeneus: pious, generous, kind, and that the image of Meleager may die as he is dead. So let it be."

THE END

59

Introduction to
"Memnon and Achilles"

GORE SCORE: <u>1</u> 2 3 4 5

I've always likened the death of Achilles with the death of Ahab in the Bible. No man was ever able to kill Achilles without divine intervention. He, like Meleager before him, was invincible, and yet, both died in battle. For Achilles, however, Paris—the comparatively cowardly brother of Hector—shot an arrow blindly, and Apollo, who held a grudge against Achilles for the desecration of one of his Trojan temples, guided Paris's arrow to the only weak spot on Achilles' entire person: his heel. Legend has it that Achilles' mother, a demigoddess, had conceived Achilles with a mortal, and she, wanting to wash away her baby's mortality—his humanity, in essence—held him by that heel and dipped him in the River Styx. As a result, Achilles is also invincible in warfare, not just because of his incredible talent and skill, but also because—let's be honest, here—what soldier in his right mind would TRY to cut a man in his opponent's heel during battle? The very notion is ridiculous. And when you consider that such an obscure weakness would likely be a deeply hidden secret, any likelihood of such a blow quickly diminishes.

It was similar for King Ahab of Israel. I Kings 22: 34-35 (NIV) has it this way:

> But someone drew his bow at random and hit the king of Israel [Ahab] between the sections of his armor. The king told his chariot driver, "Wheel around and get me out of the fighting. I've been wounded." All day long the battle raged, and the king was propped up in his chariot facing the Arameans. The blood from his wound ran onto the floor of the chariot, and that evening he died.

While 2 Chronicles 18: 33-34 (NIV) adds some detail:

> But someone drew his bow at random and hit the king of Israel between the breastplate and the scale armor. The king told the chariot driver, "Wheel around and get me out of the fighting. I've been wounded." 34 All day long the battle raged, and the king of Israel propped himself up in his chariot facing the Arameans until evening. Then at sunset he died.

So Ahab is killed by a random arrow that happens to hit him in a tiny crack between two parts of his armour, not at all dissimilar to the way Achilles' life was taken, and when you consider that Homer, like the city of Troy, was not Greek, but Turkish—telling his tales of Troy from a patriot's perspective rather than a foreigner's—Achilles would have been considered equally as evil to the Trojans as Ahab was by the God of the Bible.

But all of that is neither here nor there as far as my story goes. I note it only because of a potential deathblow upon Achilles, which didn't happen when he fought Memnon. There is an extended universe of the Trojan war, and in that arena did Memnon and Achilles meet and fight. Another Turkish poet, one Quintus Smyrnaeus (or Quintus from Smyrna), whose work is "a bold and generally underrated attempt in Homer's style to complete the story of Troy from the point at which the *Iliad* closes," wrote about the battle between Achilles and Memnon some four centuries after Christ, shortly before the fall of Rome, in fact ("Quintus"). And, while his account is the inspiration for my story, I can hardly be accused of plagiarism. First of all, his work is public domain the world 'round, and I clearly didn't retell the story.

I wanted to explore what might happen if Achilles had met his absolute match in battle—speed for speed, skill for skill, strength for strength—and tell that tale from the perspective of the Olympian onlookers, who always enjoyed watching mortals battle to the death, they, of course, having no similar outcome of their own battles, unless it is convenient for their writers to give them one, of course. So, this battle is not what you'll find in the epics, but either way, it is still Achilles' final man-to-man battle. I simply allowed the story to head in a new direction. As I was writing, I had no more knowledge of how it would end than you would before reading it, and that was certainly part of the fun. I just started writing and wrote what I "saw" as I was "watching" the goings-on. As a result, I was just as startled by the ending as I hope you are.

"QUINTUS SMYRNAEUS, "The Fall of Troy." LOEB CLASSICAL LIBRARY. https://www.loebclassics.com/view/LCL019/1913/volume.xml#:~:text=Quintus% 20was%20a%20poet%20who,at%20which%20the%20Iliad%20closes.

Memnon & Achilles

Urania is my muse. Urania, who sings of star and sky, whose heart is the heavens.
Speak to those who wish to hear, my muse.
Sing through me the song of Memnon's earthly end.
Paint his portrait in poetry, how he and Achilles came to grips before the walls of Troy.

The number of heroes on either side had severely diminished by the time Memnon came to battle for Troy against the long-haired Greeks. He was the son of golden-haired Dawn, whose rising hand, every morning, coaxes the timid sun from hiding. In that war that had lasted more than nine years, Troy had lost Sarpedon, son of ageis-bearing Zeus; Hector, son of King Priam, lord of lofty Troy; and even the Amazon queen, Penthesilea, had met her doom by the time Memnon joined Troy's ranks. Hector and Penthesilea were lost to Achilles, the greatest Greek warrior, but Greece, too, had lost a good many mighty men, including Antilochus, Nestor's proud son and Patroclus, Achilles' noble squire. Losses were numerous for both sides, and even after those many years of war, the end still stood well out of sight for everyone except for the divinities by whom the end had long before been ordained.

Even so, with Hector dead and Achilles single-handedly bringing down man after man on the battlefield, it seemed to all of Troy that their end was undoubtedly at hand. Then Memnon came on the scene. He ruled Ethiopia with an iron fist and conquered nation after nation as he made his way to Troy; he was known to dispense justice with flame and take city upon city with ferocity. He was Priam's proud nephew come to take back what had been claimed, and for a time, all of Troy breathed more easily. Nestor was the second Greek to challenge Memnon, for he had brought down Antilochus before his sea legs had regained their steadiness on land. But Memnon scorned the challenge of Nestor, who, like so many of Memnon's foes, was no match. As great a warrior as he had been in earlier days, Nestor was no longer worthy of being brought down by so mighty a hand as Memnon's. He left Nestor for the young warriors-in-training, so that they may have the encouragement of the end of a lofty name under their belts, and he sought a Greek more like himself. Like so many true warriors, Memnon lacked adversaries who matched his prowess, except in Achilles; in him, Memnon found a warrior equal to his own skill and might. Indeed, so evenly matched were they, and of such skill, that none but Zeus himself could predict the outcome that the Fates had determined. They confronted each other before Troy, each admiring the stature of the other, while many other fighting men, who could see a good fight brewing, ceased their own battles to stand amicably with their foes to study, or simply to watch, or to gamble, and, with some, to debate the merits of the techniques, weapons, fighting styles, or even the boasts of the two great warriors.

"They tell me, Achilles," Memnon began, "that you are skilled in fighting women to the death, for Penthesilea met her doom by your hand. Well done! And you accomplished such a feat all on your own! Tell me, what angered you so that you took her life, hmm? Were she and her maids laughing at that hairless face of yours, or was it that she just didn't play fair? Perhaps she stuck her tongue out at you? Or maybe she told your comrades that you like her, eh? Ooh, that's a nasty business. Tell me, pretty boy, what it was that engendered such anger in you that you had to show off your proud sword to those warrior women."

"You talk too much, Memnon. Shut up and fight. You will find out, to your own detriment, who the manlier warrior is."

"How dare you address me in such a way! I am no son of a mere nereid, such as you, but of the morning queen herself, as high above a nereid as the sun is above the water. By her mission, all gods, men, and beasts alike are blessed. Those she does not bless live in caves in the sea—dumb monsters of the deep—deedless fish. I know now the outcome of our fight; it is plain."

63

"From this moment on," Achilles declared, "Ethiopian kings will not be known for their wits, if you serve as an example. You will know of my mother's greatness when my spear makes two half hearts in your breast. It was I who avenged Patroclus on Hector, and I will avenge Antilochus on you. By this time tomorrow, your mother, if she loves you, will indeed be the mourning queen."

As they closed on each other, they drew their swords and threw such blows that the other men covered their ears for the ringing. Zeus, who loved them both, augmented their skills and made them almost tireless for the fight. Dawn, looking on from Mount Ida, folded her arms about her knees, pulling them to her breast, rocking as she watched. Thetis herself, Achilles' own mother, sat lovingly beside her, taking her hand in her own. There they comforted each other knowing that one of their two beloved sons would soon bleed his last, unable to run to his mother for the envied kiss of sympathy.

From morning until mid-day the heroes clashed. Their well-crafted shields blocked as many blows as the shore blocks the waves of the sea in a year. Their swords vanished for the speed at which each was wielded, and they whistled through the air as though a cheery song might make it plain that their tasks were no more challenging than standing guard at high noon on a peaceful day.

When the sun stood high overhead, the noble pair agreed to pause so that each might eat and drink in order to return refreshed to fight. Memnon sat among the Trojans facing Achilles, who sat among the Greeks facing Memnon. While they were each congratulated and praised by their comrades, receiving wine or water and massages on their shoulders and along their spines and arms, they met each other's war-like gaze and smiled bashfully, each in honour of his admired equal.

Meanwhile, on nearby Mount Ida, the two divinities sat relieved that their sons were both still strong. They had held each other through the long part of the early day but now sat apart, no longer at ease with each other. Finally, Thetis spoke, anxiously breaking the uncomfortable silence. "Your son fights well."

"As does yours."

Each thanked the other, then sat silent again for a long space of time, until Thetis, defeating a foe of her own, made her feelings known. "Why are we silent, Eos? Why should we, who have loved each other since before humanity, sit in such discomfort when now we each so desperately need the other's comfort? The answer is simple. I fear for the life of my son, and you for the life of yours. We are not being selfish; we are being mothers. It is right for us to care for our sons. Can we not love our sons who are enemies without being enemies ourselves? Let us continue to care for each other, especially now. Such a feat may be impossible for mortals, but is it also impossible for divinities such as ourselves?"

"Thetis, whom I have always loved as a sister, you have rightly noted our fears, in part. If that were all I fear, I would be foolish to be silent with you now. But it is not all I fear, and the thought of telling you makes me fear all the more."

"Darling Dawn, tell me your fears that I may do all I can to free you of them."

"I do not fear only the death of my son, a prospect that already tortures me beyond what I can bear. I also fear the death of your son, Thetis, for if Achilles is lost and Memnon lives, how can you and I still be close? I will have my son to love, and you will have me to watch while I love him. How will you continue to love me knowing that I love my son who killed yours? Will your love not turn on me? Are you able to imagine that I would love you if my son were lost to yours?"

"You may be right, my dear. Our sons' battle may decide even the value of our love, but consider this: my son is destined to die in this war. If he defeats Memnon, he will live for days only. Your son, too, like so many on both sides, is destined to perish at Troy, whether at Achilles' hands or at the hands of someone else. But you and I will have each other always. Rather than turning away, we can comfort each other in our pending losses. Let us rejoice that neither our sons' deaths nor their lives will separate us. What is more, look at their thoughts. They would both mourn the loss of the other, even though they don't realize it, for they, out of all those on the face of the earth, are equally matched; they are valued friends. What a blessed thing for us to see: our sons friends as we are friends."

"You have spoken with the wisdom of all the gods, Thetis. Yes, we will wait together, mourn together, and comfort each other in time, but we will always love each other. There is now only the sting of the sword for us to endure—may it be swift—and we will endure it together."

But Thetis's thoughts were not with Dawn's. "My delightful Dawn, listen to me carefully while my mind chases an idea. Both our sons are doomed, one now, one later. They are equally matched, and Zeus has augmented their skills to serve the divinities. One must win, and none, save Zeus himself and the Fates, knows who. Does anyone need to know?"

"When the end is come, all will know."

"Does it need to end?"

"You would have them fight eternally, Thetis?"

"You would have your son die?"

"If it were in my power to grant, I would have Memnon live until my time to pass is come and long since gone, but not like that! In eternal battle? Perish the thought! How could such a childish wish be made, anyway? They must fight; they must die; that has been ordained."

"Not so, Eos. Not so. What has been ordained is that Troy will fall and that neither Memnon nor Achilles will see it. If they fight forever elsewhere, that ordinance will still be accomplished, will it not?"

"Why, yes, I believe it will, Thetis, but how can we will our sons to fight for all eternity, Thetis? That is no burden for sons such as ours to bare."

"Why, Eos, you are so torn within that you examine this scene with mortal eyes rather than your own. Now, consider: The fact that they will participate in an eternal battle does not mean that they will battle eternally; the divinities are not so very different from mortals as you imagine. Our deeds are greater by far, but still very much the same as theirs. Where they care deeply, we care much more deeply; where they care little, we care not at all; where they love mightily, we love infinitely; where they burn in anger, we incite them to war; where they war for a while; we war forever, but where they take time to reclaim their strength ..."

"The Eternals take far more time."

"Yes. We recline in such leisure that humanities' most innocuous prayers make us groan with burden. So, when our beloved sons break from battle ..."

"It will be we who rub their shoulders and backs and encourage them ... and love them!

"Indeed."

"Oh, Thetis, what hope you have given me! But what shall we do? Zeus has forbidden every Eternal from clasping his knees in supplication for the mortals in these final days of Troy."

"We must try. If Zeus will not receive us, fine, but there is a chance that he will. Let us go now to Zeus to plead for our two sons. We must be submissive, reasonable, suppliant, humble, and determined as we make our demands. We must complete our task before our sons return to battle. Hurry! Come!"

Away to Olympus they fled and were instantly admitted into Zeus's presence. They approached his throne with stoic countenances until they reached the foot. Then, falling to their knees, the two spoke at once their earnest entreaties, each pleading for the life of her son and for the life of her friend's son; each trying to explain their plan; neither succeeding. Zeus, with his sceptre in hand and his golden eagle at his side, smiled at them, raising his palm, trying to calm and quiet his subjects, to do his best to listen and to attain the floor: "Ladies, ladies, please be silent for a moment. Allow me to speak. Allow me to show my favour to you and be generous. I have seen your sorrows; I have watched you dry the eyes of the other; I saw you share your fears openly with the other, ponder the strength of your bond and to swear continued fealty despite the hated outcomes that have been set. Do you not understand that love such as you have shown for each other, even before it occurred to you to ask me to spare your two sons' lives, is the love

66

that pleases Heaven? If you had been here as well as there, you would have seen how my servants wept with joy to see such love. I, too, was deeply moved, weeping with them. Such love has no equal; it has earned you my earnest desire to grant your petitions for love's sake.

"Glorious Thetis, because you love Eos so well, you have accomplished for your son something greater by far than bathing him in the River Styx; your attempt to wash away his humanity would have proved vain, but you chose a better route.

"Dearest Dawn, out of greater fear and less hope than Thetis had, you trusted correctly in coming to me, and your courage spared the life of your son. Both Achilles and Memnon will live as you have requested. Now, both of you return to Ida to see what I shall do for you and for your magnificent sons."

Together, with great, full smiles, they returned to Ida and sat arm-in-arm just in time to see their sons rise together, don their glorious armour, take up their shining swords, and greet each other's eyes for battle. They made no boasts, no taunts, no jabs or jibes, but, refreshed, once again sized the other up for long moments, neither striking nor retreating, waiting to block the blow of his foe. Circling the other. Waiting. Circling. Speeding, finally spinning around a common centre. Raising their shields, their swords, and a great cloud of dust so that every spectator covered his eyes as each had earlier covered his ears, still, the fighting pair continued to raise the dead dust. Eventually, the crowd heard the clashing of sword on shield, but none knew whose sword or whose shield. There was another blow, and another, and still another until the sounds of clashes reflected the beatings of mighty wings, dispersing the assembly as the dust quickly became a twisting storm. At a distance, the men were able to witness an enormous pillar of dense dust rising from the earth, when finally, the pillar itself was lifted from the ground, rising high into the sky, until it vanished.

On the ground, the men who had stood gazing upwards for many moments finally came silently together again on the spot where the two mighty warriors, each a battalion unto himself, were last seen. There was nothing but a crater in the sand, knee-deep at the center, the width of some twenty horses.

As he had augmented their skill, so also Zeus augmented the size of the cloud that hid the heroes, and he carried them up and away, Trojan, Greek and cloud, setting them in the heavens, among the stars, within the scabbard of distant Orion's mighty sabre. There, on fair evenings and holidays, Greece's gods and goddesses amicably assemble to study, or simply to watch, or to gamble, and, with some, to debate the merits or flaws of the techniques, weapons, fighting styles, or even the boasts of the two great warriors.

THE END

67

Introduction to
"The Judgement of Paris: A Retelling"

GORE SCORE 1 2 3 4 5

Before we talk about this particular story, you need to understand something about prophecy from the Greek epic tradition. The telling of a prophecy is nearly 100% of the time the first step in the prophecy's fulfillment. That is to say, were a prophecy never reported, the incidents it foretold would never have come to pass. Ergo, the best way for a prophecy to not come true is to keep it a secret. Once reported, however, the first thing that people in the Greek poems try to do is to take action to keep the prophecy from coming true because prophecies in the Greek epics are always negative. But trying to keep a prophecy from coming true also leads directly to the fulfillment of that prophecy. And since prophecies in the Greek verse portend negative events, the indirect murder of the person named in the prophecy is the inevitable next step.

Such is the case with Paris: upon his birth, King Priam receives a prophecy that says that Paris will cause Troy's eventual destruction. To prevent this, Priam has the baby Priam "exposed" (left alone to die) on Mt. Ida, where he is found, saved and raised by shepherds who name him Alexander. When Alexander is grown up, Zeus chooses him to select the goddess who should win the prize of "The Fairest," from the Apple of Discord (Eris). His choice leads to his return to Troy as a prince where he reassumes his royal name, and the rest is epic poetry.

In writing this story, I wanted to attempt in literature what the Renaissance artists did: combine the Greek stories and traditions with Biblical events. That's why, for example, you see Charon and the River Styx in Michelangelo's depiction of *The Last Judgement* in the Sistine Chapel. In my story, I combine the fall in the Garden of Eden with the famous (or infamous) Judgement of Paris, when he chooses who is "The Fairest" among Hera (the queen of Olympus or the goddess of "the Lust of the Eyes"), Athena (the goddess of wisdom or of "the Pride of Life") and Aphrodite (the goddess of love or of "the Lust of the Flesh").

In my story, which becomes almost an allegory of the fall using Greek characters, Paris represents both Adam and Eve. The three goddesses represent "all that is in the world" according to 1 John 2:16: "For everything in the world—the lust of the flesh, the lust of the eyes, and the pride of life—comes not from the Father but from the world" (NIV). It is these three things that Eve contends with when she grapples the apple: "When the woman saw that the fruit of the tree was *good for food* and *pleasing to the eye*, and also *desirable for*

68

gaining wisdom, she took some and ate it" (Genesis 3:6a NIV. Emphases mine). Of course, the fact that Paris is essentially forced to select one of the goddesses hints at the supposed inevitability of the fall of humanity from the Genesis account. Hermes represents the serpent, as it is he who cajoles Paris into choosing one of the goddesses and explains, "You shall not surely die."

You will notice also, in the story, that Zeus himself points out some similarities between himself and Paris, even as Adam and Eve were made "in [God's] image, in [God's] likeness" (Genesis 1:26). Finally, Paris's return to Troy represents Adam and Eve's eviction from the Garden in as much as he then needed to leave the forests around Mt. Ida, and the fall of Troy represents our fallen, cursed world that came about as a result of our "choice."

Now, one may rightfully ask, "Why would you create an allegory of an allegory with this story?" The answer is twofold: 1) I didn't set out to write an allegory at all. I set out to write a story that combines Greek and Biblical elements to retell a Greek tale. How it turned out is entirely its own fault because, as I was taught in my university writing courses by Dr. Mary Prior: "A work of art knows what it wants to be before you set pen to paper, brush to canvas, or notes to staff." I'll stand by that quote as long as I have "the breath of life" in me. 2) I didn't write "an allegory of an allegory" because I do not believe for an instant that the Genesis account is an allegory. I believe it is history. Succinctly summarized, perhaps, but historical, factual, truthful and even real, not figurative, not symbolic, not allegoric.

I wrote this story as a relatively young Christian and still a young writer, and part of me wants to rid the world of this one because of the very reason I set out to write it, but one famous poet said something regarding Homer that I can argue against with my story. He said (paraphrase) Everything literature has to offer ... can be found in Homer. I find this sentiment to be false. In my studies of both Scripture and Homer, I have found that whatever Homer might have is already found in the Bible, and the Bible has loads of stuff that Homer never dreamed of. So, while the Bible can be thought of in literary terms as an epic, since it meets all the criteria, it also is historical—which Homer may or may not be—and the Bible contains the word of life. I cannot exemplify the word of life in a work of fiction, but I can demonstrate the idea that Homer has nothing over the Bible, not even on a mere literary level. Homer is surpassed.

The Judgment of Paris:
A Retelling

Come my muse, sing to me of Eris, called Discord.
Why was it that she, of all Olympians,
was not among that happy company at Thetis's wedding?
It was that she, among all those whom the Greeks call "sacred,"
is never happy without her lover, Strife;
she has no place in marriage.
But of the fruit of her displeasure,
what became of it?
And on whom did her curse fall?

When Discord dropped her gilded fruit in Heaven's Halls at the wedding feast of
Thetis, every goddess dreamed of owning it to claim the "Fairest" title as her own.
Yet only three of these had power enough to stake a claim that held. Hera first,
as queen, thought the right was hers alone, but wise Athena, whose thoughts are
praised, sought the gold for wisdom's sake. And Aphrodite, lover of love, meekly
knew the apple hers.

In peace, they sought the power of Zeus to choose between the three, and
he, in the wisdom of the king of gods—raising palm and shaking head—declined
his right to judge. "Heavenly ladies," said he, "you have no need of quarrel. You
are Heaven's hosts, a throne for each. Such a fruit, if not beneath you, is simple
repetition."

"Not so, my lord, Olympic King," Hera entered in. "The fruit is fit for power and honour, sweetly befitting Heaven's queen."

"Aye, my lord," Athena spoke. "The fruit is ripe for giving wisdom; Wisdom earns such golden globes."

Aphrodite spoke no claim but smiled lightly in godly grace.

"My dear," said Zeus, charmed by her demure, "have you no boast for possession of this prize?"

"No, my lord."

"But you claim its title, do you not?"

"It is, indeed, most pleasing to the eye, my lord, not unbecoming Love's goddess."

"Then," decided Zeus, "if you cannot share it, I shall divide the fruit between you. Hephaestus' sword will know the mark for equal portions." But Hera spoke in haste, "You can do no such thing to such a worthy prize! Its beauty is power; to mar it, even with your great skill, will make it valueless. As Heaven's queen, your sister, and your consort, I claim the apple and its title whole. There is no prize more fitting for me than this, and there is none more fitting on Olympus for the fruit than I."

"Well have you spoken, Hera," Athena said. "There is, indeed, no one more fitting, but there are those equally fitting, and I am one. If the apple is to be left undivided and mighty Zeus in his authority will not choose between us, the fruit should either be destroyed, or we should pick a fool to choose."

Since no one wished the apple gone, Athena's second thought seemed wise to all. "Very well, then," the king of gods agreed, "there is a man who fits my plan for Earth; let him choose. Offer him riches such as your hearts might think him desirous: kingdoms, queens, strength or skill, but you must all agree that this man's choice is law and binding; he has the right, though not the might, to choose not to choose, but when he chooses, I have chosen.

"Then do with him as you will; use discretion, for you must spare his life; I have plans for him. You will find him on the wooded slopes near the base of Mountain Ida—the very area Amalthea nursed me as an infant and hid me from the wrath of crownéd Kronos. He is there, an abandoned youth, as I was, raised by shepherds and skilled in carving the wood of living trees. Paris is his given name, sentenced to death by his father, as I was, because of a fateful prophecy, which is my will for him to finish. You will know him as Alexander, the protector and protected, for that is how he knows himself, renamed as he is by the shepherds who found and raised him. He will be your judge in my stead."

71

The petitioners agreed, and with a solemn nod of Zeus's head that brought the thunder of a thousand striking gavels, his word was sealed. With reverent bows, the goddesses departed, taking Hermes as their spokesman. Together they descended on wings of lightning to the forests at the base of Ida. On every tree of more than eighty years was carved a scene. On one tall tree was a scene of sundry satyrs playing pan-flutes and dancing about three maidens who gleefully clapped their hands, tapped their feet, and sang along with joyous smiles. Above them, in the background, nearly hidden by the brush, crouched a smiling boy looking on.

Another carving showed a youthful king who held an infant high in one hand, and a mighty sabre in the other. Before him knelt two women—one with lowered head, hands at sides, palm up-turned; the other reaching toward the child in earnest supplication.

A mighty king with enormous thumbs, in yet another scene, sneered among a sea of prostrate subjects covering the land to the horizon all about him. He disdained to look on them in their humble state but turned his face to Heaven.

On the final tree the gods glanced was carved a simple portrait of a lovely woman. Her eyes were sharply focused, yet seemed to glow. Within them, one saw understanding as none on Earth possessed. Her hair was most a radiant shine emanating from within. Her lips were soft and full, yet seemed able to speak with strength. She held her head high with dignity. Hera, herself, swore the face becoming of a goddess but knew of none whom this engraving resembled.

As the four divinities remarked on the art and the beauty of the woman, Paris entered the tiny clearing where they stood. He did not know their faces, but he knew he stood among the gods. He fell to Earth in fearful obeisance, begging them to please spare his life.

Smiling, Hermes stepped forward and helped him to his feet. "Do not fear, Alexander," Hermes began. "You are highly favoured by the king of gods, for he has chosen you to judge in his own name. The three you see before you are Aphrodite, Hera, and Athena. They wish to know who among them you find the fairest—a simple task, I think."

"I am to choose the fairest among these goddesses? How can I make a choice? If I choose one, the two will surely take my life!"

"Not so, Alexander." Hermes placed an arm about Paris to speak reassuringly. "You will surely not die, but you will be as Zeus himself, with his authority to separate the fairest from among the fairest."

"I am not a fair judge. I cannot distinguish the finest gold from the finest gold; this is a job for a god, not a man."

"Do not fear to make a choice, but make no choice too soon. Hear each one speak. Listen to her words, for beauty is not just in a woman's looks, but in her gifts, as well. Be seated on this fallen trunk, beside this most exquisite portrait carved on this living tree, and hear what each shall promise you." He led the wide-eyed Paris by his shoulders to the tree and bade him sit.

Hera stepped forward first and spoke to Paris. "I am Hera, Heaven's Queen, empowered to give you all the lust of your eye—all that is pleasing to see. If you choose me, Alexander, you will conquer in the power of your youth and see the wonders of the world. Men will call you 'great,' for I will give you thrones from which to rule. Your subjects will fear you and obey. When you walk your streets, all who see will bow. Your palace will be of such quality that the threshold, floor, the very steps to your throne will seem to kiss your feet as you walk. You will rule in safety from all your enemies if you find me the fairest."

When Hera ceased, Athena stood and spoke, bribing Paris thus: "I, Athena, am given authority to grant your pride of life. I know you wish to teach a thirsty audience all that you have learned, Alexander. I can give you that. I can give you insight such as never known and with it, leadership—an ever-growing hoard of followers. They will praise you to their friends and stand in awe of you and all your teachings. All you say they will write, recite, and pass for generations. From now until the end of mankind, there will be no end of respect for you. All this, I will grant if you choose me as fairest, Alexander."

And when Athena closed, Aphrodite stood and spoke: "Regard this portrait you have carved, and ponder the lust of your flesh, Paris (for that is the name of your true self); could she not quench a manly appetite? The man who walks a city's length at noon with her, would he not be seen as wise? And he who takes her to his bed, would he not be known as great? Would he not be feared and revered, praised and powerful, Paris?" She moved behind her pet to whisper directly in his ear, calmly, soothingly—almost ... seductively. "It is the visage of Helen that you have carved following only your heart's design. She is the daughter of Leda by Zeus himself, who came to her in swan-like form; can you see the resemblance? Look into her eyes; do they know you? Can you smell the subtle perfume of her hair? Hear the praises in her voice; why, do they not speak of you? Can you feel the warmth of her touch? Taste the passion of her lips? Would any man not long for her? Is she not the fairest mortal Earth has ever seen? Yes, she is. Am I not the fairest goddess you have ever known?

He spoke nothing, nodding in dumb concession. He paid no attention when Hera spoke her curse to him: "Fool! You have chosen the fairest and your fate. The blessings I promised to you will fall to someone else in time. I can not kill you

73

as I would like, but when your family knows calamity, I shall surely side against you." Nor did he hear Athena offer her curse: "You have made your choice, but I promise, Aphrodite will be no aid to your loved ones when they come to ruin." He knew only the gift he had cherished since his youth. That he knew well.

THE END

Introduction to
"Priam and Heracles"

GORE SCORE   1   2   3   4   <u>5</u>

Of all my Greek stories, I think you'll agree that this one shows the most maturity for me as a writer. By the time I wrote this tale, I had been publishing poems and articles in various venues for a couple of years. I scrapped many of the epic conventions that I had so clung to in earlier stories, including the "invocation to the muse." I simply no longer felt that it was either appropriate or needed. In its place, I put an epigraph, as I do in almost all my stories and many of my poems. And I wrote this tale because the original is one that I found offensive. Priam hands over his sister, Hesione, to Telamon as though he was handing over a loaf of bread. In my mind, Priam is the noblest of kings in Greek mythology, and many stage and cinematic depictions of him support that notion. I wanted to see a young Priam who foreshadowed that noble king, and that is why I wrote the story—to show Priam's pain at the loss, rather than the trade, of his sister and to show her captor as a less than savoury character.

It may interest you to know that I started writing this story around 2007 while travelling to visit family in South Dakota, from whence I hail. During that visit, I elected to remain behind while my parents went to see my step-sister, family and cousins for an evening. These are people I wouldn't know if I met them on the street, which is why I chose to not attend. So I stayed and wrote the first 3/4 of this story, when my stepmother called and told me that everyone is asking for me, that they were having a great time, that I would surely enjoy it as well, and would I please come and join them?

So, I have plans for most of my stories, but I never write them down until I write the actual story. I take no notes; I do not outline. If I write down ideas, it's because a lot of diverse ideas for a number of different stories hit me all at once, but planning out the plot of a single story? Me? Never. I had an ending for this story in mind, and I was heading toward it, making great strides, when my stepmother called. And when you get such a kind invitation, it's unwise to decline, so I shut down my computer and joined "the gang" for an evening of cards and laughter and jokes and jibes. By the time I got back to my laptop, I had no clue whatsoever of where I had planned to go next. I was utterly stymied.

The story is now finished, but I have no idea if it is the same ending here that I originally had in mind. It's so odd, though, because I had the story in mind—all laid out—for months before I started writing. I had seen it all in my head hundreds of times, but just going out that evening stole the memory of that ending from me—I think, although I'll never know. The ending that is written is what came to me a year or so later, and it's a fine ending. It works; it ties everything together; it answers the big questions, and it leaves the author, at any rate, satisfied that the story is nicely concluded. That original ending, though, unless God saves such things in some sort of celestial filing system or I stumbled upon it again without remembering, it is forever MIA as far as I can tell.

Priam and Heracles

In his master's steps he trod,
Where the snow lay dinted;
Heat was in the very sod
Which the Saint had printed.
Therefore, Christian men, be sure,
Wealth or rank possessing,
Ye who now will bless the poor,
Shall yourselves find blessing.
—from "Good King Wenceslas"
by John Mason Neale

After waiting for hours alone in the deep reaches of his own city's dungeon, Priam leapt a little in his heart when he heard his name called. The voice was gruff and filled with disdain as if the mere mention of his name were beneath the use of the man's tongue. It was dark, and with no sunlight for the hours he had spent in his cell, Priam had no way of knowing if it was day or night. He could only barely make out the silhouette of the speaker of his name who now, with his armoured body, blocked the doorway to Priam's cell. Hesitating for only a moment, certain of his pending fate, Priam decided it would be better to suffer a quick death by the sword above ground than to endure the long, languishing death that lay before him someday potentially years in the distance—a death from darkness and disease in the waste left by those who had passed on before him, in which he had been sitting, in which he had even slept. The meagre lantern light that shone faintly behind the guard felt like a welcome visitor.

"Well?!" demanded the guard.

Priam, feeling suddenly very old—stiff, sore and sick to his stomach—stood and stepped forward through the slop—toward the man, toward the door, toward the light and the infinite blackness, but he squared his narrow shoulders and raised his beardless chin. The guard stepped aside to let him pass, and Priam stopped for a look up at his foe. In the dim light, he could assemble only a cursory image of the face: a scraggly beard; long, harsh hair; a massive scar down the lighted side of his face, from the temple to the lip, which sported a sneer. It was only an impression of the face, but Priam promised himself that he'd remember what little he had seen. If he got the chance, it was information he determined he would put to use.

The guard pushed Priam violently through the door: "We mustn't keep our king waiting."

Priam had stumbled, but he regained his stance and stood with his back to the man. Then he felt the sudden thrust of his clothing tearing from off his shoulders; it made a single ripping sound, and Priam found himself standing naked, his shoulders now aching, but he made no complaints. Then, with just as little warning, his body was engulfed in a wash of cold water, and, despite the chill, Priam noted with gratitude how refreshingly clean the water smelled and felt. "Scrub!" his keeper ordered, "so you can suffer a clean death before the king."

Priam complied, bathing with the rag that had been thrust at him, and he scoured away the filth he'd been soaking in, then he was doused again with more cold water. Moments later, shivering and shaking, he felt clothing thrown at him; it hit his face from the side—little more than a loincloth. He donned it, allowed his hands to be tied in front of him,—the rope was coarse and tightly applied; he accepted the sack that was placed over his head,—it, too, was rough, and he acquiesced as he was pushed forward. Marching steadily, resolutely, regally, he ascended the stairs into the halls of his own city, still keenly mindful of the sword that his guard held at his back. When they reached their destination, the guard commanded, "Stop. Wait here."

He froze, and the man pushed past him. He heard a door open. It was a sound Priam was all too familiar with—one of two doors near the front of the throne room, one to either side of the throne. There was a long pause before the guard spoke again with the distinct sound of a gloating sneer: "Your presence is required." Priam felt himself led forward some twenty paces before a hand on his shoulder stopped him again. Then someone untied his hands—he rubbed his wrists—and pulled the sack gruffly off his head from behind. The door behind him closed, and Priam found himself standing in front and to the right of the throne of his city. An enormous, burly man sat there; it was not the king he had been accustomed to seeing, even though the crown on his brow was all too familiar. Behind him stood an attendant—a scrawny, older man who looked to be far too familiar with the poetry of war to have any practical experience with the reality of war. Priam didn't know the man on the throne, but their eyes met each other's for a long moment. He leaned forward in the seat, regarding Priam with harsh intensity. Priam thought little of it but turned his attention purposely and scrutinizingly around. There was a large gathering of men at the foot of the room. One of those men held Hesione, Priam's only sister, by one arm and the opposite shoulder. She was dressed in a loincloth like his own, but, unlike Priam, she still wore her jewels that hung about her neck, draped from her hips, squeezed around her arms, wrists and fingers, and dangled from her ears. Priam could see that she had been crying and stood, now, in grave terror. His expression never faltered, though, not even to show the compassion that filled his heart for her. Then his eyes wandered around the rest of the room and came to rest on what they had just before refused to acknowledge: on the floor before the throne, before the door opposite the one through which Priam had entered, lay the bloodied corpses of his twelve older brothers and his father, the king.

Priam's first response was to allow his eyes to well up with tears, but he caught himself. Then his eyes squeezed to slits, pinching out any semblance of mourning as he looked to the man on the throne menacingly.

"Very good, boy," the man on the throne nodded. "Excellent! I can feel the chill—almost. You have learned well to choose the feelings that are best to reveal." Priam said nothing. "You are the youngest son of Laomedon?"

"I am."

"And how many years have you?"

"I have known twelve suns."

The man on the throne leaned back toward the attendant: "I'm impressed. There is no fear in his eyes, no quivering on his lips and no cowering in his voice." Then he spoke to some in the crowd: "You there, pick those up." The men to whom he spoke stepped obediently forward and began dragging away the bodies of Troy's royalty. When they had finished their tasks, the man on the throne addressed Priam again: "Do you know who I am, boy?"

"No."

Again the man on the throne leaned back to his aide: "Such strength in one so young! He never finishes a thought with 'my lord,' or 'your highness' or even 'sir,' yet he exercises excellent self-control." The aide nodded compliantly, almost bowing, as the man on the throne addressed Priam yet again. "Your father and your twelve brothers are dead; you saw the corpses yourself. There is no one coming to your aid. And I am seated on the throne that once belonged to your father. What does that tell you?"

"It tells me," Priam said flatly, "That you claim to be the king of Troy."

"And you don't recognize my claim?"

"Not at all."

The throne is mine, just the same. These men and others outside will support it should you wish to challenge."

The young Priam made no response.

"Have you a name," the man asked with frustration, "or shall I simply call you 'boy'?"

"Priam," was the only response, but it was accompanied by the slightest sliver of a smile.

"Priam," the man on the throne repeated, nodding in greeting. "I am Heracles, the son of Zeus. I killed your father right there, where he was lying. Do you know why?"

Again, Priam made no response. He stood with as much of an air of defiance as he could muster and never allowed his eyes to fall away from Heracles.

Heracles shifted slightly in the throne, leaning farther towards the stalwart child. "Let me give you fair warning, Priam: courage is one thing; I've seen it in you, and I commend you for it, but insolence is quite another thing that I shall not tolerate."

Priam's response was only to soften slightly in his posture.

"Good," Heracles said approvingly. "I killed your father for cheating. He promised to pay Poseidon for the construction of Troy's walls, but he reneged. As punishment, he was to sacrifice this young woman to the Kraken. I assume that she's a relative of yours." He indicated Hesione, who was still held staunchly by the man at the foot of the throne room.

"She is my sister," Priam confessed.

"Well, she apparently meant less to your father than even his honour did. He sacrificed her quite willingly, left her for dead until I came along. I agreed to save her, and to do so, I killed that dreaded sea monster, but as payment, I had demanded the four horses that Zeus, my father, had presented to Troy. Once again, your father reneged on his agreed payment, so I killed him. What do you say to that?"

"What had my brothers done to warrant the same fate?"

"An admirable question. I shall tell you. The elder two I killed without question. My thinking was that they were old enough to have been too heavily

80

influenced by their father; the others I chose to test. Of the next two, the elder tried to seek immediate vengeance; that fool died before he took a full step in my direction. The younger showed more restraint, but not nearly enough. In the same way, I tested the following eight of your brothers, each of whom was only slightly wiser than his elder brother, but none wise or bold enough in my estimation as king of Troy. In you, alone, I found restraint, strength and wisdom—virtually no influence of your father's rule, and yet, royal blood. I wonder if he ever even held the infant Priam twelve years ago."

Priam looked away for the first time. He swallowed, took a breath and looked back to Heracles.

"I see," was Heracles' response as he nodded in understanding. "As painful as that might be, young Priam, it is all the better for you. For had I seen any influence of your father in your character, you would have joined him in Hades by now. As it is, I have plans for you, which I shall share presently; I have other issues to deal with first. Wait there just a moment." He turned his attention, then, to the man who had been holding Hesione throughout the entire discourse: "Telamon, you were most helpful to me in taking this city; how shall I reward you, I wonder." Telamon's only response was to ripen the lascivious grin that he'd been wearing. "Ah, I see. That girl you're holding, you like her?" Telamon's debauched smile broadened as he made a grunting confession and drove his tongue in the nape of her neck. Heracles took a quick look at Priam to see his reaction. He stood horror-struck: his helplessness evident to everyone, especially to himself. "Very well, then," Heracles continued, "she is yours. Take her out of here and do with her as you will." Telamon's response was nothing more than a guttural laugh as he began to pull the girl—who had already begun to cry anew—from the room through the exit at the foot of the room. The door behind them closed with a decisive click of the enormous latch.

There was a long moment of silence as Priam began to look inward for the first time. He suddenly realized how alone he felt, indeed, how alone he had been feeling, but the cries emitted from his sister drove home the pain and the fear and the sadness and the enormous sense of loss. He felt the solitude of uselessness and helplessness. He felt the urge to try to save Hesione and the understanding of the futility of such a move. He felt the tears welling up from his heart, and he made no attempt to stifle them.

Heracles, for his part, gave the boy a moment of peace, saying nothing and letting his own eyes fall to the floor—an offer of privacy. He saw honour in the boy's character, but he also saw that he was still a boy, and so he gave him some time as a boy.

81

Presently, Priam regained his composure and stood straight again. But in those moments of tears, he had moved forward. While he yet had no control of the situation he faced, still, the glint in his eye, the breath in his torso, the tilt of his chin and the confidence of his air took even Heracles by surprise. Priam had become majestic, like a well-bred horse. "You are an impressive young man, Priam. Now we are able to take care of you. I will ask you a question: What is it that makes a king a good king, Priam? Do you know?

"A king is only a king where he is needed, Young Priam. His nobles do not need him. They honour the king—implement his edicts and carry out his commands—but only because he has the power to revoke their comfort. The king rewards them, as you have just witnessed, but the king, really, is in greater need of them than they are of him, so even the king must walk with care where the nobility are concerned. So who needs a king? Hmm? I shall tell you: The homeless, the orphan, the starving, the widowed, the aged, the infirmed, the injured, the beaten, even the foreigner who has been brought into his city's gates; it is they who need a king and thereby make a king out of the man who sits on the throne. The king who honours the least of his kingdom honours the greatest; he who honours his debtors will also honour his creditors. Therefore a city's princes must be considered expendable for its peasants, its pious for its prisoners. The nobility follow their leader; the lowly follow their saviour, and a good king must be both. Do you understand what I am telling you, young Priam?"

"I do, sir."

"Do you agree?"

"I do."

"We shall see." Heracles reclined in the throne and regarded the boy intently. "Troy is mine, Priam, but I leave its throne, and with it, its walls, homes, citadel and citizens to you. As long as I see that you are fit to rule what is now mine, you shall continue do so until she falls." Then Heracles addressed his aide again, "Where is the robe that Laomedon wore?" The aide reached behind and brought out the expansive robe that had belonged to Priam's father. Heracles took it from his aide and walked to Priam, placing it firmly on his shoulders. He took the crown from his own brow, placed it on Priam, then, with an extended arm, invited Priam to take his place on the throne.

When Priam had seated himself, Heracles smiled. It was almost a fatherly smile. "I shall now take my leave of you, King Priam, and on the morning tide, my men and I shall take our leave of this fair city. But I would like to know, first, where your rule shall start; what shall be your first command?"

Priam considered for a moment before he declared, "I shall redesign the dungeon with barred windows for air and light, and sewers for the health of both the guards and prisoners."

Heracles considered Priam's response with a proud smile. "Excellent," Heracles determined, then, waving a hand to his men, he turned to exit the throne room. As he opened the door, there, just outside the door, stood Priam's former guard. Priam immediately recognized him, not only from the vague image he had observed int the doorway to his cell but also by the prominent scar across his face and from the man's own stunned expression when he recognized Priam, seeing him seated on Troy's throne.

"Wait!" Priam called. Heracles stopped and turned to him: "Tomorrow, I shall begin work on my dungeon; the hour is late. But," he pointed to the stunned man outside the door, "this one shall spend tonight in the cell where I felt so much at ease thanks to his tender administrations. He shall be released in the morning before your departure, and with the same warmth and tenderness I received from him." The man's stupefied expression was surely no disappointment for Priam, nor was it a distraction. Heracles regarded Priam for a brief time then nodded. Priam called to his own men, "Guards, take this man below; do see to his comfort; he should be made to feel very safe with lots of well-armed company." Two guards bowed to Priam, then caught the man, each by an arm, and escorted him from the hall. Priam and Heracles exchanged glances, each with the faintest hint of a smile, and Heracles made good his departure.

THE END

PART II:
HORROR STORIES

Introduction to Horror Stories

Quality literature teaches. It doesn't matter if you're reading a novel, short story, poem, pamphlet or graffiti; if it's quality stuff that you're reading, you are being taught, and quite frankly, that's the point. So integral is the idea of teaching to quality literature that the lesson you are to learn as a reader has a separate name: It's called the theme. As French poet, René Daumal has it, "It is still not enough for literature to have clarity and content . . . it must also have a goal and an imperative." The word "imperative" refers to a command or a call to action; it requires greater specificity regarding what that theme should look like—how it should read, but he's still talking about a theme. It matters little that the theme is essentially identical to the thesis of an essay. An essay—literary or academic—is placed in a separate category for reasons that are not important for this discussion. However, as you would not want to write or read an essay without a thesis, so you should not want to write or read a story without a theme.

For a theme to be most effective, there must be two accompanying elements. First, the theme should be stated in the story rather than implied, and usually it will be stated in the dialogue of a prominent character, and yet, it must not be so clearly stated as to bowl the reader over with it. A writer must be artistic and subtle in stating the theme. Second, the story itself must act out the theme; it must exemplify the theme and support it, even as an essay's body must support the thesis. Consider Walt Disney's *Dumbo* from 1941. The theme is stated in the speech by Timothy Q. Mouse, in which he says to Dumbo, "The very things that held you down are going to carry you up! And Up! And UP!" What had been holding Dumbo down other than his larger-than-life ears? And what does Dumbo end up doing with those ears? He ends up using them as wings; he uses them to fly; they do indeed carry him literally "up! And Up! And UP!" The story of *Dumbo* teaches us that if we have been held back, we can be carried forward, as well.

I am a teacher, but my first calling is to be a writer. I didn't know for a long time how well those two callings would mesh, but it makes perfect sense that I use my writing to teach even as I teach writing. And as a teacher who is also a writer, I use anything I need to help me to teach effectively, so long as it is literary, and one genre of literature that so many people want to exclude from literature is horror. H. P. Lovecraft proved that horror is a literary genre, and he carried the genre so high as literature that his writings are often found in literary anthologies for high schools and universities. He was able to so elevate horror as literature because, unlike his predecessor, Edgar Allan Poe, Lovecraft included themes in his writings—he wrote to teach.

A story that has no theme is one that simply tepps a series of events that would be unrelated except for the characters that are involved, and while such stories are often found in literary text books, they are clearly of a lesser quality of literature, but they will often also have some other strength that helps to perpetuate them. When an alert reader comes across such a story, the reaction is unwaveringly the same: "What is his point?" Such was the case when I had my students read Poe's, "The Fall of the House of Usher," a story with no theme. I wanted my students to experience that "What is his point?" issue. Many of them, in fact, felt that they had wasted their time reading the story. But even though the story itself has no theme, my students still gleaned a lesson by reading it: They learned to appreciate the theme in literary works and to see the importance of the theme; it helped them find and understand the themes in subsequent stories they read in my classes, so reading "The Fall of the House of Usher" may have felt like a waste time, but even without a theme, the story can be used to teach that a themeless story feels like a waste of effort, and, let's be honest: despite it's Gothic melancholia, Poe's beautifully poetic writing is still a treat. Indeed, the musicality of Poe's writing, which, in my mind, far surpasses that of Shakespeare, is likely what saved him from being lost to literary obscurity.

It is for the lack of a theme that I don't place Poe on a par with Lovecraft. While Poe's writing was the most extraordinarily musical of any writer since Shakespeare, his writing consistently lacks a theme. For that, his art is forever barred from that upper echelon of literature, where you will most certainly find Lovecraft's work.

Parenthetically, while the theme is integral and ensconced with quality in literature, it also presents a danger for the writer. There is a craft to creating a story that teaches without preaching—without being "didactic." Didactic literature is also considered of lesser quality because it over emphasizes or overstates the lesson; that is, it assumes that the reader is not intelligent enough to figure the theme out on his or her own, which is understandably insulting for most people who read. If you'd like to read a decidedly didactic poem for the experience, I suggest "The Chimney Sweeper: When my mother died I was very young" by William Blake. The lesson is almost as potently presented as the moral from one of Aesop's fables, strongly detracting from the poem, ultimately cheapening the whole.

And yet, it is because of the theme that I haven't any fear of including the horror genre in my short-fiction collection. Horror is useful in putting forth

86

important ideas that Christian readers may, otherwise, never understand because it safely puts them into frightening situations without them having physically live those situations. I use the genre of horror to teach effectively and efficiently. There are plenty of Christians who will question my commitment to Christ based on my use of the horror genre, so let me be very clear. I do not use horror to glorify gore, violence, evil or death. Typically, I avoid classic monsters such as Frankenstein and Dracula, but not altogether, but I would dare to use the vampire metaphorically to ground my theme because the theme stresses the importance of literature. I use horror because we live in a fallen world in which horror becomes effective in demonstrating the power of God and God's deeds in contrast with how "good" the devil tries to appear. Horror is a literary tool that I embrace because I have witnessed its effect on readers, and that effect, in the hands of a writer bent on perpetuating God's blessing, is generally much more profound, long-lasting and beneficial than the impact of a tear-jerking story or a simple tale that has a tired and trite moral. In short, I shall always emphasize theme over genre in my writing, and I do so unabashedly and without apology.

Finally, allow me to point out that horror need not be horrific, especially in my work. I allow my stories to be what they need to be so long as they teach something biblical and godly. But not all of my horror stories are frightening. "The Old Witch," for example, teaches an important lesson, yes, but it's just a lot of fun, if you ask me. I include it in the horror section only because one of the main characters is a witch. I let my stories determine whether the conclusion is "happy" or not. If a tragic ending is more effective for the theme, then a tragic ending it shall jolly-well be. Likewise, if horror is more effective for the theme, then horror it also shall be.

For this collection, at the opening of each tale's introduction, I have placed a "Scare Score," which can help readers to determine if a scary story should be read just before sleeping, at high noon or not at all. Like the "Gore Score" from the introductions to my Greek tales my "Scare Score" is a continuum from 1 to 5, 5 being the scariest and, if it is gory, the 5 will also be the goriest. But all the horror stories earn at least a 1 just for being in the horror category, because some parents might object to their children reading any horror at all.

Introduction to
"That Which Is Evil"

SCARE SCORE: 1 2 3 **4** 5

Woe to those who call evil good
and good evil,
who put darkness for light
and light for darkness,
who put bitter for sweet
and sweet for bitter.

Woe to those who are wise in their own eyes
and clever in their own sight.

Woe to those who are heroes at drinking wine
and champions at mixing drinks,
who acquit the guilty for a bribe,
but deny justice to the innocent.
Therefore, as tongues of fire lick up straw
and as dry grass sinks down in the flames,
so their roots will decay
and their flowers blow away like dust;
for they have rejected the law of the Lord Almighty
and spurned the word of the Holy One of Israel.
(Isaiah 5: 20-24)

Decades ago, everyone in my world was pretty much in agreement about what was evil and what was sacred, what was precious and what we should scorn. There was unity and not a lot of dispute. Lately, however, the things that, at one point, we all agreed were evil, many are saying are good, even beneficial in the name of diversity. We have the mentality, of late, that we need to welcome people as they are, with no expectations for growth or change. Warm embraces for all kinds of evil in the name of a love that is only human in origin, lacking depth, having only breadth, and that, only enough to encompass those who willingly agree with their carnal, humanistic, secular, evil ideologies.

We have the arrogant, self-satisfied notion that we in our century are more enlightened somehow than people of earlier centuries as far as the good and the bad goes, but we are wrong in that assessment. As we, in our childhood, learn from adults who are here before us, so we also must learn from the generations that were here centuries before us. We may know more medically than they did, we may even know more on other scientific levels, and yet, in so many ways, scientific or not, our arrogance leads us astray, time and again. Yes, we are learning, but when it comes to morality, you cannot learn new things; there is nothing new to discover, and those things that have, centuries ago, been declared evil will remain evil regardless of how we, in our ignorance, choose to regard them. That which is evil remains always evil, and our perception of that evil won't change that reality.

With this notion in mind, I wrote the story, "That Which is Evil."

One final note of interest before you read. The story is written in the form of a sort of journal with two entries per day. In the context, it doesn't make a lot of sense for the character to begin his first entry with "Day 1" if he didn't know afore hand that he would be writing for more than one day. Further, the word "day" and the number are ultimately dropped, and the character ultimately abbreviates his titles with just "sunlight" or "moonlight." There was no way for me to explain this in the context of the story, so I didn't bother, but my assumption is that the character began his journals without the headings, adding them only after it became apparent that we would be writing the journals for more than two days, and I assume that he went back to the earlier journals and added the appropriate titles.

I strive for realism, but in a work of fiction, a missing piece of information like this can entirely undermine the realism of that work of fiction. I add this note here in hopes of replenishing that realism as you read the story.

That Which Is Evil

Now Jehoshephat kept the ways of his forefather, David,
seeking after the God of his Father, walking in his commandments
and avoiding that which is evil: the practices of Israel to the north.
So the Lord established the kingdom of Judah in Jehoshephat's hand ...
(2 Chronicles 17:3-5)

Day 1, moonlight

I am trapped. A rabbit caught by the foolishness of his own docility. The door is locked from inside, but there is neither latch nor key, and try as I might, I remain unsuccessful in picking the lock. How she was able to free herself from within a locked room is beyond me, but finally, the reality is that I am alone, and the door continues to stand closed and locked.

There is a window just below the ceiling opposite the door. I'd guess it to be about 10 by 18 inches, but it is well above my reach; the ceiling is a good 10 feet high. The window is barred on the outside and mostly obscured by shrubbery and grass. I had thought to break the glass with my shoe. I would yet be without a means of escape, but I felt that I could, perhaps, call out to passers-by. And yet, the city lies 45 minutes away by car, and the nearest neighbours live 45 minutes away on foot. It may not be winter, officially, but the weather is cold enough that it might as well be, and I would prefer, I think, to maintain what little heat I have. The outside wall of my prison radiates enough cold as it is. Sioux Falls is nothing if not terribly cold this time of year.

90

At the moment, the light of the moon is able to make its way to me, but that will soon be lost. Still, the concrete walls are smooth and light enough that, with what little moonlight remains, I can see just how horribly confined I am. My cell is roughly square; I'd say 10 feet by 10. The floor slopes to the centre where there is a circular drain about six inches in diameter. Charming. It's covered with an iron grate. The door to my cell is broad and made of wood—oak, I think, and I shall begin using what I can to scrape my way through it shortly, but I'll write as long as the light remains.

I want more than anything else to write, not so much of my present circumstances—although I cannot deny that such things are preying on my thoughts—but how I came to be in this place and why. It must be made known. People must be warned, but the light fades—more with the sun.

Day 1, sunlight

I'm not sure at all of the date. I arrived here in the evening of October 29th and, after a frightening greeting at the door, spent my first hours (or days?) unconscious in this cell, having been brutally thrust against the far wall. Since gaining consciousness, I have been fighting to maintain it for fear of a concussion, but I'm a journalist, not a doctor. Does the sleep that I've had already rule out the possibility of a concussion? All I know is that, when you bang your head, you're not supposed to sleep. I'm doing my best. I'm sure I've been awake a full 18-20 hours during which I first waited, hoping to be released. After that, I worked frantically on the door with my car keys, but have managed only to scratch it. At this rate, it will be months before I can cut a hole—if ever.

I wonder if she plans to feed me. It's looking less and less likely that she is. There is a large, black water pipe running down one corner of my prison. Its surface seems to run continuously with condensation, which has been my only source of water. I dearly wish that I had been able to wash it, but that luxury was not afforded me. I'm just glad that it's painted. I believe it's iron, and I'd hate to drink from the rough, raw surface of an iron pipe. It doubles as something of a primitive thermometer, too: With the condensation, I can be confident that the temperature in my cell is above freezing and that there is moisture in the air, more than my own body would be able to produce. Ergo, as cold as it is, something, for the moment, is generating enough heat to allow for the presence of moisture. And since I still have my coat and suit jacket, I'm comfortable ... from a liberal definition of the term. At least I won't freeze to death any time soon. That's looking on the bright side, isn't it? Can't think about that now. There is a screw loose in the grate over the drain. If I can remove it, and if it tapers ... if it's sharp, it might make a better tool than my car keys to scrape my way through the door.

It seems to be true about men in foxholes: not an atheist among them, and there's no denying that this space is a foxhole. I think a great deal about prayer recently, for the first time in a decade, and I suddenly long for the comfort of my Bible. Jonah was three days in the whale before he prayed. Perhaps my ten years or so will have the effect of generating an even more joyful reunion for God and me.

I need to write how I came to be here, and I shall begin scrawling that with the moon. For now, I shall work at removing that screw.

Day 2, moonlight

I slept, and I awoke. That's good news, right? Even better: While it was not without effort or injury to my hand, I was able to remove the screw from the grate. A layer of abrasive corrosion made the task a challenge, since the edge of the head is quite sharp. The screw has a nicely tapered tip and stretches a good two inches in length. By tearing off part of my shirt, I was able to make a safe handle, and I began scraping at the door. It seems useless, but I shall continue, at least until I'm no longer able to. But that is something I can do even in the black of night. For now, while I can see, I must write.

Let me record, then, for any who might find me—alive or dead, in the near future or many years down the road—how it was that I came to be here, not only in this house, but in this dungeon, locked away in a space that serves not only as my cell, but seems likely, might also serve as my tomb.

My name is Edik MacAber. Until I came to this place, this old house, this ... abandoned shelter for squatting witches, I was employed with the newspaper—a reporter with mediocre skills but a handsome income. It was there that I abandoned the Sunday teachings of my youth and adopted a warm and accepting attitude, which I would gladly trade now for a blanket or a cushion ... or a good meal. For the last few months, we'd been covering a series of stories on the rise of cults and covens around town: Do they pose a danger? Should people shun them? Can they be assimilated into our population? That sort of thing. Reporters went out by the dozens to interview group leaders but were all turned away, one after another after another. They surmised that the cults didn't want to assimilate. They wanted to be outcasts so that they would be feared; they wanted to be shunned. It is through us shunning them that they maintain their fear over others—and so then also their power over the populace.

That's what my *confrères* said. I refused to listen. I denied the evidence right in front of me and disdained to consider the words of colleagues and friends. Everyone needs to feel welcome, I argued. Everyone needs to be loved and accepted, just as they are. That's what ten years of distance from sound doctrine taught me, and I wholeheartedly believed it. If we were good to them there was no reason for them to not be good to us. We needed to integrate them not interrogate them. That was my argument.

The light has already passed over the wall and is being cut off—time to work on the door.

Day 2, sunlight
I discovered that I can pace across my cell 200 times in just over an hour. It does well for circulation and for keeping my mind occupied, away from the cold, away from the solitude, away from the hunger. Six paces across, six back and just 199 times more, and the hour will have passed. I have practiced counting to two hundred in every Romance language: Latin, Spanish, Italian, French, Portuguese and Romanian. Such fun. I have recited Bible stories, the 23rd Psalm and The Lord's Prayer over and over. I've even sung a few hymns that have come back to me after so long. And by the time each hour has passed, there's ample moisture collected on the water pipe, and I'm able to drink. If this situation were any different, I would be bored, but I'm not bored. I'm too hungry to be bored. I'm too cold to be bored. I'm too afraid to be bored.

It is no longer only the outer wall that maintains the cold of my prison. The floor near the wall is increasingly colder, and the cold is spreading across my dungeon with what seems a necrotic will. It can only get colder. I picked a good time of year to visit this decrepit mansion. Which is better, I wonder: to freeze to death or to starve to death? I am certain now that I shall come to know one or the other intimately.

This is not how I wanted to spend my sunlight. I guess I needed to vent. I'm feeling morose, depressed and lost. Part of me wants to feel betrayed, but I know that ultimately, I'm the betrayer, not the betrayed. One thing I'm going to do in the coming hours of darkness is sing lots of hymns, lots and lots of songs about God, hoping that there's still some power in them that will cause the old witch to writhe in her sleep, assuming that she sleeps—assuming that she's even still here. Besides, aren't there Bible stories about people singing hymns in prison? Don't they escape?

More about my life outside of this box with the moonlight.

Day 3, moonlight
I lack the energy to write. I'm forcing myself regardless. It was the same all day: I just couldn't find the strength to continue cutting the door, but I pushed

myself as much as I could. I've so far created a square of grooves that should make a good-sized hole if I'm ever able to cut through the wood, if I have the energy, and if I live long enough. I slept a good long time today, but I'm already looking forward to sleep as soon as the light fades.

It's essential for people to know how I came to be here, so I shall explain despite the difficulty. While my newspaper was investigating those local covens, I got a lead on one known witch who seemed unaffiliated with any cults as far as anyone else had found out—a lone she-wolf, you might say. I saw her as an outcast among outcasts, shunned by the shunned, and I felt sorry for her. I was going to leave my job behind for a while and extend that welcome to her on my own.

I went alone after work one day to where she was said to live—a dilapidated farmhouse about an hour south of town on such-and-such a road. I arrived late in the day, with just enough sunlight to help me find it among all the dirt roads and cornfields. I told no one where I was going.

It turned out to be no small house. It looked to be 80 to 100 years old. It was two stories with three small, gabled windows to the front, one on either side, some of which were boarded up with what looked to be scrap wood. The foundation was made of that red quartzite that you see all over town, especially up near the Falls, and it was surrounded with shrubs, around which was miles of long grass as far as I could see. Mostly the house still seemed solid enough, just terribly neglected. You need to understand: I assumed that she was having the home restored. It never occurred to me that she was living by choice in squalor.

The main entrance lacked an outer screen door but was blocked with a solid oak inner door, weather-worn and sun-bleached. There was neither garage nor driveway, but there were the remains of a wooden hitching post. Thinking it the most polite, I parked my car beside that post just off the dirt road that stretched along out front of the house.

The inside was not lighted, but I assumed that the old girl might be poor of sight, with no need of lighting a house. And with that, despite the huge brass knocker on the door, I simply entered the house.

I'm losing the light. More to follow.

94

But Jehoshaphat made an alliance with Ahab, the wicked king of Israel to the north,
through the marriage of his own son with Ahab's daughter,
for Jehoshaphat said to Ahab,
"I am as your are; my people are as your people; we will stand together with you."
(2 Chronicles 18:1-3)

Day 3, sunlight

Inside the house was a large foyer adorned with darkened wall lights and a staircase behind, with a landing at the top that led in either direction on the upper floor. There was nobody there. I promise you there wasn't, but I got three steps inside when I heard the old lady's voice:

"What do you want?!"

The voice seemed to come from no direction in particular, and certainly not from a heart of friendship. I told myself that she was lonely and hurt, in need of love. There didn't seem to be an intercom system, but the voice sounded like it emanated from very close to me. And yet, there was no one!

"My name is Edik MacAber, Ma'am." My voice echoed in the barren room.

"What do you want?!" she insisted, her voice clearly that of an elderly woman yet strong even if, apparently, disembodied.

I answered by looking all around the foyer as I spoke, both to make sure she heard me and to see if I could catch a glimpse of her. "I simply wish to try to help you feel welcome."

"Oh," she said, and she suddenly sounded genuinely touched.

"Yes, you see, many folks are coming to town who are known to be witches, and your name is mentioned among them. If you are a witch, ma'am, I want to remind you that the days of witch hunts are long passed; not everyone sees such a thing as necessarily bad."

"How nice!" she said, sounding as sweet and charming as Witch Hazel. I never thought that it could be sarcasm.

"If you need assistance, I am willing to avail myself to you. And if you would like to move into town, I would be pleased to help with that as well."

"And why would I want to do that?"

"So that you're not so isolated, ma'am. So that you have people around to care for you."

"Ooh, such a kind young man," she said. "Let me show you how much I appreciate your kindness by sharing my hospitality with you. Please feel welcome to stay here for a very long time." With that, I floated in the foyer air, was carried swiftly to the basement and thrust across the room that has become my new

95

home. It was then that I banged my head. I vaguely remember seeing the door slam closed unaided before passing out and waking up locked in. That is how I came to be here.

Darkness. More later.

Day 4, moonlight.

Keeping these journals, such as they are, helps me to keep a measure of time and gives me something to look forward to. Without them, I might very well lose my mind, so I press on with them if only to add some cheer to an otherwise decidedly dreary day.

Over the past while, I've been thinking about a story that was read to me when I was younger, when my parents used to send my brother and me off to church every Sunday morning. I remember studying about Jonah and Noah, of course, but one story stuck out to me because of the name: Jehoshaphat. I recognized it because my dad used to say that name instead of ... well, others that he might have used when he was angry. I didn't know that it referred to an actual person until one Sunday when the sermon was about this king, this Jehoshaphat. He made a pact with the devil—or the next best thing, and not only did God punish him for it, but Jehoshaphat's descendants were also cursed by it, in as much as they became like the very devil with whom Jehoshaphat had allied himself. I remember that story like it was told to me yesterday, that's how much it impacted me. So I used the first part of my moonlight tonight to see how well my storylines up with Jehoshaphat's. It's pretty remarkable in a scary sort of a way, especially since, like that Hebrew king in days of old, I, too, have a son. Will my actions impact him in the same way?

My light already draws thin.

Sunlight

When I stood up this morning, my slacks fell to my knees—no food for at least four days. Well, I tugged them back up and sat down again. What do I need to stand up for anyway? It's not like there's a big breakfast waiting for me.

My son is only twelve. He's in grade 7 at Edison Jr. High. His teachers adored him last year. I haven't heard much about them this year. He wants to be a writer like his ol' man, God love him. His mother is all he's going to have. Soon enough. It's not that she's less than adequate. She is, to be honest, quite excellent. Better than I ever deserved, make no mistake. He'll be fine, but if he does, indeed, turn out to be like his Papa, I just pray that he's not too much like him.

96

I can see my breath in the sunlight from the window. I noticed it when I tried to warm my hands. When it floats directly through the glow, it takes on the appearance of transparent marble: mutable marble in motion. Like drops of motor oil disbursed in a water puddle. It moves through the light, and then it's gone. Like it was wholly imaginary, except that I saw it. I SAW it. It was there.

I've heard it said that it can take months to die from starvation. By that reckoning, I've only just begun to starve ... to die. What they don't tell you is all that happens between your last meal and your last breath, and, unfortunately for me, I'm here to tell you that it's not fun. I've taken to "biting" my nails. Down to the nub. What can I say? I like nails with catsup. Not as filling as a hotdog, but just as much protein. Of course, it makes it all the more difficult to write.

Ah, the light fades once again. Good night, my someone.

When the king of Judah, Jehoshaphat, returned safely to Jerusalem,
Jehu, the prophet, went to meet him:
"Why would you help the wicked and love those who
ignorantly despise the Lord your god?" he asked.
"Because of this deed, the Lord harbours a great deal of anger against you."
(2 Chronicles 19:1-3)

Moonlight

I started this journal to warn people. How successful can it be? In order to read my warning, you have to already be within the very house she inhabits. You may already have been closed within this same cell—a prisoner just as I am or was. If so, then I am sorry, but perhaps there is hope for you. Perhaps you came in the summer. Break a window and call out for help or continue to dig your way out through the door, but do not allow yourself to suffer my fate.

But if by some chance you made it to this room unnoticed, that you're reading this now while kneeling beside my corpse, know that a witch lives here, and that witch is evil. Do not try to save her; save yourself. Get out! Get away while you can, and if you dare to return, then burn this house to ashes, or raze it to the earth and consider the entire area cursed. Do not think that time has changed her. If it has, then she will come to you, but do not trust to that hope while you breathe the air within these walls.

I was a fool! God, forgive me! Punish me no longer! I need no more convincing! Please take me out of here. Let me go home, God. Let me be with my family.

97

When Jehoshaphat died ... his son Jehoram became king.
His other sons were Azariah, Jehiel, Zechariah, Azariahu, Michael and Shephatiah.
Jehoshaphat had left them gifts of silver, gold, and other costly items ...
but he designated Jehoram as the next king because he was the oldest.
But when Jehoram had become solidly established as king, he killed all his brothers ...
Jehoram followed the examples of Israel's kings; he was just as wicked as King Ahab,
for he had married Ahab's daughter. So Jehoram did what was evil in the Lord's sight.
(2 Chronicles 21: 1-7)

Sun

The sun brings little light and less warmth. The cold of the concrete floor seeps through my slacks and burns me as I sit or lie. Writing is very difficult with all my shivering. But I welcome the cold. As it seems that I shall never leave this room, I find the idea of dying sooner by freezing—compared with the slow, agonizing decay of starvation—to be nothing other than an act of mercy.

Funny thing: My fingernails are gone, so I began taking on my toenails for sustenance. My toes bled even more quickly than my fingers did. I found that surprising. But my toes got so sore that I couldn't put my shoes back on. I went barefoot until they went numb, and then I could slip my shoes back on with no pain, and my feet are getting all toasty warm. Isn't that a riot? They hurt a bit now, but they're warm ... well, *warmer*.

The water on my watering-hole is no longer water. It's frozen, offering no liquid. A thin glaze coats the window, too. It won't be long now. Not long at all.

One last thing: I do not want my son to suffer the horrors of the lesson that I had to be caged to learn. Maybe in this one area I was a bad influence on him, but in many ways, I wasn't a bad father. I wasn't. He and I were very close. I can't give him the guidance anymore that I would like to, but then, without my time here, I may have messed it all up. Who knows? If I can't guide him, though, I can give him my prayers. I can do that. I will do that. What breath, strength and life I have, I bequeath to my son as an offering of prayer for him and his mother.

I don't know if I'll be able to write more. If not, then know that I leave this earth prepared to rest in it. I have not made peace with myself. Despite this concrete cave, I have made the peace that all men need: Pacem habeamus ad Deum. Amen.[1] If he chooses to not free me from this place except through my death, I can accept that. I have accepted that.

The light fades and all warmth with it.

1

Pacem habeamus ad Deum. Amen. Latin. "Peace with God. Let it be."

POLICE REPORT: Re: Case#10-30-62 MP-EAM1046
DATE: Monday, 24 June 1991
VICTIM: MacAber, Edik Alan
VICTIM STATUS: Deceased
   Case re-opened: Friday, 31 May, 1991.
   Original date: Wednesday, 31 October, 1962.
CASE TYPE: Missing Persons
CURRENT STATUS: Solved.
REPORTING OFFICER: Sgt. Terry Razka, SFPD:
PERSON INVOLVED:
   Wife of Victim:
      Sashia Marie Karn MacAber
   Son of Victim:
      Eric John MacAber

The five days of journals above were written in pencil on the concrete walls where Mr. Edik Alan MacAber's remains were found. Police officials accept these writings as Mr. MacAber's sworn testimony. There are no edits. The Bible verses conform to no known translation. Police conclude that they are Mr. MacAber's own paraphrases based on passages that he had memorized or nearly memorized prior to his captivity. The references were added to ease the police investigation. They are approximate based on context.

Mr. MacAber's testimony is confirmed, except that the door to the chamber in which he was found was not locked, as he has testified. According to the demolition team examining the house (who discovered Mr. MacAber's remains), the solid oak door was tightly wedged in a closed position, requiring them to force it with a battering ram. The door was slightly too broad to fit within its jamb. Closing it from within the room would have required the weight of a full-grown man, but then opening it again would have been virtually impossible from the inside.

Investigations revealed that there is no official record of anyone occupying the residence where Mr. MacAber's remains were found during the time frame of his testimony, but as he referred to the woman as a "squatting witch," it is assumed that there is no reason for documentation to be found.

It is evident that no one else in decades had entered the house. Dust levels remain consistent and undisturbed. There is no graffiti or evidence of any other type of vandalism. There is no significant garbage or waste or other evidence of any occupancy.

The remains of Mr. Edik MacAber have been positively identified via dental records. They are to be interred at Woodlawn Cemetery according to the request of his surviving widow, Sashia Marie Karn MacAber, upon completion of this investigation.

Mr. MacAber was reported missing on the morning of Wednesday, 31 October, 1962, by Mrs. MacAber.

The coroner reports that Mr. MacAber likely died of exposure to cold on or about Saturday, 03 November, 1962, based on the final entry of Mr. MacAber's testimony. He was, however, officially declared deceased in January of 1970, having been missing a full seven years. Mrs. MacAber received no significant inheritance or insurance settlement as a result of Mr. MacAber's absence, only the modest pension from Mr. MacAber's newspaper. An investigation into Mrs. MacAber's whereabouts during the week of Mr. MacAber's disappearance revealed an alibi; she has been cleared of suspicion.

Mr. MacAber's car, a black 1959 Renault Dauphine, was found in front of the house where his remains were discovered. It had been parked in high grass, resulting in hidden license plates that were never checked; as it is not uncommon for cars to remain with abandoned homes on old homesteads near farming communities in South Dakota, its proximity to the house would not have appeared unusual or suspicious to passers-by, which explains why its presence was never reported.

Mr. MacAber's son, 40-year-old Eric John MacAber, has requested the return of his father's vehicle so that he may restore it. The city will return Mr. Edik MacAber's personal effects to his son upon completion of this investigation. Personal effects include the car, one gold Dunhill watch, one gold wedding ring, one gold Cross pen and pencil set, a leather wallet with photos, I.D.s and $127 in cash. All dates antedate Mr. MacAber's account.

In honor of Edik MacAber's stated consternation regarding his son, it is noted that Eric is a respected, upstanding resident of Sioux Falls, South Dakota, as of the date of this report.

CASE CLOSED AS OF DATE ABOVE

Introduction to
"The Empty House"

SCARE SCORE 1 2 3 4 <u>5</u>

I'll tell you straight out: "The Empty House" is most distinctly based on actual events from my life. Indeed, it is almost autobiographical, and it was a frightening series of events. The problem with just saying that it "is a true story," however, is that it's not a wholly true story. For example, John and I are indeed friends; we did join the navy in 1983; we did attempt to make a movie during the summer before our navy adventure began; three episodes did take place at the abandoned house that we had discovered for the sake of our film; the last of those events did involve Jeanne Anne and Dave, and it did scare us all away from that house for the remainder of our lives. But the story needed certain enhancements if it was going to function well as a work of literature. No true story ever transfers directly to the page without embellishments of some sort, but in this case, the embellishments that I still feel are entirely necessary for the telling of the story, also serve, in part, to detract from the true-to-life aspect of the story, and that, in turn, tends to detract from the impact of the theme that I feel is especially important. So, to refill my theme with the power it both needs and deserves, I turned it into a thesis and laid the story out as an essay, rife with introduction and conclusion, to replenish in the story the touch of reality that it needs. Narrative essays are supposed to be, thought to be and taught to be renderings of factual events. So, "The Empty House" is a true story that's made into fiction but rendered as an essay to make it real.

I want to share in this introduction how I began incorporating those embellishments, and for that, I need to go back to boot camp in San Diego, California, in 1983, October, to be specific. John—yes, the same John who had discovered the empty house with me was now in the navy with me—and I were in our last week of boot camp then.

It is a rare thing, indeed, for a good writer to also be a good storyteller. Stephen King testified to as much in his novel, *Misery.* I am, however, one of the few blessed with both talents. I enjoy telling a good story just as much as I love to write one, and I got the chance to show off my tale-telling prowess one night during boot camp—not the regular boot camp, but an extension of boot camp called "Posmo," which is short for the ironic title, "Positive Motivation" (I'm here to tell y', though, there ain't nuthin' positive about it.)—when the guys and I were telling ghost stories. John was out on "watch," which meant that he was spending the evening alone, marching back and forth across a parking lot about the size of a standard house lot in a typical US city. He also "got" to carry a rifle that could not shoot to protect himself from any would-be invaders on a strategically meaningless target of a military base. In short, he was under orders to waste two hours marching and carrying a useless weapon.

When my turn for a story came, I shared about the empty house, but I began incorporating enhancements immediately, since I was improvising the tale as I told it. There were ten of us all together as I shared my story, and they were all fully engaged. When I finished, everyone seemed stunned. One person went to the bathroom, but when he came back, he told us that he had just told John about the goings-on with us inside, that I was telling them about the empty house. That startled me because John would have known of any enhancements of mine. I would have been found out, my story would have been counted a lie and this person would then be able to tell everyone that I was "full of it." But that's not how it went down. This person just told John that I was talking about an empty house, and John responded with, "Oh, he's telling you THAT story!" Everyone in the room accepted that comment from John as confirmation of the truth of my story with all of its enhancements. It was most gratifying.

The next time I told that story, I was teaching grade 12 English in Prince George, Canada, at a small Christian school with one class for each grade, K-12. So I had the entire graduating class for English near Halloween that year, and, as they were all a bit antsy for "tricks or treats," I "calmed" them with my scary true story with all the enhancements. They were thoroughly engaged for the entire class, so much so that they told the Grade 11 class about my frightening tale. I don't know how many of the details they shared, but the following year, when those former grade-11 students were grade 12 students in my class, they begged me to share the tale with them. Well, of course, I acquiesced, and their reaction, despite a decidedly more uproarious group of students, was similar to their predecessors' response: They were *enthralled!*

After that year, I began teaching at the college just down the street from that high school. And, as I had some repeat students, I was once again begged to tell my story around Halloween. After that, it became a tradition for me to tell the story at least once a year, but often even once a semester, and I never had a bored audience. So I told the story again and again for about ten years. At one point, I was even able to tell it to my three daughters and some of their friends around a campfire when we lived, for a few years, away from town. Eventually, I had told it enough to know which enhancements work best and to discard the others, finally settling into a consistent formula. It wasn't until then that I wrote it.

It would help if you remembered, however, that it is still a true story. I do not wish to tell you which elements are embellishments and which are not, except that John and I went into the navy in late August of 1983, not November. I stretched out the tale so that the concluding event would be nearer to Halloween in the story, but it was actually closer to late July or very early August when that event occurred.

Even many of the embellishments are still true events, just from altogether different occurrences. Still, there is enough truth to the story as is to justify the theme that I feel is so significant, to wit: that God is never in need of being flamboyant in the displays of his might. Sometimes, I suppose, he might make himself abundantly clear by making his activities grand and obvious, but more often than not, his actions are understated, as in 1 Kings 19: 11-13.

> The Lord said, "Go out and stand on the mountain in the presence of the Lord, for the Lord is about to pass by."
> Then a great and powerful wind tore the mountains apart and shattered the rocks before the Lord, but the Lord was not in the wind. After the wind there was an earthquake, but the Lord was not in the earthquake. After the earthquake came a fire, but the Lord was not in the fire. And after the fire came a gentle whisper. When Elijah heard it, he pulled his cloak over his face and went out and stood at the mouth of the cave. (NIV)

Often are we required to search for where he has been at work; his deeds do not necessarily stand out to us. Why is this so? Because he is so magnificently powerful that he doesn't need to make a bigger show—not since the death and resurrection of Jesus, at any rate, has he made such a well-known dramatic display, and there's no denying that that event was a spectacular one indeed.

104

The Empty House
(based on real events)

He who studies evil is studied by evil.
—Solbor's proverb

I need you to understand that the only reason I write this story is that I shouldn't be here to write it at all. By rights, I should have been sacrificed to some wicked thing with horrid eyes, horns, tusks and a long snout. If people are entertained by this story, I suppose that I'll be glad, but I don't write it to entertain. I'd rather forget the event altogether, except that I am haunted by it night and day, every day, and I have been for some thirty years. Mind you, it's not the evil part that haunts me—not at all—it's the idea that whatever good it was that protected me was, by far, greater than the evil right before my eyes, and it saved me, not through magnificent miracles and fantastic flashes of force, but through such inconceivable might, there was simply no need for a more extravagant demonstration of its power.

It began one summer when it was hot and altogether unpleasantly humid. I was twenty. I'd been trying to finagle my way to a music degree at a private college in my hometown of Sioux Falls for two years and was achieving very little. I was significantly less mature emotionally than physically, and, like so many young men, I simply hadn't the self-control to make myself perform my best in all my studies. While I earned "A's" of one type or another in all my various music classes, I achieved distinctly less appealing marks in virtually everything else, producing a wretched 2.5 GPA—clearly, not enough to impress my father, who had been paying my pricey tuition.

The reason for my high grades in music, though, was not that I was so very committed to it, but that all my friends were in music with me. When they practised, I practised; my only other option was to sit around bored. One of these friends was John. He was a year and a half my senior, but we'd been friends since we met in Summer Strings just before my grade-five year, some ten years earlier. He was engaged to Jeanne-Ann, a charming lady, but the prospect of marriage made John choose to seek more remunerative employment to support all three members of his pending family. So he had joined the Navy and was due to depart for boot camp the following November. Now, you have to remember that John was my best friend, and there wasn't a lot going well for me at home. So, when I learned that John had joined the Navy, I promptly did the same. That meant that for us, this particular summer, the summer of 1983, the summer of *Star Wars: The Return of the Jedi* and *Star Trek II: The Wrath of Kahn*, would be our last as independent, single, mildly mature young men. And what were we to do with our time? The South Dakota Symphony, our sole source of income during the rest of the year, had disbanded for the summer, and, since we both still lived with our parents, rather than looking for temporary jobs—surely, the responsible thing to do—we chose to find something more memorable for a summer project.

The idea came to us late one night after watching some gruesome horror movie in John's tiny apartment in the attic of his parents' house. VHS was still a novelty, but, when it came to movies, John was always up to speed no matter how far it set him back. Then, with a beer for each of us and his Ouija board between us, we asked for an idea from whatever spirit realm might be attentive as to what we might do to kill time for the summer. When we were both too toasted to wonder anymore if one us might be responsible for manipulating the handpiece across the board, the Ouija made up our minds for us: "MAKAMOVJA," it said, which we interpreted as, "make a movie" since the "j-a" at the end of this otherwise nonsensical word could be pronounced the same as the "j-a" in Ouija.

So, we decided to make a horror movie. We both had lots of experience watching them, obviously, and John had oodles of experience making little movies of all kinds—in the horror genre: live-action, claymation, two-dimensional animation, and on and on. He owned video cameras, and all the other paraphernalia, primitive as it was, and his basement was stocked with miniature sets that he'd made over the years—he even owned a coffin, an authentic prop from one of his Dracula films! I had virtually unlimited access to a car—a "virgin white," 1973 Oldsmobile, Cutlass Supreme station-wagon with that hideous 1970's lime-green interior. So we set out to make a movie, as we said, "in the tradition of the original *Texas Chainsaw Massacre*," that is to say, "very low budget:" small cast, few props, few locations and zero special effects. Our first task, we decided after I had roughed out a plot, was to find an abandoned farmhouse for our primary set. It didn't really pose much of a problem. In South Dakota, you can't drive twenty miles on any dirt road without passing one, so, in effect, all we needed to do was to head out of town far enough to find a dirt road and go. It took less than an hour from gathering John and his video equipment at his home to pulling in to the unpaved driveway of a house that immediately looked to us to be surprisingly promising—and on our first try!

Numerous dangers kept us both on edge, though. First, the outskirts of Sioux Falls were laden with Satan worshippers (that is, according to our mutual friend, Dave, who loved to frequently share stories of the many horrors he'd heard), and neither John nor I wished to be party to some human sacrifice in any capacity. In addition to that potential danger, though, there were the gangs, the bikers, the homeless people and often just other young adults looking to cause trouble or to get high or to have sex in abandoned farmhouses, especially those as close to town as this one was. None of these people, we suspected, would welcome intrusions by low-ranking movie makers such as ourselves. We chose to err far on the side of caution since neither of us was a fighter; we were musicians, after all. Our idea of winning a fight was escaping it altogether, preferably unscathed.

But we were young, and as chance would have it, I had been keeping—for what reason I haven't a clue—two three-foot sections of hydraulic tubing in my car; it was similar to the tubes used on gas pumps. At that time, my dad was a salesman of hydraulic motors and accessories, among which was this type of tubing designed to be pliable but strong enough to hold vast quantities of viscous hydraulic fluids under tremendous pressure. These two sections of tubing were of obnoxious neon orange and were light-weight but very hard, so that they were easy to wield but quite probably lethal for anyone who might have the misfortune of getting hit on the head with one. We were both comforted by having a section of this tubing to carry as we went about exploring the house.

It was asymmetrically 'T'-shaped and densely surrounded with trees, except where the driveway cut through. The front of the house stood some fifty feet from the road; it had two large windows of slightly different sizes, one on either side of the front door, which was not quite centred under the apex of the roof. A narrow, concrete path led from the dusty driveway to the door that stood atop a flight of three uneven concrete steps and a small, square-ish concrete porch. It sported a screen door in reasonably good condition that stood wired shut on the outside (a good sign), and a formidable wooden door inside. Above the door was another, smaller window, indicating a cramped upper level, and that prospect we found to be both pleasing and frightening. The side of the house to the left, which ran along the end of the driveway, also had two or three windows and, near the back, another door. To use it, though, one would require a set of some five or six steps because the ground lay at a lower level there than it did upfront. But no steps led up to it, and it, too, was wired shut (another good sign).

Looking in through a basement window, we discovered, to our dismay, that it was flooded up to the lower level of the windows. Useless. The back, however, had no barn or corral, just a dense row of trees, and on the other side of that, a vast cornfield that ended with another row of trees on the distant horizon. Yes, this house would do nicely, we decided, the flooded basement notwithstanding. It lacked symmetry, it lacked any sense of hominess; it lacked the freshness of paint or any modern siding, and it lacked any view of the city. A camera could pan a full 360° with no man-made structure, save the road, in sight. It evoked a sense of solitude, of instability, of horror.

It is with a degree of embarrassment that I tell you that it was I who was finally able to pry the wire off the screen door at the front. John was just a violist, so the calluses on his left hand were not nearly as dense as those on mine; I played the double bass. That's how John explained it, anyway. Once the wire was off, we opened the screen door and found the inner door unlocked. The hair on both our necks stood on end, then, as we readied our tubes, and I swung the door open. Inside, the air was stale but not overwhelmingly so. A small mudroom just inside the door opened to a fairly spacious living room that was littered with various types of trash, but no faeces from anything larger than mice. (It's not uncommon for boys to leave their vulgar calling cards behind as a way to claim, "Kilroy was here.") And from the look of it, there were plenty of mice around; the floor was riddled with tiny, hard, brown pebbles that rolled underfoot as we moved, making

108

a crunching sound, like coffee beans in a hand-cranking grinder. Toward the right was a smaller sitting-room with a rotten, holey sofa—not usable, but appropriate for our movie. Behind the living room was the kitchen—a frightful mess—and to the right of the kitchen, two sets of stairs: one leading down to the flooded basement, the other leading up. And it was that flight of stairs, not the one leading down, not the flooded basement itself, not the potentially weakened floor joists beneath us as a result of the flood, not the thought of what horrible diseases lie floating in that water, no, it was that flight of *ascending* stairs and the knowledge that we would need to climb them that gave us pause, for upstairs ... there is where the secret goings-on would occur. Upstairs is where any gang members, bikers, hoodlums, homeless, or—God forbid—Satanists would lie in wait, hiding from us—hiding for us—the intruders. And even if they weren't there at that moment, if they showed up while we were up there, we'd be trapped.

We discussed the next step in some detail, finally deciding that I would go up the stairs facing forward while John would ascend facing backwards, both of us with our tubes at the ready. Up we went. It was a steep stairwell with eight or ten steps that ended right below one of the small, upper-level windows, which was remarkably clean, both the pane and the sill—no dust, no grime, no dead bugs—regardless of the dust that discoloured every other surface. The room immediately at the top of the stairs was nothing more than a small entryway that seemed entirely useless for the human occupants of old, obviously the result of a bad day for whatever make-shift architect had been hired. It ran just a bit longer but was only equally as wide as the stairwell. And since much of the wall was angled with the roof, we had to lean nervously over the stairs as we made our way along the narrow stretch of floor to the back. That trek was especially frightening because there was no railing around the stairwell to help us balance and keep us from falling. We took it slow, grateful that we had no need to hurry.

Directly behind the stairwell stood two doorways, entrances to two other rooms. The room to the right sat without window or any lighting fixture. There was no flooring either, just the joists that lay between the house's upper and lower levels. The wall opposite the doorway was slanted with the roof, and in the small area where light shone in from the other rooms, we could see the pointed tips of the nails that held the shingles in place on the outside. The wall far in the back of the room was shrouded in darkness; the inside wall separating the two back rooms had no drywall, only the studs on that side, exposing the old wiring, but other than those studs, there was no wall on that side of that room.

It was the other room, though, the last room of the house that really grabbed our attention. It was well lighted by one window on the wall opposite the doorway, and that window, again, was remarkably clean for one in the upper level of an abandoned house. Every other part of the room, though—all four walls and the entire floor—was covered by 4'X8' sheets of ¼-inch plywood, loosely but neatly set in place. And in the very centre of the room, directly illuminated by sunlight shining in from the uncovered window, was a neatly-stacked pile of magazines.

One expects to find magazines in such a structure—kid-smuggled pornography for gawking at with buddies. Bikers might leave behind stacks of motor magazines, or there may even be women's magazines left behind by former occupants. But none of that type of reading material was available. Of all the literature that one might expect to find if it were any other abandoned house, what we found was odd, at the very least, but uncannily appropriate—frighteningly appropriate for John and me: It was a stack of dozens of issues of a magazine in which each issue, from the earliest one in the early 1940s to the latest in the late 1970s, focussed on a different classical composer ranging from Henry VIII to some 20th-century composers neither of us had heard of. Immediately, we sat on the plywood covering of the floor like a couple of kids trading baseball cards and looked through this treasure trove of reading material.

Accompanying each composer's detailed biography and timeline summary in each issue were lists compositions and of recordings of those compositions, information about influences, other composers and well-known people in different genres of the arts from the same era. They gave commentaries, interpretative analyses—enough to keep us occupied indefinitely, and we sat engaged in reading for some minutes, carefully setting aside issues to take with us, when John left me alone, somewhat unexpectedly, to explore that unlighted room next door.

After mere seconds I heard a noise like the sound people make when they clear their voices, a sound I hadn't heard when both John and I were together. I called out, "John, are you alright?"

"Yeah. Fine."

So I went back to reading and heard the noise again—a low, guttural, grunting noise, not unlike the sound a pig makes as it roots in its manure. And in fact, it sounded like it came from an animal just that size—the size of a badger, maybe, or a wolverine. I took a moment to ponder the idea that John might have left me in order to relieve himself in private, and that the noise I heard intermittently might also be of a more personal nature. Still, it didn't quite sound like that kind of noise either, so I finally called again, "John, are you ... uh ... coughing?" I had learned some manners, after all, and didn't want to be too crude in my query, lest I end up sounding less concerned about his well being than my own.

110

"Nope," was his response. "Why?"

"I keep hearing a sound like that coming from your direction."

"Right." There was just enough sarcasm in his response to elicit the tiniest bit of ire in me. (Incidentally, John told me later that he was in that room as long as he was because he was trying to reach the far end. He had to wait for his eyes to adjust to the ever-dimming light as he stepped from one joist to the next, but the farther he went, the larger the room seemed to be; he never did reach the far end of the room that couldn't have been deeper than, say, twelve feet, judging by the size of the room beside it.) Moments later, when I heard that noise again, I got up as quietly as I could and snuck over to the wall. Sure enough, I heard it clear as day through the wall separating John and me. I was sure that John must have been making the noise somehow, perhaps with the intention frightening me; there was simply no other explanation since no sound could be produced from inside this wall, which had gyprock on only one side. But as I left the room that I was in so that I could listen at the doorway where John was, I no longer heard the noise, so I assumed that John had heard my footsteps and dummied up. "You are too making that noise," I laughed.

"I'm not making any noise at all."

So I went back into the lighted room and heard the noise again. I talked John into leaving his task to come into the lighted room with me. I suddenly felt that I was playing the role of the stereotypical nervous housewife (if you'll please pardon the cross-gender analogy) waking her husband in the middle of the night to listen for a noise that she is certain she had heard but which never comes again, so I was half expecting the what-ever-it-was to keep quiet and leave me feeling the fool when John came to listen. Thankfully, he did hear it. We took several trips back and forth from one room to the other. Every time we were in the larger, lighted room, we could hear that grunting noise coming from the wall between that room and the dark room. It was intermittent but quite clear. But every time we were in the dark room, standing on the joists, stepping carefully from one to the next, there was nothing—no noise out of the ordinary. We separated once or twice, and always the person in the lighted room was distinctly able to hear the sound that was inaudible at the same instant to the one of us in the dark room. There were no heating ducts in the wall or the floor for some creature to hide in, but that's really irrelevant because the truth ultimately dawned on us: The sound distinctly emanated from inside the wall—from an animal that was surely too large to fit inside a wall that wasn't really there in the first place.

111

That was enough for John, and his apprehension made me nervous as well. We agreed to leave right away. Grabbing our tubes, we walked quickly but cautiously through the narrow hall at the top of the stairs, then descended the stairs more rapidly, departing the house, closing the front door behind us and replacing the wire that had held the screen door closed. In the car on the way back to John's house, we agreed that, even if we still made our movie, we'd have to find another house; there's no telling what that animal was, no telling how dangerous or diseased it might have been, no telling how it could project its grunting vocalizations from within a non-existent wall. There was no way, we promised each other, that we'd ever allow ourselves to be dragged back to that house. Huh-uh. No way.

But we were young and not too bright, evidently. After a few weeks of searching for another house and finding nothing that quite suited our needs, I started thinking about returning to the first house. Nothing really happened to us there, after all, and the place seemed sturdy enough, clean enough and unused enough that it was worth a second go; either that or scrap the movie altogether; time was not on our side. It was John, though, who finally spoke up one morning: "I really wish that we had taken some of those magazines."

"At the first house?"

"Yeah."

"Me too. I was afraid to say anything. What do you wanna do?"

He thought about it for a few moments. "Well, it's not that far away," he finally decided. "We could drive out there, taking all the necessary precautions, go in, get the magazines and leave. No delays. Strictly business."

"Mm," I started, "we could take a flashlight just to see more detail in that dark room and maybe find our creature. It might turn out to have been nothing more than a creak in the floor ... or a squirrel."

"A squirrel that sings baritone!"

"You know what I mean. Besides, we still have our movie to consider." Since the storyline was mine, mainly, and I was quite proud of it on a literary level, I was reluctant to see it go to waste.

John conceded me a point, so I grabbed a flashlight, and we were off. The tubes were still in my car. We made one quick stop for fresh batteries then found the farmhouse lickety-split. We did indeed take all the same precautions: carrying the tubes, entering the house with great trepidation, ascending the stairs with me facing up, and John facing down. We found everything just as we left it. Even the separate piles of magazines we had made remained undisturbed. We breathed a sigh.

112

I don't remember whose idea it was. It might have been mine; I was the one who wanted to find our little lurking creature, after all, but John was really the brains of our twosome. It makes little difference; the point is that somewhere along the way, we got curious about what was behind all those panels of plywood in the lighted room and started to remove them from the walls, stacking them beside the doorway. On the wall with the window and on the wall opposite that we found nothing and nearly gave up for fear of slivers (musicians, you know), but then we went on to that wall, the half wall between us and the dark room. We'd already removed one panel from it during our last visit to look for our critter, but removing the other two panels revealed an enormous mirror, clearly five or six feet from side to side and three, maybe four feet top to bottom. Like the house's two upper-level windows, the mirror was spotlessly clean. Of course, our first thoughts were to consider the value of such a mirror and that it wouldn't be all that hard to lift. What other treasures lay hidden behind these panels, hmm?

John began lifting the panels from the floor while I removed those from the wall opposite the mirror. All I found, painted on the wall in red, was a number—a mathematical formula of some sort: "$2\sqrt{231}$." John's work, however, revealed something so frightening that it made us stifle the screams that threatened to spill from our throats. On the floor beneath the plywood panels, centred where the magazines had been piled, was a pentagram that spanned the room and was accompanied by all the usual calligraphic symbols. The lower tip of the pentagram pointed directly to the centre of the mirror in which my mathematical equation stood in horrifying reflection. Backwards, the formula read as the Latin form of "Jesus," with an "I," rather than a "J," and a "V," rather than a "U." John and I exchanged horrified glances, then, once again we grabbed our tubes, John grabbed his pile of magazines, and we headed out, our hearts pounding like the timpani in the theme from *2001: A Space Odyssey*.

We made it out of the house safely a second time. A second time we secured the screen door; a second time we promised we'd never set foot in that house again, and boy, we meant it this time, yes sir. As I drove, I tried to erase from my brain the route to that house, and we both swore that, not only would we never return, but we'd never speak of that house ever again, so long as we both shall live.

But we were young and not too bright and not a little tipsy that night in late October. Dave, our friend whom I mentioned earlier, had joined us for a quiet evening of wine and music, as did Jeanne-Ann, John's fiancée, although she didn't drink. We were celebrating the aftermath of my twenty-first birthday, so the music of my favourite composer, Alexander Borodin, played quietly on John's stereo. The four of us sat around swapping stories. You know how it goes: you each tell stories on a given topic until the topic expires, then you start exploring other, more thrilling issues, and each person's account has to be just a little better—more exciting, more intense, more frightening—than the last. Finally, Dave told a story about his recent encounter with a Satanist. They'd met in the mall or something, and the guy had tried to convert Dave: "An evangelical Satanist," Dave remarked, "Lucifer's Witness." He continued telling how these guys lure people to sequestered areas for their rituals. It happens in a way that seems like it's your own idea, "although sometimes it might take just a bit of additional coaxing," he added. I remember vaguely thinking that his tale was vividly detailed for a second-hand report and decided that he was embellishing, albeit, not ineffectively. But once he got us on to the subject of Satanists, I became impatient for him to shut-up so that I could share our "secret" tale, despite our vows. The moment he paused, I jumped in: "I can top that." John gave me an angry look, but I was too toasted to care: "I can top that by a long shot!" So with sporadic punches and jabs from John, I told Dave and Jeanne-Ann about the empty house. In all honesty, it wasn't long before John stopped hitting me and started adding details of his own. Jeanne-Ann was horror-struck by John's irresponsibility and the fact that I'd been aiding and abetting him. Imagine putting your life in danger when you have people who depend on you.

Dave sat confidently incredulous: "It's a crock," he concluded.

"No. Really! I can prove it!" I objected.

"How?"

John interjected at this point: "I can diagram the layout of both floors."

"So, I'm supposed to believe you because you can draw a floor plan?" Dave argued.

"I can drive you there without even taking a pause," I offered.

"Oh, so you can drive directly to any one of hundreds of abandoned farmhouses south of town. You'll have to do better than that."

"Well," John said after a few nervous moments for thought, "if I diagram the first floor, and we show it to you, too, that should be pretty convincing, right? But I'm not going upstairs again." Jeanne-Ann nodded approvingly.

That plan satisfied Dave, and he was quite eager for us to be off right away. He even seemed somewhat annoyed when John and I insisted on bringing a flashlight. "It's pitch black outside, and there's probably no lighting in the house," I argued. "How are you going to be able to compare John's diagram with the actual house without light?"

114

"Fine," he said. "Whatever, just hurry up." So the four of us headed out in my car. I look back on this incident and shake my head. There's a certain bravery accorded young adults—a bold tenacity, if you will—that wanes after an all-too-brief period of time. It is, after all, the young adults who seem always to be more willing to take a stand, to block oppression or fight against corruption. It was, perhaps, that same fearlessness that led John to join the Navy. In any event, we need that crusader's attitude to help us carry through some of the more difficult growing times in life, but it's also a source of some of the stupidest acts among humanity, this one included, and it's underscored by the appearance of an owl.

It was an enormous brute, fully two feet tall, and whiter than sheets, whiter than mist, whiter than Fear or Disgust or Death. And there it stood, right in the middle of the road, right where we were to turn onto gravel. I have never seen an owl that size, especially not in South Dakota. His torso faced the direction opposite our turn-off, but his eyes were fixed on us as we approached. I slowed. It stayed. I shut off my headlights. It stayed. I pulled up to within six feet of the thing and stopped, and it just didn't budge; it stood there looking at us for the longest time, and the four of us in the car made no noise other than the sound of our quick, deep breaths as we huddled together.

Finally, after what seemed like minutes, the bird hopped and turned its torso toward us, and then—Yes, I am fully aware of how crazy this sounds—it shook its head at us in a sort of resigned frustration and flew away. The first flap of its enormous wings lifted it higher than the roof of my car so that we all had to bend down and lean in to see it fly out of sight.

At the farmhouse once again, this time a sense of foreboding caused, perhaps, by how very dark it was, prompted us to make sure that the car doors remained unlocked, since we, undoubtedly, wouldn't be in the house for long. We walked apprehensively in single file toward the front door. Dave took up the rear with John just one or two steps ahead of him, and those two carried the hydraulic neon-orange tubes whose colour stood out like beacons in the dark. Jeanne-Ann walked behind me, and I was the idiot leading this expedition armed only with the flashlight and a pocket knife so dull it would more likely have bruised than pierced. I got as far as the concrete steps when I noticed that the screen door was not wired shut and that the inside door stood open. My mind raced: We wired the door closed. I'm positive we did. Didn't we wire the door closed?

115

Behind me, my three comrades huddled together at the bottom of the steps, leaving me to ascend them alone. They said nothing. My heart thumped; I breathed uneasily, and I could feel sweat collecting on my brow. Swallowing hard in response to stress, I reached for the handle, pulled the screen door open and shone the flashlight inside. Everything appeared to be in order. I took another step so that I had one foot and my forearm just inside the doorway, the screen door braced against my hip, and that's when it happened. A sound—a shuffle just past the mudroom. It was the unmistakable sound of a shoe scraping the floor with perhaps a half dozen mice droppings rolling underfoot. It suggested to me that someone decided at the last instant to double-check that he was entirely cloaked in darkness. I felt myself freeze for an instant, then I turned to my entourage and yelled, "Run like Hell!" The four of us scrambled for the car. Jeanne-Ann sat shotgun while I raced around to the driver's side, pulling the keys from my pocket. Dave and John took the back. We slammed the doors and locked them while I started the car, put on the headlights, threw the car in reverse and backed out of the driveway as fast as I knew how. But as I was backing onto the road, turning the car on to the highway, the back end leapt up, and we came to an abrupt stop with the back end sticking up in the air as though the car were in heat. I had been looking at the road as I backed up; to this day I swear that there had been nothing on that spot while it was in view, but something held us in place with the back end suspended in mid-air and with the headlights illuminating the entire front of the house. I tried speeding forward but just spun the tires in mid-air. That's when Jeanne-Ann screamed; I looked up, and I think we all froze for a spell. There, in the window, dressed in a robe with an over-sized hood that pointed up and back, stood an intimidatingly large man, an odious parody of Obi-Wan Kenobi. He simply stood and looked menacingly out at us. And there was a feeling—oh, yes—there was a sinister spirit, a malevolence washing from him. We stared at him in shock and disbelief until John finally grabbed my arm: "Drive!" I only ended up spinning the tires more, and that's when I noticed movement among the trees surrounding the house. Hoards of hooded figures, like scores of over-sized Jawas, stepped out from hiding and came walking into the light with all the speed of hunters who stroll leisurely about the woods checking their traps. I tried backing up more; I tried speeding forward; we weren't going anywhere. That's when Dave spoke up: "We're completely stuck, guys; we might as well give it up."

Then an amazing thing happened: the back end of the car simply fell with a thud, as though whatever it was under the car had vanished, leaving the vehicle

116

to drop like Yoda's blanket after his demise. Everyone outside froze, stared at us, then scattered like a flock of hens when they've spotted the fox. That's when Dave started to panic: "Oh, God! What was that?! What happened?" he cried. We all turned to try to calm him down. He got the question out one more time before he, too, faded from sight the way a puff of thin smoke dissipates in a closed room. I looked to the others for a moment, but none of us said anything. I suddenly felt quite at ease, remarkably, and backed the rest of the way on to the road, pulled the gear shift into 'Drive,' and rode away in a surprisingly calm manner.

That was thirty-three years ago now. None of us ever saw Dave again, and as time progressed, we simply stopped inquiring about him altogether. John and I never made our movie. I've never returned to that house; I doubt that I'll ever try to. John and I spent four years in the Navy and were both able to grow up quite a bit. I put that time to good use, deciding that I didn't want a degree in music after all. I left the Navy, knowing that I would major in English and that I would do well, so I ceased taking music courses, and my GPA climbed during my second attempt at a degree. John and I slowly parted ways, and I haven't seen him now for ages. He and Jeanne-Ann were married and had two children. It's strange to think that those two kids are older now than I was when this all happened. Isn't that odd? It seems to me, even thirty years later, that they should still be kids, presumably the age that their own kids might be.

But that empty house changed the way I think about life and death, the here and the hereafter, Heaven and Hell, that sort of thing. I think John and I were selected for some type of ceremony, that we were led to that house, that we were lured to that unholy upper room. I suspect that there was a great deal of planning went into this scheme because think about how elaborate such a plan would have to be, what patience someone demonstrated in trying to claim us: the Ouija board, the perfect house, the magazines, the solitude. I look at that and conclude, that, despite all the awful things we see daily in life, there is something good around that is immeasurably more powerful than the evil that seems to prevail, because look at how this being who wields such extraordinary power demonstrates his superiority: Does he wipe evil out of our way with a wave of his mighty hand? Does he cause the earth to open and swallow his enemy's followers? No. But what does he do to foil his enemy's plans? He causes me to hear one of them scrape a shoe across the floor, and that—with all of its understated confidence—spells power even more than great storms with blinding bolts of lightning. I suppose that, every once in a while, there will be a need for a Mt. Carmel event—magnificent miracles to force open people's eyes, such as the apostle

117

Paul's experience on the road to Damascus, but such is not the norm. After all, why bring a tanker of water to flood a desert when all you need is an eyedropper? That's what my mind insists on concluding every time I think about this incident; it underscores the whole event for me, and it's for only that purpose that I write it.

THE END

Introduction to
"The Ghost and the Zombie"

SCARE SCORE 1 2 3 4 5

"The Ghost and the Zombie" is, perhaps, the story with the most literary origins of any in this collection, and as one in the category of horror, there is, in reality, nothing horrific about it. I do not wish to malign horror by saying that it is less than literary. Horror can be intensely literary on a scale of Oscar Wilde and Richard Wright. I only mean to say that I wasn't trying to write horror when I wrote "The Ghost and the Zombie." I was trying to create a work of art that introduced something new for discussions regarding the roll of the narrator in fiction.

For years I taught high school and university students that the narrator in a first-person story is always a major part of his or her own story. That is, when the narrator is identified as "I" in the story, then the narrator is usually the protagonist or at least a major character. As such, the narrator will have a story arc in which he or she develops or matures. Protagonist or not, the narrator in a first-person story is an integral part of that story. That's the rule. Now let's discuss some exceptions to that rule. Stephen King, in his written original version of "Rita Hayworth and Shawshank Redemption" makes fun of his own first-person narrator when that narrator, Red, accuses the reader of complaining that Red is a minor character in his own story. Even though Red argues against that stand for a couple of lines, it's still a fascinating point with some weight to it. I know that I was thrilled to read that idea at the young age of 15. Since then, I have wanted to move my first-person narrators out of the way of their respective tales just to see if it could be done.

My story, "Onessimus: Troy's Fall Denied," is the earliest in this volume and the first attempt to keep my first-person narrator from being a part of his own story. I used him to introduce each segment and comment at the end, but that is all the reader sees of him. "How Meleager Met His Maker" is much the same. The narrator shares events that he has witnessed but barely, if at all, participated in. As early pieces, I'm not entirely displeased, but there is still something missing. First-person narrators must still be "round" characters who develop during their narratives, and these two do not. It's not just a matter of them not needing to grow. The problem is that they are two-dimensional characters—"stock" or "flat" characters is the term used in most literature classes. Flat characters are background beings. In movies, they are the characters you see, but who have few if any lines, and as a result, we learn nothing of them, nothing of their backgrounds, their thoughts or their feelings. Flat characters are there to fill the screen so that a gang looks like a gang instead of just the leader and his friend, or so that the army troop looks like a troop rather than just a captain and the sergeant, or so that the city is populated with people, even if we never get to "know" any of them. That's what my two narrators are ultimately. I wanted more for my narrator of "The Ghost and the Zombie."

My goal for "The Ghost and the Zombie" was to have a first-person narrator not even remotely associated with the events of the story except in the relating of those events to my readers in my stead. And yet, this narrator must still be a three-dimensional character with his own story arc: he must grow and learn and develop during his story.

I had made several attempts to achieve these goals with other stories, but they failed in many cases because I got so emotionally invested in either the characters or the storyline that I was trying to pretend that I hadn't created, that I had to finally admit that I had, indeed, created them, so I could take over as narrator. Some of those stories I was able to save in revisions, but most I ultimately scrapped. What I needed in order to have my narrator utterly separate from his or her characters were characters that I—as the writer—could not invest myself in. That is, I needed characters in whom I could not believe. And since I utterly cannot believe in ghosts or zombies, mainly because my belief in the Bible precludes a belief in nonsense, I selected one of each for protagonists. Then, to keep the narrator out of the story, I imagined, as I wrote, that my narrator was part of a gathering of people who were playing a game—something akin to charades, but in this case, instead of silently describing a title of a known book or movie, my narrator, whom I imagined as the one who is "it," had to improvise a story on the spot. I imagined that he had to select a style and a pair of characters blindly in separate draws from bowls or hats and then extemporize with perhaps a few moments of quiet thought for preparation. Then I imagined how I would open such a tale, and once I "heard him starting to tell it," I had my story.

I believe that I succeeded. I achieved my goals. I have two characters in whom I cannot believe. I have a narrator who learns and develops during the story, which gives him an arc and a higher degree of believability as a character. It was enough believability, at any rate, that the theme of the story centres around the narrator, which it should when you have a first-person narrator. Indeed, it was that point that indicated success to me. While the two mythological characters also develop

120

and change and perhaps even draw out a minor theme or themes of their own, they and it are overshadowed by the narrator, as they should be.

It is, indeed, a whimsical tale, hardly frightening at all, and it's not meant to be. Even the theme has nothing to do with horror and has everything to do with art. As I have said, the story's real purpose, so far as the writer is concerned, is to be a tale in which the first-person narrator stands apart from, not as a part of the action of his own story, almost becoming a 3rd-person narrator—almost omniscient, but not quite, but still having his own story arc as the narrator of any first-person story would have. Therefore, my story cannot be autobiographical, as first-person narratives usually are, nor can it be pseudo-autobiographical as are the most of the remaining such stories are. It is a tale created entirely on the fly, and even the flies have nothing to do with either the ghost or the zombie.

The Ghost and the Zombie

A work of art knows what it wants to be
before you set pen to paper ...
—Dr. Mary Prior

I'm going to tell you a whimsical tale of a ghost and a zombie. A ghost, as you know, is the incorporeal remnant of a living being—a spirit. It could, perhaps, be an animal's spirit, but the ones most corporeal people are concerned about—the ones that scare them—are the ones disembodied from other people, so this latter type of ghost is the type I shall use in my story. A zombie, on the other hand, is the animated, flesh-eating physical remnant of a living being, again, in most cases, a HUMAN being. What animizes the body without its spirit? Who's to say? I know of none that have been captured and studied to discover the cause, as fascinating as that might be. Only this I know: I believe in them: zombies, vampires, ghosts, goblins, ghouls. Some people believe in Santa Claus, others in angels. I can accept them, but it's more fun to truly believe in the macabre. It does, after all, make for wonderful stories that have a life all their own, engendering gasps and embraces among audiences, especially around a campfire, doesn't it? There are, of course, those who do their best to remain aloof to the possibility of phantoms for whatever reason, but they cannot do so in this story, for they are already caught up in it, you see, and must continue their way through it, for even if they were to leave it now, it would not leave them. They are very much trapped, not unlike the spirit in the body or the ghost and the zombie, if you will.

I open the story some fifty years ago. Let's just make it 1965—nice and easy—right near Philadelphia. It was early evening, as these stories are wont to be set. The ghost found itself floating along in the fashion ghosts are, likewise, wont to float in stories such as these. It blew through a wooded area in the very early spring, not in the fall. The trees were yet bereft of leaves, but Hope, recently emancipated from its ancient prison, waited in the proverbial wings. After all, what is a story of death without some hope of hope, may I ask? Well, the ghost breezed through the trees while the trees, in turn, also breezed through it, and it spied a man. Or what it thought was a man. It honestly looked to the ghost very much like a man, and so it elected to "spook" the man, for that is what ghosts do, you see. I suppose it makes them feel alive. Or perhaps it gives them a sense of superiority, for surely a man would never frighten a ghost. The ghost placed itself directly in the path of the man and ... stopped moving. Well, I can't really say that it "stood there," now, can I? Certainly not! A ghost, this one, in particular, has no legs. It's little more than a mist, a floating vapour that is only dense enough to be perceived when the failing light hits it at just the right angle, with not too much intensity, lest it instantly dissipate. But the man, you see, taking no notice of the ghost at all, kept lumbering his way through the woods and the ghost, grinding to mush the decaying leaves under his feet, his back rolled forward, his arms dangling lifelessly to his sides, as though they were too heavy to be swung in the usual manner for a man. He was a somewhat smartly dressed man, apparently in his early 30's, with blond hair—slightly ruffled, parted just off centre, and with a heavy sport coat that indicated a particular flair for fashion ... for the day.

The ghost was surprised but not deterred by the man's lack of response. It was, after all, just fog, and not at all terribly discernable to a man who appeared to be distracted by some critical thought, as though he were late for some important date; the ghost tried again with its "Boo" thing, you see? But the man appeared to simply have no time to trifle with being frightened at all; the idiot kept right on going, to the great frustration of the ghost. "How dare he be so bloody bold?" the spirit wondered. So it sped again in front of the man, placed itself directly in his path, and the man, unfettered by any fear of anything—or thought of anything, for that matter, truth be told—plowed directly through the spirit a third time without so much as a flinch.

Well, I do believe that the ghost got a bit peeved, ultimately. It brought out the "heavy guns," shall we say? And delivered a goose-bumping, spine-chilling, will-melting barrage of scary screams, and THAT finally got the attention of the man. Mind you, if a spirit could be out of breath, this one surely would have been at this point, but, as a spirit is a breath, and one cannot be "out of one's self," as it were, the encounter proceeded unencumbered. The man stopped suddenly in his steps and seemed to freeze. "Now, there's a good little man!" The ghost thought aloud, smiling smugly, although, you'd never be able to tell. After a brief while, the man turned his head slowly around, eyes wide, jaw dropped with just a little spittle spilling from the corner of his mouth, and that's when the ghost noticed it. "Finally!" You might say to yourselves, because, even though you may already have "gotten it," the ghost hadn't understood until just then that the man wasn't a man at all; hadn't been for some hours, you see.

This story doesn't take place in a cemetery because such a setting would be what we in literary circles call "cliché;" that is to say, a cemetery would be an old idea, overused, commonplace, even. There is, however, a cemetery in the back story, just a hundred yards or so ... in back of the "man." He had come to place flowers on his mother's grave, when—long story short—he fell, bumped his head on a tombstone, made a nasty gash, and died. In no time at all, he was back on his feet in search of supper, for, you see, this man was now a zombie, and zombies need to eat, or ... well, since zombies are dead, I suppose they don't need to eat in order to live, they just need to eat, if there is, indeed, something around to be eaten. It actually makes perfect sense if you think about it. Our bodies' natural and initial instinct is to suckle—to eat. When a zombie becomes a zombie, that inclination still exists. Mind you, if there is no food, a zombie continues on not living anyway. After all, it can't exactly starve to death, now can it? Certainly not.

So, as I was saying, the ghost looked into the eyes of this "man," seeing the lifelessness there, seeing the coagulated blood that had been spilling from the mortal wound, seeing the reason for the dangling jaw and arms and contemplating the lumbering stride, and ultimately, albeit slowly, these ideas came together into one coherent moment of realization for the ghost that this "man" was no longer a man at all, but was, in fact, deceased. What the body was doing up and around in such a state was beyond the understanding of the ghost, but being deceased itself, it really gave that particular question not much thought at all. But since the ghost was lost in contemplation, it was actually the zombie that first connected the proverbial dots, believe it or not. Yes, you see, the zombie—conveniently not so vacuous as one might expect—was able to set aside its fixation for food for a moment and see that its own eyes were focussed on a familiar spirit, after all. It turned its entire body to the apparition and said—and I quote, "Uuuuuuuh huuuuuuuungh!"

"Excuse me?" the ghost moaned, because, you see, a ghost wouldn't just speak. It must, after all, sound like a ghost, mustn't it?

The zombie took a clumsy, heavy, laboured step toward the spirit, bent one arm at the elbow, then bent it again in the correct direction, tapped its chest with its palm and declared again, "Uuuuuuuuh huuuuuuuungh!" And since the ghost was still not perceiving, the zombie repeated itself with yet greater emphasis: "Uuuuuuuuh Huuuuuuungh!"

Strangely enough, if not merely conveniently, the ghost finally understood the zombie and so was able to understand the situation, too. Now, don't start thinking Deus ex Machina. It's not, I assure you. Bear with me. But, you see? Here's the hope that I promised you!

The zombie had "recognized" (for want of a better term) the spirt as its own spirit. And, after a time, the ghost also understood that it was, itself, the spirit of what had been THAT man. They knew each other, and THAT is also why they were able to understand each other. Now, you see, if I had told you that was foreshadowing before, I would have destroyed this surprising plot twist; am I right? At one time—one very recent time—the ghost and the zombie had both been one complete man—part and parcel of the same person, separate entities now: one without substance, the other without depth. It's actually quite sad, come to think of it. Imagine a child finding his lost dog that had, for some many months, or perhaps even years, been loved by another child who had rescued it, and the dog had, subsequently, become fully devoted to the second child. You see how sad that might be? Both the ghost and the zombie felt a bit like that first child and regarded the other as something akin to its own long lost dog. How very sad, indeed. You know, this isn't at all the direction I had wanted to go with this story. Well, I'll keep going and try to get back on track.

The zombie hobbled again toward the ghost—one, two, three very awkward steps and reached a heavy arm out. In response, the ghost floated down to the zombie and stared for a long moment, blank eye to darkened eye, and if you were to have listened very closely, you might have heard the theme from "Romeo and Juliet" playing softly in the background. The question that hovered between them like an invisible bubble from the comics and held them in such a long, visual embrace is this: "Can we be spliced back together? Can the two halves be made a whole again?" My! How touching! Oh, dear! This isn't the story that I set out to tell at all! Well, I guess we'll just see where it takes us.

The zombie reached out with both arms in a vain attempt to stuff the spirit back into itself, but its arms simply passed through the ghost very much as we move through the air. The two remained in place, neither one closer to the other than it had been. The ghost, perceiving the zombie's desire and seeing it fail in its endeavour, moved into the zombie like a cold gust of wind into a drafty old house. But, even though the spirit could, in fact, move into the body, there was nothing for it to use to attach itself within; no locking mechanism to hold them together as one, you see? As quickly as it had blown into the zombie, the ghost blew right back out again, and neither one felt more or less alive than it had just moments before. The two entities, dejected and forlorn, resigned themselves very soon after.

Now, let's just think about this for a minute; this must have been a painful experience. I suppose it may have been a situation very much like a person experiencing a phantom limb after an amputation, maybe, or... well, perhaps not. You see, a person can recover, actually quite quickly, from the phantom limb once he knows that it is, in fact, a phantom. No, it's not like that at all. It's more like ... It's like a large, deep incision on the inside of a joint, such as the underside of the toe right near the pad of the foot, so that the wound takes much longer to heal because it's always being stretched and turned. The toe isn't severed; there's still a connection, but because of the wound's location, it's much more difficult to hold the two edges together to aid healing. Consider for a moment, the death of a spouse rather than a divorce from the spouse: There's nothing easy about losing a loving spouse to the Grim Reaper, really, but, as awful as it is, it's easier to recover from a death, because, with divorce, the wound of loss is continually torn open, again and again. Every time you see your former spouse, you're reminded that you're no longer the same person you had been, but try as you might, you can't reattach yourself. There is the person that, just yesterday, you loved, but today, you're no longer allowed to. There's still a connection, but there's really no way to bandage it, and healing is prolonged. Yes, this situation is more like divorce than death: here are these two entities who were, just recently joined, but were suddenly thrust apart—divorced, as it were, through death. And, as the ghost and the zombie were both deceased as a result of this divorce, there was no healing for them at all. In a way, then, the ghost's appearance for the zombie is more like that of a wraith—a harbinger of its own end, I suppose.

Oh! Goodness! this is bleak! I'm not happy with how this story is turning out at all, but, it very much seems that I shall have to finish it now that it's come this far. Complete what I have started? Where shall I go from here, I wonder. What else is there that needs telling? Give me just a moment, please.

126

Well, the spirit met its end quite swiftly after that, actually. It began backing away from the zombie but eventually began to float up, up and away, quite literally, allowing itself to be carried on a friendly, warm, easterly breeze. Higher and higher it flew; faster and faster it sped on its way, little by little losing parts of itself, leaving droplets of itself behind until finally, there was nothing left but the breeze that had taken it, and so the ghost met its end in a matter of minutes.

The zombie's end was much more protracted, for his particular breeze was less stiff than, well, than the stiff—in comparison to the ghost and the breeze that carried it away. The zombie watched his former other half move off into the heavens like some child watching a kite flying away after the breaking of its string, then walked away in an oblique direction from his original course. As fate would have it, it was the direction of desolation—of non-habitation. Long he wambled, by chance avoiding populated areas for many days, into weeks, skimming city limits, never purposely but always successfully avoiding living people.

As he moved, since he was not living, he grew gangrenous. It became visible first around the wound on his face and then on his hands. Of course, he gave it no notice at all, but he, nonetheless, became zombier and zombier as time went on. Ultimately, he began losing pieces of himself—a hand first, then the arm below the elbow. Finally, his very jaw became unusable, dangling to the side of his face like the excessively long tongue of a slobbering canine, and he ultimately abandoned his mandible in a field, just northwest New York—the city of lights. When he lost his leg below the knee, he crawled on what was left of his "all fours" until, finally, the weight of decay worked its way through the neck bones, and his jawless head fell to the earth, severed from the body by the dull, slow slicing blade of decomposition. It rolled back a few feet down the hill that he'd been slowly ascending. He crawled no more then, and no one can be certain just how very long he remained undead after that, but, in time—after his few remains were scavenged by critters and the skeleton picked clean by worms and ants—a pile of dried human bones, minus one leg and one arm, was discovered by a pair of nature-loving hikers, guy and gal. They had planned a year-long trip cross-country along the 49th parallel to Mount Baker because, in those days, you could do such things in certain parts of the world without having to worry about family posting your picture at every corner store in town. The spot where the bones lay in the sun was only their first stop, not even a full day into their journey. The skull, minus the jaw, was lying separately, just a couple of feet to the south, the eyes gazing to the West. The leg, arm and jawbone were never recovered, but no one really gave their loss much thought, to begin with.

There was an investigation. Some suspected foul play. After all, what would a body be doing "out there where there's nobody?" The hikers were never suspected because, clearly, the bones had been there for some time, but they were never really looked on the same after this incident, either. Of course, nothing could be proved about the remains either way, and the investigation eventually lost momentum. It was finally declared an "Unsolved Mystery," as redundant as that might be, but one that no one cared to read about in the tabloids. It simply lacked glamour. The case's file has since collected many years' worth of dust, buried in what has ultimately become an unmarked cabinet in a musty, unused basement in a little-known, seldom-visited adjunct office of the police homicide division, and such is the monument that remains for this poor fellow: unvisited, virtually unknown, decidedly forgotten.

And now, I suppose, you want some grand finale? Some surprise discovery that ties everything together for your satisfaction, hmm? Well, I'm sorry. There is none. There would have been had this story not spontaneously taken on a life of its own. But now, it appears that, rather than a tale with a nicely rounded conclusion, apparently, you'll have to accept my long, sad, tapered end.

THE END

Introduction to
"The Old Witch"

SCARE SCORE 1 2 3 4 5

I am 1/4 Irish, and I love that part of me. I'm not saying that I don't love the other parts, but in recent years, I have learned to appreciate the Irish-ness in me in ways that the other parts of me just don't quite measure up, at least not yet. So, I wrote "The Old Witch" for two reasons, and only those two: 1) To write something as wholly Irish and authentically Irish as I was able. 2) To have fun doing it.

Don't get me wrong: The theme is still an important component, and it may even be one of the finer and more important themes I've ever explored, but without the theme, it wouldn't be literature. It MUST have a theme, but no rule says that I have to have as much fun writing as I did while writing this story. In fact, the only reason that it's in the "Horror" section is that there is, in fact, a witch in the story. He's one of the significant characters, and he's a favourite character.

There are, really, only the two characters, and both of them are Irish. The Narrator's Irish accent I modelled after Miles O'Brien of *Star Trek* fame; his accent comes from the north and isn't quite as prominent as that of the witch. The witch is from the south of Ireland, so his accent is thicker, but since I only know that I'm 1/4 Irish, and I don't know if that part of my heritage comes from the north or the south of Ireland, I wanted to represent both in this story.

The Old Witch
The Story of an Irishman

There was an old witch.
Believe it if you can.
—Children's song

The funny thing about him is that he's really a nice guy. It's even easy to like him, which can be a bit scary, if you ask me. But that's how I recognized him. By all reports, he's a friendly, charming fella who's even a bit of fun to have a drink with. But y'can't let yourself be fooled: while he is gregarious—and there's no denyin' that he is—he's also a bit solitary and menacin', and while he's handsome, he's also ... vile. I mean, he may be a nice witch, but, let's be honest, here: He is a witch.

He's an Irishman, too. Still carries the accent even after all this time. By all appearances, he's a man in his early thirties—about ten years my junior—dark hair and eyes, and, while distinctly Caucasian, he's darkly complected. But'e claims to be a mere thousand years old, while some of the accounts regarding him predate The Battle of Hastings by a century or two. I guess even witches lie about their age. If it were me, I'd be bragging it up a bit: "I'm twelve ... HUNDRED years old," that sort o'thing. But that's just me.

His game is poker, but he doesn't play for money. Y'see, he puts a hex on the chips before a game, and they become numbers of years that you're gambling with—years of your life. If you lose, y'might have time enough to say goodbye to your loved ones before those lost years catch up with you. But make no mistake, by night's end, you're a corpse—if you lose. If you win—well, that's what you're there for, isn't it? Y'come in at ninety years old. Maybe widowed. Kids all grown and gone—left y'for dead in a nursin' home, maybe. Y'win a lucky hand with this fella', and the next day, you're out chasing chicks again, no way for anyone to know that you're starting a second life. But y'see, that's the trap. Y'win enough, y'can live forever right here on good ol' planet earth.

The thing is, I can't understand anyone wanting that—not really. Terra Firma isn't so "firm" when you look at it. I mean, really look. Why would you want to live forever in a life that's filled with sickness and loss and pain? Don't get me wrong: There are wonderful things in this life, but I know where I'm goin' when I die, and I want to go there. I'll not hurry the process along, but why purposely delay it? I mean, why would you go through twelve years of school just to get to your senior grade and start it all over again, especially if you know that better things'll folla' going forward? My school years weren't that spectacular, thank you very much. The next time I hear "Pomp and Circumstance" playin' on a loop, I won't be marchin' up t'get m'certificate for a second time; I want it to be when I'm ascending Jacob's stair, marchin' up t'Heaven t'get m'crown.

So, you'll meet this fella in a bar on a weekend night. He'll buy you a drink or two, tell you what he's about, and challenge you to a game. Mind you, he's good, so he doesn't go for the easy marks—not often, anyway. Like anyone else, he enjoys a challenge, so usually, he goes for the brainy type: those who can play the game well enough, but who are arrogant enough to think that they can win enough to keep their brains and their looks for an extra decade or two. But then, like I said, he's also a nice guy. One time when'e had a winning hand and knew it, he bluffed—let his opponent walk away with some fifteen extra years, and the ol' guy lived to see his great-grandson graduate. If he loses, he's not known to welsh, and people have come away 'feeling young again.' But mostly he wins, and, well, that's why he's as old as he is, isn't it?

I've known about'm most of m'adult life. I teach British History at Queens University Belfast, and I did my dissertation on'm—believin'm to be a myth, o'course. Now, I haven't taught anything about'm. I mean, it's not like there are long accounts of'm to have students read and discuss in class. He's more of the type of thing writers mention in passin': "I know a guy who knows a guy," if you

131

see what I mean. Even so, like Scotland's Loch Ness, y'read about this guy from about 850 AD and into modern times. But like that one famous picture of Nessie in the 30s, the accounts of this witch seem to end abruptly just before the second world war.

Then, about a month ago, when I was visitin' family in London, I overhear people talkin': "There's a bloke at the pub last night. 'E says 'e wants to play poker, but not for money, 'e says, but for time! I says, 'Boy-o, if y'wanna spend some time playin' a game, 'ow's about some darts? I says.' 'E says, 'No, no, no, mate. Let's play poker.' Then 'e says, 'If you win,' 'e says, 'you win years added to your life.' An' I says, 'wha' if I lose?' An' 'ere's wha' he says! 'E says, 'If you lose, I win years taken offa' your life.' So I thinks. An' then I laughs, an' I says, 'Matey, if you think I'll be playing you for years, y'might'a been drinkin' too much,' that's wha' I says."

Well, it was enough to get me thinkin', y'know? If there's already a thousand years of stories about this fella, scattered here and there all throughout British literature and documents, isn't it possible, just ... y'know ... possible that the person they're talkin' about is the same fella? If the stories have any truth at all, I decide it is possible. So I go to the pub and wait, hopin' t'see him. Hopin' t'recognize him.

Turns out that I'm there about three hours before he shows up. At least, I think it's 'im. I work my way around the pub until I find a place to sit near him so I can listen in without bein' noticed.

Now, don't go on talkin' stalkin' t'me. We're talkin' about a twelve-hundred-year-old witch, here, not some helpless waitress headin' home at two in the mornin'.

Anyway, I hear him talkin', and I get the confirmation I need. I even get his name. It's him, alright. So, the next day I'm stunned, right? I mean, on the one hand, I've spent my life studyin' this fella', and there he is. It's like meetin' Elvis or the Queen on the street, and all I can think is, "What does this ... bein' ... have to say about the last thousand years of history? Have you ever wondered things like that? It's pretty compellin' stuff for an history buff like me. I remember going into Westminster Abbey in London and wondering pretty much the same thing there: If this place could talk, oh, the things it could teach us! The events it would have witnessed, the atrocities that took place within its own walls and the horrors outside o' them. The weddin's, the interments and the coronations. The preachin's and the teachin's, the truths and the lies, the wars and the truces. Listenin' to somethin' with that kind of learnin', that kind of wisdom, it would make me feel like Mary in the Gospels sitting at the feet of Jesus, just takin' in all that he had to say. I'd take in all that the Abbey had learned and all that it could share. An' this fella's older yet! The insight, the perspective of someone like that. I was mesmerized; I really was!

On the other hand, this fella IS a witch, and he's twelve hundred years old, even if 'e does lie about his age. How easy would it be for'm to out-think me? An' if I make'm mad? Can 'e hex me out of existence? No, really? Could he? He's the first witch I ever come across. How do I know what he can and can't do?

I'm there three nights before we finally talk; I'm still payin' off the tab. He comes to m'table with a toothpick in his mouth 'n'tells me that he's seen me around the past while; can he share a table with me? So, I tell'm, y'know, have a seat; he buys me a drink, and we make small-talk for a while before he asks if I play poker. Well, short story made trifle, we retire to a private antechamber where he has a table all set up—rife with a bottle of my favourite Scotch, I might add. How he knew my favourite, I'll never get. It's Canadian. They don't serve it at the pub.

In this room the light's different from in the bar: it's brighter. He tells me t'have a seat, and while I'm waiting for him to set the chips on the table, it's the first chance I've had to really look at the guy, and what I see is ... how should I say? ... less than impressive, I suppose, and I start havin' doubts—second thoughts. He sets the chips centre table and kinda' waves a hand over them, and while he does, he closes his eyes and chants something in old Gaeilge. I don't speak it m'self, but I've heard it plenty.

So, he sits across from me with a fresh toothpick in his jaw. He holds the deck of cards to his chest an' smiles in a friendly manner: "As host, I reserve the right to deal first," he says.

"Fair enough," I say, smiling back at him, an' he starts dealin' the cards an' says, "The game is five-card draw. Nothin' wild. Ten-year limit. The ante is one year."

I ante up an' look at m'cards. I know what I have, but m' brain suddenly shifts away. In m' mind, I'm seeing image after image of Saint Martin's Church in Canterbury, England. It was like being forced to watch a slide show of all my memories of the structure. I've only been there ... what, three times, I think, but my mind is suddenly revisiting the buildin' in incredible detail. I see dozens of images in just a second or two, an' they leave me with a sense of inspiration, even ... insight, I think. "Do you mind if I tell you somethin'?" I say.

He looks at me with surprise for a second, then he smiles. It's one of those grinnin', confident smiles, an'e says in words exactly what that smile already said: "I know precisely wha' you'll say, Pal, but I'm not changin' the chips back."

"Wha'?"

"Y've committed to playin' this game, so, like it r'not, y're playin' fr' years."

I smile and chuckle, then shake me 'ead. "No, that's not what I was goin' t'say."

"What, then?" he asks, an' he seems genuinely curious.

I think about it for a moment. It seemed a long time then, but I suppose, looking back on it now, it was only two or three seconds. But I finally say, "What can you tell me about Dublin when it was just a Viking port?" "Anythin'?" I ask.

He pulls the toothpick from his mouth, shakin' 'is head. "What's this about, now?" he asks with a grimace.

"What about King Cenwulf, or Egbert of England?" I ask then. "Any insights there?"

He shakes his head again, like he's confused, but his expression is that of a person who's frantically searching for a lie as a cover-up, but with anxiety preventin' success. "Y'see," I say, "I actually came to this pub to meet you, not to play poker."

"Y' wanted to meet me," he says with a laugh. "What am I then, the Pope?"

I chuckle again. "No. Not at all."

"What is it yer after, then?"

I take a breath. "It is you whom the chronicler, Bishop Asser, mentioned to King Alfred The Great in the context of discussing Cenwulf, isn't it? Cenwulf played a game with you, didn't he, the last king to rule before Egbert ruled a united England. He played against you and lost. Didn't he?" It really isn't a question I'm askin', but it comes off as more of an accusation than I intend. I only mean it as a statement.

"I'll put it to you again, then:" he tells me, "what is't you're after?" He leans over the table toward me. "Are y'thinkin' to blackmail me?"

"Nothin' like that."

"What then?"

"It's hard to describe," I tell 'm. "I wanted to talk to you, is all. At first, anyway. I wanted to see if I could gain some ... understandin'. Y'see, I've pretty much made a career out of you. There are accounts of you throughout British history in letters, chronicles, courtly documents ... you're even briefly mentioned in some obscure medieval Romances and lais: 'The witch with the crime / To taketh or giveth thee time, / while you decay either way.' That's you, isn't it?"

He nods thoughtfully. "Aye, 'tis. What is't you're wantin' to talk about?"

I look at him, almost staring at him for a long moment. "I'm not sure," I finally say with a frustrated laugh.

"Y've obviously waited quite a while to speak with me, and when the moment arrives, y'can't think of a blessed thing to say? C'mon, boy-o: Opportunities like this don't come along every day. What is't that's holdin' y'back?" he asks.

"It's different," I say, but it's not even clear to me what's different, not yet, anyway.

He smiles incredulously, shaking his head and thrusting forward a bit. "What could possibly be different?" he asks, and I allow myself a good few seconds before I respond. I think back to just days before, when I wanted to meet him: What was I wonderin'? What was my urgency? In a few seconds, I see a mental picture of Westminster Abbey in London, and it dawns on me: This is a man, not a buildin'. That's the difference. As obvious as that may seem, it hadn't really occurred to me. I had wanted to hear from ancient structures that had witnessed history, t' hear history taught by a two-thousand-year-old witness, like a tree or an ancient buildin'. That's the sort of thing I wanted, but before me was not a tree or a buildin'. He's a man. Maybe he was also a witch, but when all the excess is carved away, he's just a man. When my mind had assembled all the separate parts, I nod m' head slowly with comprehension. "Y'present the appearance of a man of about 35 years or so, wouldn't you say?"

He nods first, then tips his head back as if in understanding, pullin' the toothpick from his jaw, "Ah, I get it," he declares. "You think that, because I look a little younger than you, that you have an intellectual advantage. Is that it?"

I tip my head to the side. "Never occurred to me."

"Well, please feel free to clarify," he insists.

"In my forty-plus years, I've known a great deal of goodness in life. Clearly, you have too," I say.

He nods and shrugs with a contemplative frown.

"But I've also known m' full share of grief and loss," I add. "And I'm not talking about the usual loss of grandparents and parents at my age, either. Sorrow and I know each other well enough to be besties, it's just that we also don't like each other very much. An' you can't tell me that, in all your years, you haven't gotten cozy beyond comfort with it, y'rself, 'ave you?"

"I suppose," he says and puts his toothpick in a nearby ashtray.

"And yet you still gamble for years, and you've prevailed!"

"Aye, of course!" he says. "The alternative is certainly much less appealin', wouldn't you say?"

"No!"

"No?"

"That's right."

"And yet, you've not yet slit those smooth-skinned writs of yours, have y'."

"No. You're right. I'm not eager to end my life. Neither am I willing to prolong it, not when I know what's comin'."

Then he rolls his eyes at me, long and slow to be sure I get the point. "Boy-o," he says almost with a groan, "in my years on this earth, I've heard many-a-time what you're proposin' to tell me: Salvation or damnation, heaven or hell, life or death, up or down—that's it, isn't it?"

"Y' forgot 'blessin' or cursin','" I say.

"Aye, that I have." He sighs and shakes his head, and while he pulls another toothpick from the plastic wrap, he says, "If I haven't bought it yet, what's t'make you think I'm interested now?" An' he puts the pick in his teeth.

"Nothin'," I say. "But that's precisely why my initial conversation with you has lost its appeal. In all your centuries on earth, you haven't learned a blessed thing. Leastwise, nothin' that holds any interest for me."

"I see."

"I seriously doubt that."

"Let's not be forgetting that, compared with me and my years, you're little more than an infant." He leaned forward. "I'm the adult in the room, ... Laddy."

"And yet, the adult is entirely unfit to teach the infant. You've used witchcraft to extend your natural life by more than eleven hundred years, and you still haven't learned to look beyond what little your craft has taught you. If I'm right, then all of creation, as vast as it is, is only temporary décor. The day will come when the plug on your power will be pulled. And, even with centuries left in your account from your poker-playing prowess, your life will come to an abrupt end. You're goin'a look back over your twelve hundred years and realize, it was all a waste, and all because you never tried to peer behind the veil. There are glimpses of a sort available y'know."

"And just what would I see if I were to take a peek?" he asks.

"But y' know that already, don't y'?" I say. "An infinite number of years, with no fear of losin'm to a random opponent with a lucky hand." I pause and pull my chair in. "No disease, no loss, no grief, and if there is poker, it will only be for fun, but it will always be fun."

136

"As wonderful as that sounds, it still leaves us with the problem of me having to die to get there, doesn't it?" he asks.

I chuckle and gather my thoughts while lookin' at the tabletop. "When you know your future in the afterlife is secure, then the absolute worst possible thing about dyin' is that you feel so stiff the next day," I add with a chuckle.

He smiles at my joke and nods, indicating that he gets my point, too. Then he pulls the toothpick from his mouth again and nods. "Well, that's something worth considerin'. then, isn't it?"

"Aye, boy-o," I say, "I'tis."

We sit silent for a spell, an' he seems to really be takin' it to heart in a way that I found gratifying in a hope-for-the-future sort of way. Then he says, "So, how 'bout you and I play a hand anyway—a gentleman's game: no money, no years, just for the sport o' the game? I know that I'd enjoy that, an' I 'ave a feelin' that you might as well."

Well, of course, I acquiesced, and it's a good thing we weren't playin' for time!

What on earth would I do with fifty extra years?

THE END

Introduction to
"The Pit"

Spoiler Alert!

SCARE SCORE: 1 2 **3** 4 5

Sadly, we have, all of us, met that person who works in the church, devotes time and energy and funds and belongings to the church, and yet, displays no change in lifestyle by the indwelling of the Holy Spirit. This person's life is not moving forward, but has stagnated along with those of the folks who live to the right and to the left, influenced by the world, not by Scripture, not by solid teaching and doctrine and not by rebuke, regardless of how frequent it may come. This is the type of person who is the inspiration for "The Pit." For these people I wrote "The Pit."

I believe in a living Hell, that it was prepared for fallen angels, but that humanity gained access to it through the fall in the Garden of Eden. I believe that a huge part of the descendants of Adam and Eve will spend their eternities in Hell where they will be forever tortured by a physical pain that I am at a loss to understand or explain, and by a solitude so profound that typical, earthly loneliness would be infinitely preferable. There will be no company, no commiseration of one of Hell's inmates with another. Each person will suffer in an aloneness that defies imagination and description.

It was for the prayerful benefit of those unsaved who believe themselves to be saved that I wrote "The Pit." I wrote it to remind us all that salvation is not inherited from parents or friends. We must each—individually—accept that Jesus, when he was on Earth, was God in the flesh; that he lived a perfect, sinless life; that he taught his followers that the way to heaven is only through him and his actions (our actions come to nothing); that Jesus died in obedience to his father having taken onto his mortal body the immortal punishment that we each have earned and deserve; that he paved the way through his resurrection for us to also be resurrected, that our belief in all these points is imperative and that we must confess in the name of Jesus that we do believe him, at which point and only upon reaching that confession we are guaranteed our spots in heaven. For these reasons, I wrote "The Pit."

On a more literary level, there were parts of this story that were inspired by Edgar Allan Poe's "The Pit and the Pendulum." My story has no pendulum, but it does have a pit. There is a line near the end of Poe's story when the narrator says, "I struggled no more, but the agony of my soul found vent in one loud, long and final scream of despair." The power of this thought has haunted me since I first read it back in grade-7 English class. And there is a fascinating conflict because, in the absolute knowledge of his impending, his imminent doom, his soul did "find vent." That is, there was still a sense of relief for Poe's narrator, however minute. But that character, so far as Poe's story is concerned, is not about to drop into the pit of hell, but just into the pit of his physical death, and there is a distinction that I felt a need to emphasize. I realized as I wrote my story that I must reference Poe, but to offer my readers that sense of doom with no sense whatsoever of any type of "vent" in the least. This is eternal despair from which there is not a breath's worth of time spared. So I turned the quote on its head making the reference somewhat more oblique: "And with one loud, long and final scream of terror, she found no sense of relief or vent."

Of all my stories in the genre of horror, none is more horrific than this, for me. It is coated with baked on sorrow, remorse, grief and loss that has been flavoured with fear such as cannot be known on earth. Imagine, though, believing yourself to be saved, having the knowledge of Hell and its various characteristics and finding yourself standing before God knowing that, with all you knew, Jesus himself never knew you. My belief in the Bible and its teachings prevent me from being frightened of man-made monsters and terrestrial events. Such things, if they existed, can only take my physical life with me ending up in eternal bliss. What's the big deal? "Just a little pinch" as the nurses say before giving you an injection, "and it's all over." But possessing the knowledge for any length of time, no matter how fleeting, that you are to be continuously, continually burned alive for eternity—while I can only imagine it and will never experience it—that is a fear that could wake me in the dark watches of the night in a bath of my own sweat and tears. It is my hope that there might be someone who fancies himself or herself saved but lives in need of such a reminder. God willing, my story will be a ministry for such as those, and that brings me to my final thought.

Originally, there were two versions of this story. I didn't know if a happy ending or a "less-than-happy" ending would be more effective and beneficial—not for the story, so much, as for the readers. I wrote one version in which the protagonist wakes up and gets saved, the time spent trying to avoid the pit of hell having been just a dream. The other version ended as this one does.

Once both drafts were complete, I left them alone for a few weeks and came back to read them. I found that the happy ending actually served to undermine the reality of Hell, making it seem as though it is certainly something to fear, but no more than you might fear The Mummy or a Martian. So obviously, I chose the not-so-happy version as the more effective, but I added the dream sequence to it, except that the dream is not of hell, but of being back on earth, alive. The idea is to raise my reader's sense of doom by throwing in a red-herring for a line or two before closing the story as a tragedy. This new dream sequence seems to re-emphasize the reality of hell, making its presence all the more threatening. I wanted the hell from my story to be something that would stay with the reader, even, to a certain degree, feel threatening to the reader, so that its reality would loom over the soul of the unsaved and push that person to the Lord.

The Pit

That if thou shalt confess with thy mouth the Lord Jesus,
and shalt believe in thine heart that God hath raised him from the dead,
thou shalt be saved.
—Romans 10:9 KJV

And then there stole into my fancy,
like a rich musical note,
the thought of what sweet rest there must be
in the grave.
—Edgar Allan Poe,
"The Pit and the Pendulum"

She found herself in an enormous hall. So large it was that she saw neither walls nor ceiling. It was lighted from above, but there appeared no discernable light source. There were two visible details of note: One was the floor: smooth and black as pitch, apparently made of homochromatic stone. It was the only thing she could think that it could be, but it was a single sheet of it—entirely seamless—yards long and yards wide. Were it not for her reflection on it, she could have been made to believe that she was standing on nothing at all, and as it was so mysteriously dark, she began to wonder whether the floor was opaque, like highly polished marble, or if it was as purely transparent as crystal, and the black she saw was the vacuum of a starless space beneath.

141

The other feature was a circular wall of masonry, hip-high and about two feet thick, but the inner circle was no less than twenty feet across. As she gazed over, she saw that there was no floor inside: giving no reflection. It was, in fact, a hole, deep and dark enough to make her wonder if it might even be bottomless. She considered dropping something in to hear it hit, but there was nothing, save herself, that could be dropped.

It was upon completion of that thought that she saw him approaching. She regarded him with neither fear nor hope, suspicion nor assurance. It's just that he was, and that was all. It was as though he was made of light, for he glimmered and yet illuminated nothing.

He had no discernable face, like he was wearing a sock over his head to hide his appearance except that this was his appearance. He wore a long, dazzling robe of white with a blue satin sash starting over his right shoulder and downward across his chest; crisscrossed at his middle on his left, then tied on his right at his waist, leaving ends that trailed toward the floor ending in tassels of sparkling electrum. "Greetings," was all he said as he approached. His tone was checked but not unfriendly.

"Hi," she said, her southern, U. S. accent still apparent in her speech.

"Do you know where you are?" he asked.

She shook her head with a pleasant smile. "All I know is that a minute ago, I was dyin', and now I'm here. I was on Earth, but now I'm … somewhere else," she shrugged. "That's about it. Am I in Heaven?"

"No," he said. "Heaven itself is a brief walk in that direction," he told her, pointing. "This area is a … parlour of sorts: more than a foyer but less than a living area."

"What am I doin' out here?"

He didn't look at her. "Some people are granted a preparation time before they enter eternity," he answered.

"Hmm. Well, I don't remember reading nuthin' 'bout this in my Bible," she observed, looking over her surroundings.

"Well, it's hardly an integral component of creation," he said.

She nodded with a frown as she continued looking about, and she locked her hands behind her.

"So, You know your Bible," he said.

She nodded again. "Mm-hmm! Sure do. M' Daddy was a preacher man all his adult life," she said, turning back and forth on her hips as she stood, still gazing about.

"Ah, so you grew up in church."

"You bet I did. I went to Sunday school then I taught Sunday school, and I spent nearly my whole life working at church."

"I see, then perhaps you know what this is," he said, indicating the circular wall that stood nearby.

She shook her head. "No. I don't remember reading nuthin' about that, neither."

"Mm," he observed, looking over the edge. "This is the other entrance."

She stopped swaying as she stared, horror-struck at the masonry. "Y' mean the entrance to hell?" she asked, instinctively backing away from it.

He nodded. "Yes."

"Y'know, I always had my doubts about it bein' a real place," she said.

"Well," he said slowly, "it *is* a reality."

"Why would God make such a horrible place?"

"He didn't really make it, *per se,*" he responded. "He ... *provided* it. He removed a part of himself from his own realm to give to those who do not wish to live under his rule."

"Okay, so he didn't actively create it. He's still responsible for its existence, isn't he?"

"No. The Lord never wanted anything, any place like that to ever exist. In fact, in some ways, its very existence is contrary to his nature, but supplying it is an act of love."

"'Of LOVE?!'" she protested with a grimace. "How could such a place come from love?"

He shook his head, and his voice was low and monotone. "He prepared it for rebellious angels. Even so, those on Earth who refused to submit to God's rule would find Heaven equally unbearable to live in as hell, so he grants them eternity away from his rule." He paused and gestured toward the inside of the wall. "In there, they may reign as they choose."

"But it's so terrible," she commented. "Pain, fear, grief, sufferin' ... agony for eternity." She shook her head in disbelief, her eyes wide, regarding the entrance. "There's nuthin' good about it at all."

"No. Because there is nothing of God about it at all," he said.

She shook her head, demonstrating her lack of understanding. "I guess I have eternity to learn to understand, right?"

He sighed deeply. "Yes, you are right," he said.

143

The ambiguity of his response caused her to react with fear, and she backed farther away from the entrance. "When do I go into heaven?" she asked, but it was more of a demand. "The Bible teaches us, 'absent from the body, present with the lord,'" she argued.

"The Bible also teaches, 'Blessed are the pure in heart for they shall see God.'"

"Right," she said. "So when do I get to go in?"

He said nothing.

"What are you telling me?" she asked.

"I'm telling you nothing."

"You're scaring me," she said. "Why are you doing that?

"I'm doing nothing."

"Are you saying I'm not pure?" she demanded. "I'm pure! I'm pure!" she said. "I lived in church. I prayed, I took communion, I taught Sunday school, I ... I ... I ..."

"Yes, you did all those things. But did you ever ask the Lord Jesus to add your name to his Book of Life? Did you ever tell him that you believe in him and what he did for you? What he did in your place? Did you ever confess the name of Jesus?"

"I'm pure of heart," she proclaimed. "I am! I'm pure!" she stopped speaking as tears began to overwhelm her eyes.

He shook his head. "It's even as the Lord said: 'It is easier for a camel to pass through the eye of a needle than for the rich to enter the kingdom of God.'"

"What are you talkin' 'bout?" she asked, sensing a possible loophole. "I was never rich. Maybe you got the wrong person." She nodded and forced a smile. "Yeah, that's gotta be it. You're mistakin' me for someone else. Someone rich."

"There is no error," he assured her. "You said yourself that you were raised in church. How many times did you hear your own father preach the Good News? Can you even guess how many still never even get to hear it?" he asked, turning on her. "And how many years were available to you to make peace with God through his Son? You died at the age of thirty-nine, when some people die at five, or two, or in the birth process or even earlier. But not you. You had a good thirty years of hearing the Good News with all those chances of putting it into effect in your life. *That* is wealth. But did you ever let the Lord Jesus deal with your sin?"

She was sobbing at this point. She looked over at the circular entrance some twenty feet in front of her, then she looked back at him. "I was pure, I tell'ya. I'm pure of heart!" She turned and ran away from him and from that horrible, unholy

144

hole, running in the direction he had indicated for Heaven's entrance, but it was like running off the eastern edge of a flat map. As she faded from view in that direction, she came back in sight from the other side of the hole, and she screamed in terror, now only ten or twelve feet from the entrance. She looked to him again, her eyes wide with alarm. The compassion in his heart was visible, but so was the sense of forlorn hope.

She ran off in another direction, but, like running off the northern edge of the same map, fading from view there, she reappeared again from the south, no more than five feet from the hole. She screamed again and dropped to her knees, understanding taking hold in her mind.

He turned from her, resting his weight against the circular wall with both hands, and the wall depressed in height into the floor until it was no more. Then the black floor where the wall had been, began to sag, like the floor around a drain, as though the material that made up the floor could no longer support its own weight without the added strength of the stone wall. It continued to incline around the hole as the hole itself continued to sink, and the incline to spread outward from it. While he maintained his position through no effort of his own, she saw the trap reaching outward to her. Were she to run away again, she knew that she would reappear even closer to the hole. And yet, the gruesome truth of the inclining floor continued to spread outward in every direction, creeping closer to her, crawling like a pestilence from the centre toward a victim. There was nothing for her to reach for but the slippery smoothness of the floor. Nothing to move toward but the hole itself.

She stared now, eyes wide with the dread and panic of the sinking hole in life—the abyss that went from everything good to no good at all, and yet continued existence in the eternal evil of an unholy domain. From her knees, she sat—a vain attempt at moving away from the inching, impending doom that sought her—that reached out for her.

The floor now tipped away from beneath her feet, and she pulled back. That is, she did everything a person could do to back away, but she didn't move. The hole continued to widen beneath her knees, and she felt the lower part of her legs drop. She pinched her eyes closed and turned her face aside, desperate to move away, but it was as if the wall itself had moved behind her to keep her stationary as the droop in the floor continued its menacing widening until finally, the greater portion of her weight slipped away. "God!" she screamed. "I'm sorry! Oh, God, I'm sorry! Please help me! Save me!" she cried. There was no response. Had she only made such a plea even minutes before ...

In a last, desperate hope of escape, she willed herself back to her dying, earthly body. She thought—she hoped—that she could return to her mortal self for one last moment, awaken herself and make her repentance known.

She felt her eyes open and found herself, once again, in her hospital room, awake and lucid, and surrounded by her parents, her siblings, her husband and her babies. She felt herself begin to cry rich tears of joy and relief, realizing that it had been a dream—just a dream—and she asked her entire family to pray for her as she gave her heart to Jesus, to beg for her name to be recorded in the Book of Life, and for just that moment she found one last, fleeting sense of hope in a final fantasy. But whatever awakenings she might have been allotted were now in her past; she would have no more awakenings. She felt her fingertips alone at the cusp of the slope, and she opened her eyes one last time, seeing first, her fingers losing what little grip they had, then, turning her eyes forward—downward, she looked into her entire future: darkness, blackness, aloneness, pain, sorrow and loss without end. And there stole into her mind, like the harsh clang of a discordant bell made of the grave itself, the awareness that there will never again be even the remotest, faintest, slightest rest from searing, agonizing pain, for all such gossamer frailties have long since burned in there and have been carried away and disbursed on the rising heat of those infinite, black flames. She felt herself slip to where she finally fell straight down. And with one loud, long and final scream of terror, she found no sense of relief or vent. The sound of her scream died with her.

Throw this useless servant into outer darkness,
where there will be weeping and gnashing of teeth.
—Matthew 25:30 KJV

THE END

PART III:
SCIENCE FICTION STORIES

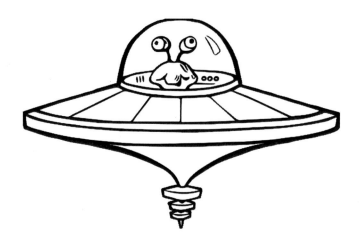

Introduction to Science Fiction Stories

Well, there's not a great deal to say here. For my Sci-Fi portion of this volume, there are no "gore scores" or "scare scores," just plain, old-fashioned good literary reading, great themes and what I feel are just nice, pleasant-reading stories.

I started loving Sci-Fi when my brother—bless his heart—got me hooked on *Star Trek* as a kid, no older than 9. Since then, I've simply loved the multiplicity of universes that Sci-Fi has to offer. Consider what all is part of the Sci-Fi genre: time travel, space travel, the future, aliens, alien worlds, anything dystopia, shrinking in size, growing in size, giant anything, technology, discoveries of ancient civilizations ... The list goes on and on ad nauseam.

Indeed, when looking for a symbol for each literary genre for this book, Greek and Horror were quite simple to find, frankly. There was still a breadth of symbols for both, but no breadth like symbols for Sci-Fi. In fact, every symbol that I considered for this section left out more than it included—represented far less than the whole. I considered making a symbol-montage, but even then there were so many symbols that the image just became an indiscernible mish-mash, and I quickly abandoned the project, finally settling on the stereotypical Sci-Fi symbol: the flying saucer, which still leaves a lot out from Sci-Fi, but I find it to be the most inclusive symbol. It represents technology, aliens, space travel, the future, the past (in some ways) and even the film *Fantastic Voyage*, about travelling through a human body, required a sort of space ship, so then the saucer also then represents shrinking in size, and by extension, growth to a giant size.

I have three stories in this genre, two of which deal with time travel, but only one of those has time travel as a major component of the plot. The other is more relationship oriented. The third story is a space-faring story. I do hope that you enjoy the read in any event.

Introduction to
"All In Good Time"

This story started as a letter of affection for Queen Elizabeth II. It is a story I conceived in 2010 or so when I realized that her time on the throne was not far from surpassing Queen Victoria's, and I imagined then that we might be living in an alternate timeline, and I wanted to address what the real timeline might have been—in a work of fiction, of course. I had wanted to finish the story by her Diamond Jubilee. I even had some romantic notions about sending a copy to Her Majesty in England, but a severe onset of depression forced me to miss my goal by about eight years. I wasn't able to even begin writing the story until well into 2014, and even then, I only finished the part called "History," and there it remained for several more years, during which I wrote my *Star Trek TNG* novel.

Once I realized that my grandson, who was the inspiration for the grandson in the story, was very nearly the age in real life that he is in my narrative, I forced myself to finish the story, not so much anymore to express my affection for the British Monarchy—although that's there, too—as to write a letter of affection to Dallas, the grandson whom I regard as my son. So that's what the story has become. And, in the words of Forrest Gump, "That's all I have to say about that."

All In Good Time

When you love someone—I mean truly love someone—
nothing can ever really separate you.
You're always together because you're always in love
despite separation by opinion, by culture, by tradition or by creed,
and despite distances of miles or distances of years ...
—Liberace (?)

*   *   *

HISTORY

*   *   *

The last time I saw my grandfather was on June third, 2012. I remember because it was the day after the Diamond Jubilee Celebration of Queen Elizabeth II when she was also formally declared the longest-reigning British monarch in history, even though the official date of the former had been several months earlier. Advisers, Ministers and Parliament all agreed that combining the celebration of the two events would seem more dignified, as I recall. Once she had been on the throne longer than King George III, whose reign lasted just shy of 60 years, her supremacy was assured. The event was commemorated with a limited-edition portrait of Her Majesty with an inscribed brass plate that read,

Long live *Elizabeth the Second,*
by the Grace of God, Queen of Canada
and of Her other realms and territories,
Head of the Commonwealth, Defender of the Faith,
on her Diamond Jubilee, June 02, in the year of our LORD 2012,
the longest-reigning British monarch in history.

My grandfather had gone to great lengths to procure a copy of that portrait for his house in Victoria. It hung in his living room on the wall opposite the main entrance so that it was the first thing you'd see upon entering, and, in fact, it was quite impossible to miss, so grandly arrayed and framed it was: in mahogany and gold filigree. It cost him $2500, but, by the time it was on its way to him via Federal Express, he had already set aside a substantial sum for a portrait commemorating Her Majesty's Sapphire Jubilee a mere five years later. She would then be the first British monarch to commemorate 65 years on the throne.

The day he got the portrait, he read the address label to me over the phone, of all things: "To Sir Dylan Thomas Walker," he quoted, "2-0-2 Government St, Victoria B. C., Canada." He repeated, "SIR Dylan Thomas Walker! What an honour," he proclaimed with jubilee. "I've been knighted!"

I don't want you to think that Grampa spent such monies out of some kind of blind obsession. Certainly, he was fixated, but not out of mere obsession. Even if he were, he's not exactly a poor man. He has a large income yet, and he is good with handling money. He was in love, though, and that's how he justified such investments. He had fallen in love with Queen Victoria when he was a teen living in Toronto, even though she had already been dead for some eighty years by then. He admired her a great deal for her wit, her charm, but above all, for her strength, which he thought manifested itself in so many varying avenues of her life. He became a devoted fan, and as a result of his affection for Queen Victoria, he became equally devoted to her offspring, thinking of them, as he told me once, as children of his own, just not so emotionally close as he would like.

I'll tell you how devoted he was to her: Most Canadians enjoy a respite from work during what is commonly known as "the May long weekend." They might sleep in that extra day or take the entire three days to head out camping or visiting family and friends. But the vast majority of Canadians will have to stop and think when asked the reason for the extra weekend day in May, and most of them won't remember that it's Victoria Day. Instead, they'll shrug and frown and give no verbal response. For Grampa, though, Victoria Day was a holiday to be honoured. He didn't hold it in as high regard as Easter or Christmas, both of which he honoured devoutly every year, but he did honour it more than his own birthday—or even my birthday, truth be told. He celebrated Victoria Day—"the penultimate Monday each May," as he said, and in point of fact, that's where I learned the word "penultimate"—by making great preparations with decorations and having friends and family over for cake and his sharing of an anecdote about the Royal Family that he had learned that year. It was usually a fanciful tale of humour and insight during what was annually an altogether joyous event—at Grampa's house, at any rate.

Grampa commemorated Victoria's death every year, too, but that was a sombre and solitary thing for him, like December 7th for U. S. veterans. He was never able to truly settle himself with her 1882 assassination. He often told me that he thought it would've been so much more appropriate for her to reign a full 63 years than for her to have lived a mere 63 years, especially after having survived seven previous attempts on her life. Sedately honouring that event every March 2 was one of four times every year Grampa would have a drink: specifically, a single shot of Canadian Crown Royal Rye.

Another of those events every year was Christmas Eve. You see, Mr. Death had been inordinately generous with his visits to Grampa during his life; his parents—both literature professors—were killed in a plane crash on Christmas Eve, 1968, when Grampa was only 20 and a fourth-year student at U of T. How he decried every year that they hadn't lived just six months more to see him graduate with honours. Grampa became a physicist and an engineer, both mechanical and electrical, and very gifted at all the above. When I was a kid, he'd boast how he could teach *Star Trek*'s Scotty a thing or two, both about engineering and good whisky.

A month after he graduated, he married my grandmother, Mary Rose Price, named for the 16th-century British warship. They moved to Ottawa, where, just shy of a year after their marriage, my mother was born on March 20, 1970—they named her Vicki, after Queen Victoria. Obviously. Grampa worked on his M. Sc. then his Ph. D. at the university there, until Mom was seven or eight. He apparently never told my grandmother about his passion for the queen. She thought it was just natural Canadian patriotism, bless her heart. She was killed three days after Mom turned ten, and Grampa has a drink every March 23rd to commemorate Grandma's passing—with the same solemn sobriety as for Queen Victoria and his parents.

Mom got married on April 4, 1989. Grampa told me that he didn't mind his daughter getting married, but when he was asked, "Who gives this woman in marriage?" he fell into tears. He had never thought of it in terms of "giving away" his beloved daughter, and when that idea imposed itself on Grampa's heart, it was more than he could bear. But on June 13 of the following year, I was born. Grampa was only 42. Talk about a young grampa! And I understand that he celebrated the event with the gusto of a grampa his age. But on my birthday in

1992, Mom died suddenly and somewhat unexpectedly of cancer, and my father, whoever he was, ran out—vanished like Amelia Earhart: without a trace.

Mom's death felt for Grampa a bit like a verdict from the Inquisition. It was like losing his beloved Victoria twice; he loves them both that much. So, yeah, Grampa has a drink on my birthday every year. He'd tell me that it's to celebrate me. I never told him—even when I had grown up enough to understand the drink's connection on my birthday with those on Christmas Eve, March 2nd and March 23rd every year—that I understood the real reason for that drink. He still celebrates my birthday with cake and song. And yet I know, as I depart his home and he's alone in the evening when the noise of the traffic outside his house has died down, the indoor lights have come on, and the curtains have been drawn, that he takes a shot of his esteemed Canadian Crown Royal and tells his beloved daughter that he remembers her and still loves her, even as he loved her the day when Grandma told him that she was pregnant and on the day that Mom was born. How could I possibly be offended by that?

In January of '93, Grampa adopted me. I became his son. And while I've never called him anything but Grampa, I really do think of him as my dad. We moved to Victoria, B. C. in the summer of the following year, and Grampa started teaching at UVic at the ripe old age of 46. He was 60 when I graduated from high school in 2008, and he was 64 when I graduated from UVic with a history degree in time for Her Majesty's Diamond Jubilee.

*   *   *   *

CURRENT EVENTS
*   *   *   *

The day after the Jubilee, Grampa called and asked me to come to his house. There was some urgency in his voice, so, of course, I made my way over immediately after lunch. At the door, I was instantly greeted by Mudgod, Grampa's canine friend whom he had adopted after I moved out. The name comes from the miniature schnauzer's penchant for lying and rolling in the mud, particularly in Grampa's garden, regardless of the weather, but the sloppier, it seems, the better as far as Mudgod is concerned. For that reason, we had considered calling him Pig-Pen, after the Peanuts character who is always walking on a decidedly earthly cloud. But Grampa wanted something more original. Ultimately, we discovered that "Mudgod" also happens to be the words "Dumb Dog" pronounced backwards. That phrase had been Grampa's dad's favourite

153

appellation for their dog when Grampa was growing up, and when you consider that Mudgod is a dog who insists on rolling in the mud despite hating his daily baths that come about as a result of it his mud-rolling propensities, the name, in both permutations, seemed appropriate for Grampa's new side-kick.

Mudgod was Grampa's second attempt at having a roommate. His first try was a synanceia—a stonefish—that he named Livingston in honour of Captain Picard's lionfish (so he said). Unlike Picard's pet, however, Grampa's guest only lived a year. Grampa had the carcass stuffed and mounted. Since then, Livingston—no longer living and never a stone—resides on a spruce plaque above the kitchen entrance. The plaque is adorned with a brass plate that bears the fish's name. It hasn't been cleaned since Grampa put it on display, so, if you look very closely at Livingston's belly, you can make out the face of da Vinci's Mona Lisa peering at you in a sort of optical illusion, but the face shows through on Livingston a bit more clearly than the real face does in the original painting in the Louvre.

When Mudgod was satisfied that I was a safe visitor, he pranced into the living room, returning to his daybed from which he was able to watch all the goings-on of the house. I took a moment to admire Elizabeth's portrait on the wall ahead of the entrance then noticed that Grampa's computer and much of the work that normally cluttered the desk in his office was now, oddly enough, cluttering his dining room: the table, the hutch and the sideboard. But I dismissed it. Grampa is, after all, an adult.

Finally, I turned my attention to Grampa sitting on his sofa. He wore only a muscle-shirt style top and shorts, which was understandable given the temperature outside. He sat looking through his Monarchy Scrapbook, a multi-voluminous photo album in which he kept pictures of everyone from Henry VIII to Elizabeth II. In previous decades, he'd tear images out of magazines from doctors' offices or wherever else, but with so many images being propagated on the internet, he began printing them himself, and his collection, especially of Queen Victoria, is impressive. He had saved images of paintings and drawings of her from her childhood onward. And even old photographs show up in his Scrapbook from 1845 on. Since he gets them somewhat randomly, they're not stored in precise chronicle order, but close enough. He had the book lying open on his coffee table as he carefully examined one image that he held in his hand and paged through the last few pages of the book.

"Grampa?"

He didn't turn to face me but just said, "Did you see the portrait on the wall?" Grampa was a stout man, not lacking any midriff, if you know what I mean. His face was still impressively young looking, and he had very little gray in his hair. He'd often say—somewhat boastfully—that all his gray grew in his goatee, which, of course, he never wore. But he was intelligent and looked the part, especially with his no-longer-receding receding hairline.

"Of course," I said with genuine enthusiasm. "How could I miss it?"

Smiling, he stood, arms outstretched, to greet me. "Ah! Come in, m' boy! How good to see you!" He hugged me like he hadn't seen me in a month. "Come n' sit. I want to show you my most recent acquisition," he said, leading me around the back of the sofa. "I pulled this off the internet today," he said with childlike enthusiasm. "It's one of the last photos taken of Queen Victoria before her assassination," he added.

"But Grampa, I think you already have this image," I said as I sat on the chair kitty-corner to the sofa.

"Quite right, m' boy! I do, but it's been colourized! I'm putting the two copies side by side, if I can find the black'n'white." He continued paging through his book as he spoke. "Ah! There it is!" he said, and he slid the colour version of the image beside its mate right near the end of that volume of his Scrapbook. "Paintings surely do her justice, but photos ... I dunno," he shook his head. "They tell a different story. A truer story." I looked at the two pictures side-by-side silently with Grampa. "Y'know, this is one of the last pictures taken of her," he said.

"Yeah, I know, Grampa," I said, smiling. After all, he had just said that moments before, but he had also told me that more than a few times in the years before.

"And with each assassination attempt, she grew to be more popular," he said, focussing on his photos.

"I remember, Grampa."

"I can't help but wonder just how much more she would have been loved if this attempt had also failed."

"I guess we'll never know."

He didn't say anything for a long time, and I even began to wonder if he was holding back tears, although he wasn't. He was restraining enthusiasm, not tears. "I think we *will* know," he said at last, but still, without turning to me.

"What do you mean?" I asked.

"I'm going to save her, m' boy," he announced.

I was a bit stunned. That kind of comment is not what you expect to hear from someone who still has a full bottle of Rye. "What do you mean?" I asked again.

"I've found a way," he said.

"'A way?' Grampa? You found a way of what?"

"A way back," he said, smiling.

That's when he turned to me, looking me straight in the eye. He said nothing for a long moment, gathering his thoughts, I suppose. "Listen to me very carefully," he finally said, "your mom died of cancer, and I still have no way to save her," he explained. "A cure is likely a long way off, and I just don't think that I'd be able to find it in my lifetime even if I searched every day, which ... just wouldn't be ethical." He stopped and pulled a picture of Gramma out from beneath his Scrapbook. He looked at it intently for a long, quiet time. "I had really wanted to save your gramma, m' boy, but she's my inspiration. If anyone's going to saver her, it can't be me. That'll never work." He smiled at the picture in his hand and gently caressed the edges of Gramma's face. Then he shook his head rigidly, as if returning himself to the present from some memory long since past, and he set the picture back on the table. "Of course, I also thought long and hard about saving my parents from that plane crash. I could do that easily enough, but I have healed quite well from that ... incident, tragic as it was. I just don't feel a need to go there anymore." He chuckled to himself. "How sad is that?" he said.

My heart had begun to race. I'm sure I was staring. "Grampa, you're not making any sense."

"It will all make sense in a little bit," he said with renewed energy, then paused, but when he spoke again, his tone was more sedate: "I want you to understand that I tried to save your Gramma first thing. I did, but it's impossible. The very notion is paradoxical; it simply cannot be. I can save no one in my family."

"Grampa, no one can save Gramma or Mom. They're dead. It's hopeless," I said.

"I realize that, m' boy, but there is a way to save the Queen."

"Save the Queen?" I asked. "Save the Queen from what?" I hadn't heard anything regarding the Queen on the news.

"From her assassination, m' boy."

"The Queen was assassinated?" I asked, feeling both stunned and suddenly very emotional.

"Right, my young historian." I missed the sarcasm.

156

"And you're going to save her ... now?"

Grampa nodded. "That's right."

"From her assassination," I fumbled.

"Yes," Grampa said, mildly annoyed that I wasn't keeping up with him. I'm not sure he understood that I hadn't even gotten out the door with him on this. "It's my duty, it's my responsibility, and it's my pleasure and honour," he said as though he had practised saying that hundreds of times in front of a mirror.

"It's your responsibility to save the queen from her assassination that happened today?"

"Not *today*," he said with a crust of disgust. "Her assassination was in 1882. You know that!"

"Oh!" I said as I began to understand. "You're talking about saving Queen Victoria!"

"Right," he said with a self-assured smile, and that's when I began to get confused again.

"Wait: You're talking about saving Queen Victoria?!" I asked, completely confused.

"Now y' got it," he said.

"You're really scaring me, Grampa. What exactly are you talking about?"

He whispered to me then. I'm not sure if he was trying to protect his secret or if he had found something that was so overwhelming that he felt constrained to speak of it with serene reverence: "I discovered how to do it, m' boy. I can change history."

Well, of course, that's when the bomb exploded in my mental magazine, and my brain began to capsize. I mean, talk about the fear of your only living relative going bonkers! I was on my feet and delivering diatribe that Hitler himself would have had a hard time besting. I thought Grampa might be deluded, perhaps even demented in the extreme. I went on and on, fear driving my thoughts, choosing my words for me and pouring them out of my mouth like water over Niagra.

Finally, I stopped, out of breath, and stared at him while I wondered what I should do. Part of me was still panicking, but there was another part of me that realized I should listen carefully—allow him to explain. Had it been any other person in the world before or after, I might very well have had him immediately committed, but Grampa had three things in his favour that made the situation altogether different: Brilliance, passion and loving affection. In my mind, these were enough of a counterbalance to keep me from reaching an unyielding conclusion. But even then, it wouldn't have taken much from him to push me over

157

the edge. Having paused in my rant, I started up once again, and had he said anything at all while I was proclaiming him unfit for everyday living, it would have been over, I think. But he said not a word during my entire invective, and I ran well out of energy long before Grampa had even begun to use any of his. When I finished, tired but still very fearful, I sat beside him, massaging my temples. He still said nothing: no defensive arguments, no acerbic retorts, no Wilde rejoinders. He patiently waited for me to initiate the calm, cool and collected continuation of our discussion.

And just how was I supposed to do that? The only thought that my mind allowed me to rest upon was to gently ask him to let me take him to see a doctor, and I didn't mean next week or even tomorrow. I wanted to take him that minute to the hospital for an examination, and I wasn't going to let him talk me out of it, but I also knew that that was no way to handle the situation, so I sat and thought, breathed, calmed and just let my brain land on its own solution, and it finally came to me: "Okay," I finally said, "prove it to me."

"Gladly," he said, then he looked up toward the ceiling as though he had hidden the answer up there. "Umm, tell me about Troy, m' boy. Or, better yet, the Trojan War's close. You're an historian; how did it all end?"

I didn't respond right away. My head was still spinning quite a bit, and I think that I might have been hyperventilating moments before as well, so I felt a little dizzy. Eventually, though, I was able to be civil and continue. "Well," I began. I shook my head sharply, trying to get back into the moment, "that's more a literature or archeology question than an historical one, you realize."

"Oh, well, if you don't know, then ..."

"I never said I didn't know," I argued. "I'm just saying that it's not really in my field," I explained, and Grampa waved his hand to concede. "Lessee," I began, "the Trojan War ended when the Greeks realized that fighting was getting them nowhere, so they chose a new tactic: the ruse, one that was the brainchild of Odysseus, if I recall correctly," I said, and Grampa said, "You do," so I went on. "They built a giant horse out of wood and left it on the beach, then sailed their ships away, hiding them behind some nearby island," I said, waving away the name that I couldn't remember. Grampa said, "the island of Tenedos." I nodded acknowledgement to him. "They left a man behind, Simon or Sinon, whose job it was to help the Trojans believe that the Greeks had given up and departed, having left the horse as a gift to the goddess Athena. The Trojans believed the Greeks' story, mainly because of a series of non-sequitur events, and took the horse into the city while patting themselves on their backs for ending the war and their nine-year siege. What they didn't know is that inside the horse were some of the Greek's greatest generals, and that night, as Troy was asleep after an evening of drinking and debauchery, the Greek soldiers snuck out of the horse, let their comrades inside the city, and they sacked Troy that night. End of story, essentially, unless you want me to go into the aftermath with Achilles' armour and Odysseus's voyage home and all that stuff that happened as the Greeks disbursed."

Grampa waved his hand to stop me, then conceded, "Not bad for an historian, m' boy! Not bad!" He raised his index finger. "Now, suppose I were to tell you that, if you had talked about the end of the Trojan War just three weeks ago, you would have recounted an entirely different string of events that led to a completely different conclusion to the war. What you say to that?"

"I would suppose that three weeks ago, I was an historian who had shared too much of his grandfather's Rye than I have today, evidently."

He laughed with a quick snort. "You always have had an acerbic sense of humour."

"Flattery will get you nowhere, Grampa," I said.

This time he laughed with his wonted belly-style laugh, head thrown back and jaw fully dropped. "Ah, bravo, m' boy. Bravo!" He paused to catch his breath, and when he had, he turned serious. He leaned forward to me. "I tested my theory three weeks ago. I went back in time to change the event altogether to see how doing so would change history for our present time."

"You did what?!"

"I changed the end of the Trojan War."

I said nothing. What could I say?

He went on. "Originally, the war was ended by a man named Onessimus who came to a point where he just didn't think it was necessary for the war to go on. He single-handedly ended the war with neither side the victor. Even that was a magnificent story."

"Uh-huh," I said, the sarcasm flowing from my voice and expression like the molasses from the Boston tank. I went on: "and you, who never fought a war—who were never even in the military!—you, all by your onesie, talked this man out of ending the war all by his onesie. Is that right?"

Grampa cocked his head to his side and scowled. "I may never have been in the military, m' boy, but it wasn't for lack of trying. A pacifist I am not," he proclaimed. Then he added defensively, "I was rooted out for health reasons," he explained.

159

"In any event," I argued, "you spoke to some dude in biblical Greek ..."

"*Ancient* Greek," Grampa protested, indignantly.

"Ancient," I conceded with my palm raised, "Ancient Greek some three thousand years ago and persuaded him to not end the Trojan War single-handedly by ... by doing what?"

"Oh," he said, tapping his pate with his fingertips, surprised that he had left out such a vital detail, "by not killing Helen of Troy," he finished, nodding with a smile.

"You're saying that he originally killed Helen."

"That's right."

"With all those soldiers around."

"Right."

"Uh-huh," I said, and I do believe that I was quite rude, but, I mean, how would one soldier get close enough to Helen to kill her from outside a fortified and well guarded city during war? I found it to be an improbable history, at best. Then, I suppose if he were an archer and an expert marksman at that—and I'm talking Artemis and brother Apollo combined with a bit of Odysseus, William Tell, Robin Hood and King Arthur thrown in for good measure—with an absolutely perfect tailwind, then perhaps he could kill someone within the walls of a Troy, but I'd never bet on it. "That must have been some speech you gave," I said.

"Well," Grampa said, shrugging modestly, "I'm a logical man; he was a logical man. I argued logically, and logically, he listened."

"I see," I said. Then I thought about the possible consequences of what Grampa claimed to have done. I wondered if Captain Picard would have approved. So I asked Grampa, "What about the timeline? Is it ... different?"

He looked down and nodded. "Yes, it is ... a little, at least."

That's when I sensed my opportunity. If Grampa were speaking facts and truth, it would be hard to find holes in his story, but if he were delusional, as I still wondered, or even if he were just creating fiction for my entertainment, I should be able to catch him on the details. So I decided that I'd check to see how vividly Grampa had rehearsed his tale for me. "So, what's different? Are we some deformed horrific version of our ancient selves as a result of your incursion into the past, or are we more godlike?"

He scowled at me and shook his head, and I felt those pangs of remorse, making me draw in my attitude just a bit. "A month ago," he began, "no one but exceptionally well-read scholars knew of Troy, and even they might have felt compelled to consult a text before offering any information on the subject—it was

160

that obscure. It was a virtually unknown little town even at its height. Fortified? Yes. Strategically located? Yes, I suppose, on the mouth of the Dardanelles, a place of trading and commerce. Absolutely. But its lasting influence was still negligible."

His eyes widened as he considered a new thought. "Consider the Greek city of Corinth, m' boy, located on the isthmus between the Peloponnese peninsula and mainland Greece. It was a city of commerce, too. Everyone going from north to south had to pass through Corinth, perhaps stay the night quite often. There would be a need for restaurants, shelter, safety, storage; you name it. It was a city of culture, of custom, of influence, of wealth and luxury. It was second only to Athens, and yet, today, only those who read their Bibles remember Corinth, and then, only because of the name 'Corinthians,' which many Bible readers might not even understand to be the name of people who lived in Corinth.

"Troy was like this, but worse. At best, it might have been a footnote in scholarly works. In the arts, it was much the same. A month ago, Troy was a vague nugget amid the remains of a great body of distilled and diffused Greek literature and other art forms with no unifying feature like what you're familiar with now. A month ago, Heinrich Schliemann was a scientist in a field so new that there was nothing for him to discover because no one had heard of Troy. He remained as unknown and obscure as Agamemnon himself. What is different, m' boy, is that a city that had been utterly unknown is now—3000 years after its demise—a powerhouse of influence on literature and art in hundreds of cultures around the globe." His eyes looked aside for a moment as he frowned, shrugged slightly and shook his head. "But you and I are the same. Our country has changed ... not at all. History overall is virtually unchanged."

"Huh. Interesting," was all I could find to say.

"You see, m' boy, Time is a living thing. It can be wounded, and it can heal. And as it heals, it tries to reclaim the form it had before its injury, but there are always scars; it's never precisely the same." He looked up at the ceiling again and scratched his chin, and he suddenly looked very professorial. "But if I were to use a single idea to describe this creature to help you understand," he said, "I'd have to compare time to a living river."

"A river?" I asked, and he nodded.

"Think of a river with a consistent flow, no rapids, no bayous. Just breadth and serenity and constant flow. Now, if you throw a small rock into a large river the size of, say, The Amazon, would the river notice it at all?"

"I guess not," I said.

161

"You guess correctly," he nodded, looking me in the eyes. "But if a rock large enough to stand above the surface of the water were thrown in, would the river's appearance change?"

"Of course," I said.

"In what ways?"

"Well, the rock would stay visible, obviously, and the water would always break around it."

"I see," Grampa said meditatively. "And the water breaking around the rock, it leaves a gap in the water flow for a great distance downstream?"

"No," I said. "The water flows around the rock and leaves a wake that flows downstream for a few feet, I suppose, at most."

"A larger rock leaves a larger wake, though. Am I right?"

"Yes."

"How much larger is the wake of a large rock than a smaller rock?"

"Not much larger at all. Even a massive rock would leave a wake that could be measured in a few feet, maybe yards."

"But then ..." Grampa began, but, seeing where he was leading me, I jumped in: "... then the river regains is initial appearance," I conceded.

Grampa shrugged again, "Yeah," he said, trying his best to keep control of his enthusiasm. "except that this river is a living entity that has been wounded, and the wake is the scar. In a living river, it never completely heals. There is always some remnant of the wake."

"Such as a famous ancient city where an obscure ancient city had been before."

"Precisely!" Grampa nodded, smiling.

I admit, I was impressed. He made a good case so far, and I nodded in concession. "It's a fine theory, Grampa. It's logical, it's certainly entertaining and intriguing, but you have yet to present a shred of evidence to support this somewhat outlandish notion."

"You have a point, m' boy, and there's a very good reason that I haven't presented any evidence."

"What's that?"

"I don't have any."

I raised my brows to object, but he raised his palm to stop me from speaking. "No tangible evidence yet, anyway."

"Then how are you going to prove this to me, or anyone?"

"I don't care about proving it to "anyone," just to you, m' boy." As he said this, he pulled a very old Gladstone bag of heavy, coarse leather from under his coffee table, and judging by the pull on the bag and his relative effort in lifting it, it was not empty. Now, Grampa did enjoy antiques. His coffee table is a fine example of that attraction. I mean, who has a coffee table these days? Especially one of such elaborate design among unmarried men? But this bag raised some serious fears in me.

He smiled. "This bag was old in 1880," he said, "even a bit out of style by then, I might add." And judging by the metal components of the bag—the frame of the mouth, the clasps and lock and the hardware attaching the handles—it was decidedly a 19th-century piece. It was, in fact, a beautiful thing to behold. It was shaped like an oriental vase from the narrower sides, narrow at the bottom, growing wider toward the top and finishing with a wide rim. The longer sides were pretty standard, except the front—the side with the lock—had Grampa's initials, D. T. W., embossed in gold, but it was also clear when you looked closely that another set of initials had been skilfully removed before Grampa's were applied. Gold from other letters had been removed, leaving behind some faint, ghostly impressions. It was a deep bag, twice that of a typical doctor's bag that you'd see 50 years after the creation of this bag. The thick leather had been refurbished and the metal polished so that the whole looked like a relatively new bag except in its design. It had the appearance of being, say, ten to fifteen years old, rather than 150 or more years.

Grampa opened it, and I admit, I lost it again. Inside the bag were stacks upon stacks of British banknotes of varying denominations, all from the 1860s and '70s! Some coin was included, but mostly it was filled nearly to absolute capacity with banknotes—paper money! Grampa let me look through them for a few minutes because he could see how stunned I was. He had thousands of pounds sterling in that bag. I reached to lift out two hand-fulls of bills—leaving at least that much in the bag—and I stared at him.

He nodded with understanding. "It's taken me about four years to buy all of those bills from collectors the world round, and I always bought lower-quality notes to stretch my finances as far as I could."

"Grampa!" I started to say with no knowledge of what I was going to say next.

"I know, m' boy, but don't worry. There's still plenty of money set aside for your inheritance."

I shook my head. "But this is a waste," I said.

163

He leaned toward me with a finger pointed at my chest. "You won't think so in a few minutes," he said as he stood and picked up his Gladstone bag. "Follow me."

I followed him down his hallway that sported doors to the bathroom, the linen closet and three bedrooms, one of which operated as his office. He had always kept the door to his office closed. Whenever he wasn't in it, the door was shut. But he never used to lock it. It had been a couple of years since I'd been in his office; I had no use for it anymore. What I used to use in Grampa's office, when I occupied the bedroom in the basement, I have since purchased for my own. What I don't own, the school library has been able to supply, so I hadn't even tried to go into his office for four years by then. The office was the room farthest down the hall: past the guestroom, the bathroom and across from Grampa's room: the last door on the right. He unlocked and opened the door and walked in with me right behind him. It was pitch black inside. I assumed that a shade was drawn over the window, but it wasn't covered by just a set of blinds. It had to have been a blackout shade, I thought. It was *that* dark!

He flipped on the light. The office had been entirely cleared of everything that I knew to be Grampa's. His entire library was gone. His Tiffany lamps, his globe (and its contents, presumably), his art and even his antique desk were supplanted by a card table on which he deposited his key as he entered. What remained was just the room. The bald floor was cleared and clean. The shelves were gone. The ceiling light in the centre of the room sported a single, bald but certainly modified bulb, but the socket, the ceiling, the walls and the floor—everything that he couldn't remove from the room, he covered by a layer of dull, grey monochrome lead. In fact, the window that I had thought was covered by a blackout shade was actually boarded over, and it, too, was covered in a layer of lead. As it faced the neighbour's house rather than the street, few people, if any, would have noticed the oddity from outside. I know that I never did. It wasn't a think layer of lead that coated the innards of the room. I mean, through it I could still see the texturing of the gyprock wall and the pattern of the fibreboard Grampa used to seal the window. In some places on the floor, the grain of the underlying hardwood was still visible. The lead coat could be no more than a couple of nanometres thick, yet I could smell the musty, metallic odour and feel its dampening effects on the room's acoustics, like winter's first heavy snow.

Grampa just watched me take it all in for a few moments. He said nothing during that time, but finally, he turned toward the part of the room where the closet used to be. Of course, the doors were gone with all the shelves, poles and

164

supports you'd expect to see, and even the upper part of the wall that would top the closet doors had been dismantled. The closet was now just an extension of the room. But Grampa had also walled off the closet in his room and added that space to the room that used to be his office, all lined with lead. The closet area stood to the left of the entrance in what might be considered an alcove within the room, so it wasn't readily visible upon entering. But within the leaded walls of the closet sat a mechanism of unknown purpose. In the centre of this odd-looking machine stood a tall, clear dome made of lead crystal. It was quite narrow—decidedly standing room only within, but it stood to within six inches of the ceiling and contained two hand-level panels, one positioned for each hand very close to the legs. The dome was criss-crossed with a metallic web-like design that I supposed was used to strengthen and support the crystal. It had two guides, sets of tracks, along two opposite sides. These guides were accompanied by sturdy looking arm supports that reached upwards from below the dome; on these supports, the dome could ascend or descend on the guides to accommodate a person within. Outside the dome on the right-hand side, stood a third panel like the two within the dome.

The dome rested on a raised, circular area of a lead platform that sat directly on the floor. The raised area, centred on the platform, was topped by a grate or vent. The platform itself, shaped somewhat like an eye with the raised area standing in for a large pupil or small iris, was roughly four feet long and maybe two feet wide. It also sported three arms about three feet high, supporting nozzles that I learned later were emitters. They looked every bit like ray-guns right out of a 1930s sci-fi movie, complete with five art-deco-style rings around each tapered spout. Two of the emitters sat on stationary arms set on either side of the dome but reached toward the back. In front, the third emitter sat on a pivoting arm that now stood front and centre, so all three arms, spaced equally around the dome, formed an equilateral triangle, and all three emitters pointed toward the centre of the dome. On the platform, on either side of the dome, were two cylinders about six inches high and maybe four or five inches in diameter. Each had a series of small tubes leading out from them. One tube from each led to the raised area of the platform below the dome. Three others each led to the arms supporting the emitters.

I was more than a little stunned. With my jaw dangling, I stared at Grampa, who chortled good-naturedly and walked over to the machine. "This is my magnum opus," he said almost mournfully, "the culmination of all my education and expertise, all my aspirations and ambitions, and years of planning and

165

preparation." He gazed for a time at it, finally resting his hand on it as he would a son who had just graduated top of his class. "Yessir, this machine goes way back. In some ways, it goes way back before my own University education." Then he smiled again and looked at me. "Well, what do you think?" he asked, almost sardonically. If you're anything less than blown away, I'll send you to your room without supper."

His humour brought me back to the present in a hurry. "I'm 22 years old!" I gibed.

"Fine," he said with a light tone, "I'll send you to your old room," and he smiled at me. "You seem to be ... not entirely unimpressed," he said and, apparently no longer interested in my opinion, he walked to the card table, picked up the key and handed it to me. "Put that in your pocket for now, will you?"

I accepted the key without saying anything, and obediently dropped it into the pocket of my jeans. Grampa tipped over the table, folded the legs and carried it out of the room, setting it in the hallway. He came back and stood in the doorway. "Grampa?" I said, not sure of what I wanted to ask.

He smiled at me again. "I'll be back in just a few minutes," he said, then departed into his bedroom and closed the door. Moments later, he returned wearing a suit of a style befitting his Gladstone bag. His hair was parted down the centre and lay flat against his scalp. He wore a handsome white shirt with a high collar and Ascot-knotted cravats adorned with a handsome, decorative pin. Over that, a grey waistcoat and striped slacks over button dress boots. On his arm, he had draped a frock coat and dress gloves, and in that hand, he held a collapsed opera hat. All very Victorian, all very authentic but all obviously new. He came into the room and closed the door. When he spoke again, it was with the most remarkable English accent I've heard. I wasn't sure if the picture was charming or ludicrous, but the effect was certainly surreal.

"On the kitchen table," he said in his new English-ness, "you'll find all the information you'll need to become the executor of my estate, my good man. Despite appearances," he went on, " everything is organized and clearly labelled." He stood before me, looking me over. "Yes," he said thoughtfully. "Yes, I believe you'll do quite nicely on your own. You've done remarkably well up to this point, you know. No reason it shouldn't continue. None attol. You've grown into a capable, intelligent, formidable young man."

"Grampa?" I stammered.

"You'll be fine at this point. I'm certain of it. Just fine," he insisted.

"I don't understand," I said.

166

"Oh, do forgive the new locution, my good man. I am in desperate need of getting into character here, so that I don't drop out of character at my destination. You can see that, can't you?" He closed the door to the room, and I noted that the inside of the door and the knob had also been coated with lead. Then he stepped over to his machine and pushed a button on the panel outside the crystal dome. When he did that, the front emitter swung slowly left on its arm toward the other arm on that side. While it did, he continued speaking to me. "I do realize that this has all come upon you rather suddenly." The arm and emitter stopped pivoting. "But fear not ..." he said as he punched what seemed like a code into the same exterior panel so that the crystal dome began to rise on the two guides that ran along either side. "... in time, you'll recover yourself and get along with your life swimmingly." The dome rose nearly to the ceiling but tipped to an angle to avoid it. He stood and watched it. "You know, the first time I used this contraption ..." He cut himself off and cocked his head. "Con-traption," he repeated then turned rigidly to regard me, as though proud of himself for having said such a word. "Now, there's a term you don't hear every day!" he observed. "It's a sorry thing, indeed, that we ceased using it. It's quite befitting, don't you agree? It connotes a certain ..." he spun his hand vaguely in the air while looking for the right word, "... mystique about a machine, as if to suggest that one doesn't quite know its purpose, but it also connotes a healthy degree of frustration with the mechanism, as if afraid he can't fully understand its function." He waved a hand in the air to bring his thoughts back on track. "At any rate, the first time I used it, I programmed it to come with me so that I could return to you." His voice softened. "I wasn't ready to leave you just then, even though I do believe that you've been ready to live on your own for quite some time. Still, I came back for my sake, just as well. You've no idea how proud I am of you. How pleased I am with you. How much I admire you and respect you." He shook his head as if preventing me from protesting, even though I don't remember beginning to protest. "I know that you know of my fondness for you. I love you mightily, indeed, you know that, but I needed to be sure myself that you knew. There are, after all, some things that must never be left unsaid. Wouldn't you agree?"

It wasn't a question ... not really, but still, I answered: "Yes."

"But there is a problem, you see," he said as though I'd had no need of speaking at all. "Of all the people in this world whom I have dearly loved, the only one whom I can save is the one I have yet to meet. For more than sixty years, she has lived in my past, but tonight, she stands in my future, and this machine is the key—the way back. Do you see?"

167

I nodded. My heart raced. I think Grampa could see that. He smiled at me again, and when he spoke again, he spoke as Grampa. He stepped out of character. No accent. He stood toe-to-toe with me, man-to-man. "But this time, there will be no returning for me. This time I'm programming the mechanism to send me, not to carry me. The machine itself shall remain here when I am gone. Do you understand?"

"Gone?"

"Yes, I'll be gone, m' boy."

"But why?"

"Because Time is a living being."

"So it heals."

He smiled at me again, and, closing his eyes, he nodded. "Yes, it heals. You're right, but we don't really understand whether the use of my mechanism is akin to tossing pebbles or heaving boulders," he said. "Since we don't know how injurious the effect is, it's wise to ere on the side of caution. It's best to respect living creatures. You see that, don't you?"

I nodded, but I couldn't hold back the tears any longer.

He hugged me then, and we stood in a long embrace. "All that I have lost, m' boy, amounted to nothing once you became a part of my life. In you there is more gain than one can really understand. You have made my life rich and full. I am simply too grateful for you to be able to express the notion to its fullest."

I wanted to speak, but I found nothing to say.

Again, Grampa shook off the emotion and reclaimed his new persona. "In any event, my good man, the house is yours. All the paperwork is there. Everything you need from banks, lawyers, stockbrokers and so on." He picked up his Gladstone bag, set it on the platform's raised portion, and then slipped his top hat under his arm. "If you do sell the house, though, you have to promise to dismantle this ... contraption ... first."

"I ... do I?"

"Come, come, you must promise me that you'll destroy my machine. No one must know of it, what it is, what it does. Destroy it, now. Do you promise?"

"I promise," I said, but I was so dazed and confused that I'm not convinced my oath would hold up in court. Not that it would matter.

He pulled one glove onto his hand. "Now, after I am gone, I want you to live well. Find a wife, raise a family. Take pride and joy in all that comes from your own hand." He flexed his newly gloved fist, then began pulling on the other glove,

168

and he flexed that fist. "I feel very much like a character in *Mission Impossible.* You know, I do!" He stood to look at me again, and we both smiled.

"Now," he said, "I need you to stand in this corner." He said this as he pushed me at my shoulders into the corner. "Stand very straight," he said, then he pulled another door from the wall. It, too, was coated with lead. The bottom of it scraped against the floor as it closed, forcing me into a tiny corner area. "You see, the lead in the room will protect you from the radiation," Grampa explained, "but it will also protect you from my changes so that you will remember all that you have learned in your past 22 years and all that you're about to learn in the past 22 years. That is to say, you'll remember both histories, and that shall be my evidence, my proof for you."

"But Grampa ..." I said, but he cut me off as though I had said nothing.

"Stay behind this door regardless of anything else," he said, then he pointed to a small hole in the door. It was eye level, and just off centre. "The glass in this lense is lead crystal. You'll be able to see me through it. Watch the lights of the machine. Stay behind this door until they stop shining. It will be only about three minutes, but you must wait until they've all died. Is that clear? It will get very bright. You might have to look away momentarily, but you won't miss much if you do."

I nodded as best as I could in the tiny corner.

"When the lights have died, I'll be gone, and you'll be safe. You can come out then." He closed the door all the way, and from above, he dropped two triangle pieces to cover me. They simply rested on the door that closed me into the corner of the room. It was like a triangular Iron Maiden without the spikes. I looked through the small crystal window and watched Grampa don his frock coat. Then, with his opera hat under his arm and gloves in place, he picked up his Gladstone bag and stepped into its spot on the platform, balancing the bag cautiously between his knees. He pushed some buttons on the panels at his hands, and the crystal dome began to slide down the two tracks on its sides. The lower it got, the more it began to set itself upright. Grampa had to bow slightly to accommodate his height into the dropping dome. Once it had sealed itself against the platform, Grampa could no longer drop his head to look at the controls, but he kept his eyes on me, anyway. Operating the machine from then on was evidently done all by feel. He moved another button, and the third emitter swung forward, stopping when it was pointing directly at Grampa's torso. All three emitters were, once again, evenly spaced around the dome, and Grampa was centred among three points of an equilateral triangle. There could not be a great deal of air in that

169

dome, but I noticed that, after Grampa moved a switch, air began fluttering the hems of his slacks from the grate beneath his shoes.

He took a large breath and smiled at me once more time, then, with a decisive gesture, he pushed one last button, and the emitters began glowing at the ends. The two that faced Grampa from behind were most visible to me. The nozzles shone brightly, and the rings around the spout seemed to vibrate sympathetically with light beams that shot from the emitters, hitting the dome and spreading out all around the entire crystal structure starting with the centre and stretching both upwards and downwards. I saw Grampa begin to squint, finally closing his eyes altogether. I thought then that maybe he was in trouble. The machine wasn't working right, I thought. I have to save him! And just as I was about to step out of my led casket of protection, he managed a smile, and I knew then ... I don't know how, but I understood that he was ok. Then the light grew too bright for me, and I was forced to look away from my peephole.

Moments later, the light died enough for me to look again. The entire dome was still aglow, but it was dim enough for me to see that it was empty, which led me to two conclusions: First, that Grampa was just "gone" as he said he would be, and I still had only a vague understanding of what he might have meant, but there had been a great deal for me to take in, so my thoughts were neither precise nor reliable. The second conclusion, however, is the one that claimed the greater part of my mind: Grampa was dead. I mean, for me, even if he wasn't really dead, he might just as well have been. He was, after all ... *gone*.

When the light had faded fully, I withdrew from the shelter and made my way with great trepidation to the mechanism in a state of disbelief and denial. What was I supposed to think? Grampa was gone. Not "gone" as in *gone* to the store and "back in a while" or *gone* to work and "be home tonight." Not *gone* as in saying that you still knew where he was. Not going, going, gone; He was *gone*; gone away; gone ahead; gone sour; gone along; gone the distance; gone to pot; gone for the kill; gone with the wind, gone for good; he was gone, baby, gone! I couldn't see him, and by all accounts, I wouldn't see him again. I couldn't touch him, and by all accounts, I wouldn't touch him again. I couldn't talk with him again; I couldn't listen to him again. Not ever. That's the kind of gone Grampa was. So far as I was able to determine at that point, Grampa was dead, and "gone" was merely a euphemism. That's what my heart was telling me; that's what my mind was telling me, and that's what the evidence was telling me. I dropped to my knees and wept.

170

*   *   *

AFTERMATH

*   *   *

I fell asleep in that room. At least I think I did. When I came out, it was dark outside. I briefly considered what danger there might be in the act of sleeping on lead, but then I realized that I really didn't care; the thought was little more than a point of interest just then. I started toward the sofa to sit in the spot Grampa had been sitting when I came over to his house. On my way there, though, I passed Grampa's portrait of Queen Elizabeth, and my mind told me that there was something different about it. I wasn't sure how it was different, so, after looking over the picture good and hard for a few seconds and finding nothing, I chose to disregard it as I had disregarded sleeping on a lead-covered floor. I finally made it to the sofa and sat by Grampa's Monarchy Scrapbook and just stared into space for ... well, for a long time, anyway. I finally found that I couldn't keep that up anymore, either, so I rolled onto my side and slept for the night right there on the sofa.

The next morning I called in "sick." I didn't lie and say I was sick, but that my grandfather was missing. I was surprised that they were so very understanding. Then again, Chapters is a huge bookstore with a huge staff. They wouldn't miss me. My boss told me to just take that day and the next off unless Grampa was found. I agreed and thanked her and for the rest of the day, I did nothing else to speak of. I did less, essentially, the following day, except that I did take a long, hot shower letting the water just run down my head and face. It was better than tears. Other than that, I slept and stared. I fed the dog and let him out when he needed it, but I didn't bathe him. I just let the mud dry. I went to "bed" early, and I stared and slept, both intermittently. The next morning, though, I began to feel a sense of strength returning to me.

I woke up on the sofa again and opted to shower, and this time to actually get clean. On my way, I passed Grampa's portrait of Her Majesty, regarding it only in passing and smiled, remembering how proud Grampa ... *had been* of his new prize. But no more than two or three steps beyond the portrait, I stopped. The same notion returned to me that had come to me before: Something was wrong with that portrait. I didn't see anything or note anything specific. I only knew that something about it was different. I went back, stood in front of it and examined it closely. Nothing stood out on a second viewing, but I kept looking over the entire item with nothing established. Still, the feeling nagged. It felt like those times when you watch a movie, and you recognize a certain actor. You know that you've seen that guy, heard that guy's voice, experienced his person in another film, and yet you cannot place the actor, his voice, his name or the movie that you know you've seen. I read the inscription and stared at the photo; I looked the entire picture over in detail. The more I looked, the more frustrated I grew, so I finally gave up. "Whatever!" I said to no one and tried to forget. After all, I did have plans to enjoy a shower and make myself presentable again.

I was in the shower with my mind in neutral when the tears came again, seemingly out of nowhere, but they lasted only a few seconds because a thought occurred to me; I heard it in my head in Grampa's voice, but it was about me. It was this: "In time, I will heal just like all living beings heal, including time." Then, speaking quietly, I said to no one, "Time heals, but there will always be a scar." Then, as though someone had just handed me new insight, I knew what to look for regarding that scar in Time, at least in part. I still had shampoo in my hair, but, forgetting that for the time being, I shut off the water, wrapped a towel around me, exited the bathroom and went to examine the inscription on the portrait once again as it hung on the wall:

Long live *Elizabeth the Second,*
by the Grace of God, Queen of Canada
and of Her other realms and territories,
Head of the Commonwealth, Defender of the Faith,
on her Diamond Jubilee, June 02, in the year of our LORD 2012.

"It's not there!" I whispered. I reached out to touch the plate, but it was under the glass. Then it occurred to me to examine Grampa's Scrapbook more closely. If everything is consistent—consistent in the new way—then Grampa's Scrapbook should also be different. Holding the towel tightly about me, I moved swiftly to the album still lying on the coffee table. It was open to the last picture that Grampa had put in, and, even though the chronology was never entirely rigid, it was still, decidedly, right near the end even now. The Scrapbook hadn't changed. If everything held, I thought, then I should see images of a Victoria much older than the 63 years that ...

But that wasn't the problem. The problem was that I was having difficulties learning to integrate two histories of the same period. On the one hand, I remembered that Grampa collected images of Queen Victoria all the way up to her 1882 demise. On the other hand, I also remembered that the same Queen Victoria died in 1901, and that 1882 was simply the year that filled this particular

172

volume of Grampa's Scrapbook. He had intended to begin another volume for her final two decades but simply never got around to it with his focus being divided among Victoria, Elizabeth II, Elizabeth I, all six Georges and a plethora of other British monarchs. Plus, he couldn't find a matching album. It was almost as though one Grampa in either history knew both histories and worked to prevent a horrible paradox. But I also soon realized that this was all irrelevant for now. I needed confirmation not mental ramblings on ideas that may or may not have any basis in history. That is to say, I realized that I could have been simply losing my marbles altogether.

I stood, tightened the towel about me and moved to Grampa's computer. It was in sleep mode, so just moving the mouse got it going again. I typed "Queen Victoria Years" into a search engine, expecting, of course, to see the same years I had known of her since I was old enough to understand: 1819-1882. But the computer told a different story, and I was dazed for a long time. But here's the extraordinary thing: Even though I was expecting the same years as before, I knew at the same time what the computer was going to tell me even before it showed me the year of Victoria's death. I remembered both histories as though I had lived my 22 years a second time. The difference is that, while one had been true, the other was true now, having supplanted the previous.

That brought up another even more serious issue in my memory, or memories: My mind's strongest memory at that point was that Grampa had gone back in time to prevent Victoria's assassination. Apparently, he was successful. So then, where was he? I mean, in this timeline, he wouldn't need to go back in time to save her, so he should be here, because, now, Victoria had lived to the ripe old age of 81, dying of natural causes. I had to dig deep to dredge up the memory of Grampa confessing to me that he simply wanted to meet Victoria whom he had loved for so long. It was a solitary memory, with great emotion but little action or impact. It's almost a miracle that I remembered it at all, but, oddly, the things he said to me just before his departure in both timelines are word-for-word identical. The memory of Grampa's confession and the memory of Grampa never finishing his Scrapbook, I began to realize, were more scars left behind on Time's being—scars placed there by Grampa's attack on Time. Not huge scars, it seems. They were little more than pin-pricks, but they remain, nonetheless.

I sat stunned, for a long time not noticing that Mudgod had been rubbing his muddy body against my wet legs. It wasn't until I finally put the "scar" into words that I came to myself again: "He did it," I said aloud but somewhat meditatively, like a man talking in his sleep. "Grampa saved her; he saved Queen Victoria!" I stayed in that chair in the dining room in my towel, reading for the first time what I had clearly read before. It was both new and not, simultaneously.

After some time, Mudgod made it clear to me that he was uncomfortable. While I continued to mindlessly scratch his chin, neck and ears, that was not the attention he wanted or needed so badly, and I realized that he had rubbed off a great deal of mud onto my legs that were now coated with what had been covering Mudgod. I smiled at him—my first smile in three days. Mudgod wagged his tail and barked. Still in my towel, I took Mudgod for a bath. The soap remained in my hair, but I'd pretty much forgotten about that because Mudgod was so uncomfortable. He ran ahead of me to the shower, setting his front paws on the tub's edge and looking up at me with those sad puppy eyes pleading with me. So I washed a small truckload of dirt down the drain, finished cleaning myself, got dressed and realized then that I felt better. I went back to the computer to find what other changes there might be for my new timeline. I had a lot to sort out in my mind and found it confusing: separating what had been confirmed from what seemed to me at that point to be current events, of a sort. It was like rebooting my brain after an overnight update.

It turned out that changes are few. King Edward lost some 20 years on the throne—years usurped unknowingly by his mother from one perspective, but years that belonged to Victoria from another. Most of the decrees and decisions by the crown or the crown and parliament remain the same. Those that differ are too minor and too few to bother with. I decided that I would be able to adjust to my new histories.

In 2017, in Grampa's honour, I followed through on the purchase he had wanted to make: A portrait of Her Majesty, Queen Elizabeth II that commemorates her Sapphire Jubilee. It now hangs in the same spot where the portrait for her Diamond Jubilee portrait had hung. With a full 65 years on the throne for Queen Elizabeth, Time had healed. Grampa's beloved Queen Elizabeth II had surpassed her predecessor by nearly two years on the throne. If all goes well for her, as I understand things, some time quite soon for me now, in June or July of 2024 Queen Elizabeth will not only be Britain's longest reigning monarch in history, but history's longest reigning monarch, period, and I, quite honestly, believe that she'll make it. Here's hoping, anyway.

So I now live in a world in which Queen Victoria survived eight assassination attempts. Originally, Roderick Maclean had had quite the perfect shot before the boys from Eton beat him nearly to death with their umbrellas. I "wondered" with a smile what had thrown his aim off in this new reality. What was the new element?

But of course, I knew. I imagine that Grampa had identified the pending marksman from photos and drawings of him and knocked him off balance with a jab of a walking stick, perhaps. Then, when the errant shot flew out, creating its natural confusion, Grampa slipped away from the crowds and let the Eton scholars do their thing with much less violence in this case. In both realities, though, Roderick Maclean lived the rest of his life in Broadmoor Asylum, dying in 1921 at the age of 67.

While I'm convinced that Grampa did change history in his own past, there's nothing else of him to report. There is no evidence of him anywhere else in 19th century England that I can find. I assume, since his initials were on the Gladstone bag, that he retained his name. One day I might look through records from cemeteries. Perhaps I'll be able to find his resting place. Perhaps not. It's good to know that he stuck with his own ethics and made no more scars on Time.

That's all well and good. History has regained its natural, calm, steady flow. It might be a point of interest, however, that I found Grampa's Gladstone bag for sale on eBay. I asked the British owner for high-definition photos of the gilded initials and confirmed before making a purchase that the markings are the same. The seller sent me some 20 photos with different angles and lighting, all quite professionally done. The bag cost me $100 plus shipping. It remains in fine condition, but the question stands: how old is it? Having been owned and re-owned by the same folks, presumably, is the bag just 150 years old or is it 300? I suppose that the idea that I, at the age of 22, having 44 years of memories does not make me 44 years old might answer that question.

But there is one alteration that few shall know of, and it's in me. Grampa "vanished" (for want of a better term) several years ago, at this point. I live in his house; I teach in his school, and Mudgod, old and frail now, has become my friendly companion. The four times a year that Grampa, by strong emotional tradition, enjoyed a shot of his beloved Canadian whiskey, I do so now, but I've added a fifth date to commemorate the man who was my grandfather and who became my adoptive father. Five shots of whiskey annually by tradition for love and for memories.

But you need to understand that I discovered Grampa's changes to Time after his reappearance into time in the past. That is to say, the very things that Grampa has done that are now many decades in the past are influencing my life even now, and he's been gone for many a-year. The fact that these actions occurred well over a century ago—well over Grampa's lifetime ago—render them no less impactful on me than if they'd happened today—this minute, even.

Quantum physics discusses time as a three-dimensional thing that they illustrate with a globe. Time moves about the equator, but all events that occur in time converge into a dot—an instant—at the poles, which you might think of as God's perspective. At the poles, there is no time between events; there is no time; all events occur simultaneously. This is the best description of how I see Grampa now. It explains how his influence is just as poignant for me now, at this moment, as it was before his "disappearance" and as it very well might be as Time flows onward. Grampa is still able to touch my life, communicate with me and even direct me to some degree. Grampa is alive, right now, at this moment, even though he is living more than a century in the past. I sense no separation, no paradox; there is no division of Time between us. What he has already accomplished is still just occurring in my life, even as I speak. Can you see the comfort that I find in that? There is solace that can in no other way be explained. Grampa cannot be "gone" if he's still right here. I am still guided by his wisdom ... by his intelligence, his wit, his example. Even if his example or learning is decades—or centuries—old, it is current and relevant.

Now, I may still shake my head when I think about that; I shake my head as if trying to get the contradictory elements of this truth to settle evenly in my brain, to level out and pack together, but they won't have it, and I think that I'll be shaking my head regarding this for whatever years remain of my life.

Of course, Grampa's disappearance had to be investigated. The police looked askance at me because I had called in to work with the news of his disappearance without calling the police to report it. Logical. Since there was no evidence of foul play—mainly because there had been no foul play—their doubts came to nothing. And while I showed that I was telling the truth, it was also apparent that I wasn't telling the whole truth, even though I told nothing but the truth. They saw Grampa's machine, but I had removed the power source, so, while certain portions of ground in the mountains on Vancouver Island may glow at night for the next few years for those few who might happen upon the right spots, the machine itself was seen as nothing but an oddity, which led them to believe that Grampa's mental capacity was also something of an oddity, and all that helped them move toward closing the case on Grampa's disappearance all the more swiftly.

I did, finally, dismantle Grampa's mechanism. The lead—which has a value of about a dollar per pound—I just donated to the first people who would please take it off my hands. As for the crystal, well, I cut that up into small chunks, many with a little hole, stuck a chain through each and sold them as jewellery: brooches or pendants at $60.00 apiece. I sold all but one that I have kept. I stored it away in the safe that I use to guard important documents. Since I still have plans and hopes of taking a bride at some point, I have a unique gift for her when I do, and a story to accompany it.

THE END

Introduction to
"Time Out of Mind"

The original vision for this story was to have my Jack Henderson character send three time travellers to different times on earth, but as the time machine began to fail, the travellers, each, in turn, would see a portal appear near them. As it grew progressively more consumed with fire or heat, readers saw it disintegrate from the perspectives of all three travellers in tandem. I wanted to illustrate the idea that, from God's perspective, all points in time, from creation to time's own demise, all exist simultaneously. This point explains, in part, why the story, as it stands today, is rendered mostly in present tense—to demonstrate that all times are "now." Indeed, Jesus said, "Before Abraham was I am," which, while a distinct claim to his divinity, is also, grammatically, a claim that while he is speaking with contemporaries of 2000 years ago from our perspective, he is also, simultaneously, walking and talking with Abram some 1500 years earlier, and he is also at all points earlier in time, and presumably all points in the future from that perspective in time. Time, from Jesus's perspective, is without points or eras or ages, but is all an instant. This is the point that I strove to illustrate, but succeeded with it in the story "All in Good Time." My original storyline for "Time Out of Mind" was a flop, especially since Quantum Physicists illustrate the same point far more eloquently, succinctly and clearly with their own diagrams.

So, here I am, stuck with three time travellers stuck in three different times and a person controlling all of their time-travelling events. I liked the characters, and I liked the setup. I didn't want to abandon them just because I felt compelled to abandon the one storyline. It didn't take years or even months, this time for me to find a way to conclude the story. What I came up with you can read on the following pages.

An added point of interest, however: Jack Henderson's surname comes from a character in a made-for-TV movie called *The Henderson Monster*, which aired in 1980. I saw it the year before I graduated from high school. I enjoyed it immensely, and it had a profound impact on me. It is available on YouTube currently, if ever you're interested.

My point in naming my lead character after this movie's lead character is not just that I enjoyed the movie, but that my character also creates a sort of monster. It's not biological, but it is potentially enough of a monster to warrant investigation by the government in my story.

178

Time Out of Mind

The things that are deeply hidden belong to the Lord our God,
but the things revealed belong to us and to our children . . .
for all time . . .
—Deuteronomy 29:29

Brian Guo sits near the vineyards in Sian, in the Yellow River Valley of China, observing the area of night sky between the horns in the constellation Taurus. He is making mere naked-eye observations because, aside from the tiny note pad and writing utensil that he can easily hide, he is allowed only contemporary instrumentality—a restriction of Henderson's devising that was an immediate frustration for Guo.

"How many times will we be able to observe the greatest supernova of recorded history?" was Guo's argument. "Plenty," was Henderson's reply, and Guo found himself strangely disappointed by it. "If we're careful," Henderson continued, preoccupied with his computers and other sensitive equipment, "we'll send hundreds of observers, each to different areas to keep their observations independent ... and to keep them from meeting each other—it's confusing enough as it is. Imagine meeting someone who was sent there twenty years after you were. Plus, there are dangers to consider." He continued without meeting Guo's eyes: "The Administration will find out about this, and if they think we've been the least bit careless, they'll shut us down, posthaste."

179

Judging by the movement of the stars, Guo estimates that he's been observing for roughly four and a half, maybe five hours without any sign of the illusive "guest star" that he's been waiting for. *There are only so many hours to a summer's night,* he muses. *I won't have to wait much longer; the star visits tonight—July fourth of this year.*

Having grown up loving stars, Guo could identify the planets and all their major moons by his eighth birthday. He paid for half the cost of his first telescope when he turned thirteen, and one of his greatest joys after that was hearing people's delight when they saw Saturn up close for the first time, or the Orion Nebula, or just the surface of the moon. By the time he was twenty, he could locate hundreds of celestial objects, so he spent many clear evenings sharing space with his friends. He earned his Ph.D. in astrophysics before he was thirty and spent the first ten years of his career looking for and hoping for events just like the one he now waits for in China. Even though he's forced to observe without even a pair of binoculars, at least he is here, and this is an extraordinary opportunity.

Imagine, Guo smiles, *a man comes to witness the astronomical event of recorded history more than a thousand years after it occurred! It's a wonderful time to be alive!* And reclining on the grass, folding his hands behind his head, Guo realizes how nice it is after all to have to observe without aids. Gazing at the sky, he remembers the last time he simply "look'd up in perfect silence at the stars"—ages ago. Pity. Every once in a while it's good to forget that we're trying to learn and allow ourselves to simply enjoy, because it's the enjoyment, after all, that got us wanting to learn in the first place.

Then, like the strike of a match and growing discernibly brighter, the nova makes its presence known, and Guo stands as though thinking that he might get a better view. Within seconds it's brighter than Sirius, and shortly after than, brighter than Venus, and Guo notices that in its light he casts a visible shadow. He sits again while the star continues to grow. "Even brighter than what was recorded," Guo whispers while trying to both hide his eyes from the star's light and record all the pertinent information on his note pad. *The ancient Chinese must have an over-developed gift for understatement; this can never be outdone!*

While he continues to watch, Guo notices another object appear beside him—a red, glowing rectangle about the size of a household door. "The portal!" Guo whispers. "But I should have lots of time!" Despite his intense desire to stay, Guo realizes that Henderson wouldn't have sent for him yet if there weren't a problem. Disappointed, he shakes his head and steps toward the glowing door.

*　*　*

180

Daniel Kauffman would never have guessed that Jerusalem during Solomon's reign would've been so large or the people so friendly if he hadn't seen it with his own eyes; it's hard to imagine a city in which gold is so plentiful that silver is looked on with disdain. Even Babylon in all its storied splendour wasn't (or won't be) dressed half so well. *So this is the city,* Kauffman muses, *that was "the perfection of beauty, the joy of the whole earth!" I can understand why,* Kauffman notes. *The streets are clean and well maintained; the people are happy and comfortable, and even though the city is walled, it feels open and welcoming.*

Even as a boy, Kauffman had been proud of his heritage. Longing to visit the Holy Land himself, but never able to, he developed a profound jealousy for any of his friends who made the trip, be they Christian, Jew or Muslim. All their comments about standing where Jesus had stood, or walking where David had walked had made him shake with envy, but now he has his revenge; he's not standing where Solomon *may have stood,* he's standing where Solomon *might stand*—tomorrow! and where Jesus *will walk*—one day.

He stands, now, fifty yards or so from Jerusalem's recently dedicated temple. He longs to go nearer but cannot consider himself to be ceremonially clean according to the standards of Solomon's time. Besides, there are lots of people around to hold him at bay, each equally as enamoured with the new temple as Kauffman. They each take a moment to stop and admire the structure, pointing and marveling. *It is wondrous to behold,* Kauffman decides. He looks around again at the city, then back at the temple. *Nothing compares with this!*

He walks to the front to examine the *façade* for any detail that he might take with him. The architecture is utterly unique. *It has a humble feel,* Kauffman concludes, *unpretentious. It fits aesthetically with the rest of the city, and yet no other building resembles it. And what's the precedent for the architecture?* Kauffman wonders, turning his attention to the two bronze pillars. *With the exception of the fact that they are pillars, they are entirely unique. The flutes run in intersecting spirals rather than straight up and down the shafts. The bowl-shaped capitals are accentuated with ornate festoons of flowers, involute maple leaves, and the four hundred pomegranates that made them famous—marvels of hand-crafted design.*

What amazes me most, though, Kauffman decides, *is that they built the temple and its columns wider at the top than at the bottom! What culture dares defy the laws of physics so blatantly? Plans for a building like this would be rejected by every inspector in the 22nd century.* At that moment Kauffman notices the narrow filament of Henderson's portal suddenly appearing to his left; he breaks his silence to hiss, "It's still daylight, Henderson!" He glances around; no one seems to notice. Taking one last look at the temple, realizing that there must be a problem back home, he reluctantly moves to the door.

*   *   *

The year for George Sipiros currently, is 285 B. C. He stands, awe-struck, at the foot of the "brazen giant of Greek fame" that he had studied as a boy—the now five-year-old, 105-feet-tall Colossus of Rhodes created by the hand of the artist, Chares. Sipiros's grade-seven teacher had required his class to memorize all seven Wonders of the Ancient World for a test in history—a task that had thrilled Sipiros. When he was young, most of his friends loved dinosaurs, old cartoons, cars or space ships, but Sipiros loved the Greeks, from Troy to Rome. He memorized every detail he could find on the seven Wonders; eventually, Colossus grew to be his favourite. As a young man, Sipiros visited every imitation of it: the Statue of Liberty, the remains of Mt. Rushmore, The Motherland—the sword-brandishing sculpture in Volgograd; he'd even visited the enormous bronze Buddha in Tokyo—four times the size of Colossus— each very impressive, but nothing beats the original, and—oh, yes—he got an 'A' on that test.

Sipiros originally wanted to sketch all seven Wonders, but certain constraints necessitated the visitation of only one. He found little difficulty deciding which it would be, and he wasn't disappointed. *This is a fairy story of a mission!*

He stands now, holding charcoal and a crude form of paper, frozen in a pose of one who is drawing, as though he were the model rather than the artist. His goal is to draw the Colossus, but he only moves his head, looking up and down the sculpture as he takes in every detail, just as he had in grade seven. It, too, has a crown of seven rays, but they're longer than those of Lady Liberty. The nude figure doesn't straddle the harbour, thankfully (in grade seven he and his friends wondered how any self-respecting sailor could pass under a nude Colossus without gagging); even so, the feet are set apart from each other. The statue stands in a pose that gives it the appearance of ... a dancer, perhaps, or a gymnast—frozen in an elegant mid-stride, the engaged leg requiring understated contrapposto since the heal of the rear foot is lifted, and the back arches as the figure lifts his lamp toward heaven. This isn't the static Colossus Sipiros had studied as a boy; *it's far better! ... and the detail—the tension in the muscles, the protruding veins, even the elegant stance—exquisite! But for all that,* Sipiros notes, *there is a distinct hint of facial expression, well beyond the typical poker face of other classical sculptures such as* The Discus Thrower, *although still clearly less expression than* Laocoön. *Colossus has only little sense of movement*

182

in keeping with the more static stances of many classical sculptures, and it has, to a small degree, the taut and twisted torso of Hellenistic sculptures. It has the delicate elegance of the Classical era in its pose with the robust details of the Hellenistic era in its execution. I'll be! Instead of straddling the harbour, Chares' work straddles the line between two artistic styles; the Colossus stands on the cutting edge of art for its day—right on the cutting edge!

Sipiros is standing in the same place when the sun sets and Henderson's neon-like portal appears beside him. Its ominous significance wakes him with dismay from his study. "Not yet!" Sipiros cries, "I just got here! I need more time!" He waits, almost expecting a reply from the portal, but knowing it wouldn't have appeared if there weren't a problem at home, either with the computer or—God forbid!—the Administration! "Henderson is recalling me for a reason, I suppose. Maybe it is time." He takes one last look at Colossus, then grudgingly makes his way to the door.

*   *   *

Jack Henderson sits alone in the Audience Hall of the Administration, the governing body of the Conjoined Nations of the Western World (CNWW). It's a room similar to a court room but without the seating areas for jury and observers. The only notable features, in fact, are the uncomfortable, non-form fitting, archaic wooden chair on which Henderson sits and the looming bench of the Council of the Administration accompanied by plush, leather seats and a small microphone centered in front of each. Like that in a court room, the Council's bench possesses stately construction of dark wood but in a triangle with the bottom corners curving around Henderson, forming a semi-circle along the base. The twelve-foot peak is the post of His Lordship, the nameless—and for most people, faceless—leader of the Administration's twelve elders who sit at lower posts beside His Lordship, six on either side. The elders and His Lordship comprise the Council, the august body that heads the Administration, which governs the CNWW from Chicago.

In this hall that he and his compatriots have always feared, Henderson sits and rubs the side of his index finger nervously across his thick moustache. It used to be dark as well as dense, but he's been too busy in recent years to notice that it is now almost entirely gray. He had spent several minutes looking about the Hall, but since he's already taken note of the details of the chamber, there's nothing else to see, so his deep brown eyes stare ahead through the unkempt gray bangs that fall nearly to his cheek bones. His anxiety is steadily mounting. Soon the Council will enter from the door that stands behind His Lordship's post, and then ... what? What is the basis for his appearance? Has he been arrested? On what charges? "What have I done?" he asks aloud, and in the Hall, his voice echoes around the room. In what might seem a response to his question, the door behind the bench suddenly opens, and twelve middle-aged citizens, men and women apparently from every corner of the earth, wearing dark, ceremonial robes, enter. Henderson immediately sits up from his slouched position as the elders take seats behind the bench with little more than emotionless glances in Henderson's direction. They say nothing.

Moments later, as if by some invisible cue, the elders stand; Henderson himself, for reasons he doesn't quite grasp, stands with them. His Lordship then enters through the same door the elders had used and stands behind the more throne-like seat of his post for just a moment, and Henderson feels the stun of seeing His Lordship's face for the first time; there are never any clear pictures of him published, and when he's quoted on the news, you only hear his voice—no one *sees* him—and here he is, in the flesh. He appears to be in his late sixties, say, ten years Henderson's senior, but it's impossible to identify any one race in his visage; his face has the complexion of Europeans with the features of Blacks, the dark, straight hair of Arabians and the intense eyes of Asians. Henderson is embarrassed to acknowledge that the only adjective he could think of to describe His Lordship is "beautiful," like the face of an ancient sculpture in a museum. After a few moments of what might be a ritualistic pause, His Lordship, the elders, and Henderson sit simultaneously. But as the Council members shuffle papers, sip water, and settle themselves, Henderson's posture begins to droop again under the weight of his own insecurity and the tension of the silence. Finally, the elders fold their hands in front of them, look directly toward Henderson and remain entirely silent as and His Lordship clears his throat and opens the meeting:

"Very well, I call this meeting to order." Henderson notes that His Lordship's voice echoes in the chamber as his own had moments before, and he reasons that the microphone before each member of the council is not for amplification, as there clearly is no need, but to record the events. "Everyone is represented," His Lordship continues, "and I remind you that these proceedings are classified." His Lordship pauses and glances at some papers in front of him. "Now, uh, Mr. Henderson, I appreciate the fact that you were brought here without any warning—at best, a very disconcerting situation for you. Am I right?"

As His Lordship speaks, Henderson notes that, with the echo—is it His Lordship's voice or his words?—there flows to Henderson a wave of calming reassurance, and he can feel his spine begin to straighten. "In all honesty, Lordship," Henderson begins, so dazed by the company he finds himself among that he feels almost whimsical, "'disconcerting' is as much of an understatement as I can imagine."

His Lordship muses on that comment briefly. "No doubt. I do apologize, Mr. Henderson, but it was necessary." He regards the documents with greater intensity as he continues. "You are an inventor, of sorts, an engineer, and a bit of an electronics genius. Correct?"

"The Administration has provided me with an excellent education, yes, Lordship."

"And I see that you have taken wise advantage of your education, Mr. Henderson. You've earned titles, and been presented with awards and honouraria in the form of degrees and grants, not to mention your extensive list of varied accomplishments in the sciences. That is how I like to see an education appreciated." His Lordship wipes a tentative hand over his face showing what might be embarrassment, if it were anyone else. "And I don't want to put you on the spot any more than you have been, but it can't be avoided, I'm afraid." His Lordship pauses, putting his weight on his elbows. "We are aware that among your many and varied achievements, especially recently, is the discovery of how to travel through time. Am I right, Mr. Henderson? Please be honest."

Normally, Henderson might have lied without compunction, but he feels no need to, even though he is understandably stunned by His Lordship's discovery. "I have achieved a ... *basic* ... understanding of the principles involved in time travel, yes, Lordship. I must admit my surprise by Your Lordship's wealth of knowledge."

His Lordship waves a hand in the air, as if to say, "Fiddlesticks." "Don't think of us as 'Big Brother,' Mr. Henderson. We haven't been spying on you. There was ..." His Lordship considers his terms and finally nods slightly to the side, acknowledging that there is only one term, "... there was an informant."

Henderson's mind races, searching for who might know about his research. There are only three people who are aware of his experiments, and none of them are ... present. He was careful to maintain absolute secrecy. *There can be no informant!*

"Please, Mr. Henderson," His Lordship continues, "don't trouble yourself with trying to figure out who the informant might be. There are so many details in a person's life that no one can possibly secure everything. As a matter of fact, I'm surprised that you were able to keep your research a secret for as long as you did. Chicago is the capital of the world's largest nation in history as measured by population, prosperity and even by geography. But, while we can track, even from

185

the moon, mind you, the movements of ... an amoeba ... if we were so inclined, you stood right in sight, and the Administration never noticed you." His Lordship leans toward Henderson. "I want to dissuade you from thinking of this informant as some tattling little brother: This was information offered entirely unwittingly. I brought you here, Mr. Henderson, so that we might reason together about this, as I feel we must. If I need to make decisions at these proceedings, I shall, but that's not my initial purpose." After a space of time for emphasis, His Lordship confesses, "I am truly amazed. You have found what every great literary and scientific imagination has sought for centuries. Tell me, what is it about time travel that motivated you to try to make it possible, Mr. Henderson?"

Henderson isn't sure if he's frightened, but he's certainly dazed from learning about an informant and therefore entirely unaware of what he's saying when he responds to His Lordship's question: "Jack."

His Lordship sits forward in his seat, perplexed. "I beg your pardon?"

"Jack is my given name," Henderson says, almost whispering. "Your Lordship may call me Jack."

His Lordship, pleased with Henderson's gesture, responds amicably: "Why, thank you. I shall then, Jack."

"Would Your Lordship please repeat the question?"

"Of course. What is it that compelled you to research time travel?"

Still climbing out of his daze, Henderson responds, "Questions."

"Questions? Please explain, Jack. What questions are you trying to answer?"

"The mysteries that can be explored only through time travel. The questions humanity has pondered for centuries but can't answer because we've been unable to access the past."

"To what mysteries do you so desperately need answers, Jack? Have you any examples?"

Henderson feels the fog beginning to lift. As his presence of mind slowly returns, he responds with continuously increasing clarity. "Yes, Lordship. Troy."

"Troy?"

"Specifically, Schliemann's Troy. Did he discover the Troy that Homer talks about or some obscure city? There are only two ways of knowing: either find, in what we believe to be Troy, an artifact that tells us definitively, 'This is the Troy of Homer fame,' or travel back to 1200 B.C. to see if Schliemann's Troy and Homer's Troy are one and the same." As Henderson's mind continues to clear, the passion from his time-travel research returns, and the questions that he'd almost forgotten spill from his mind and shoot from his mouth with rapid-fire succession. "Or what about the pyramids, hmm? When were they built? and how? and by whom? Lordship, we have theories that have responded to these questions, but no answers, no real explanations. And what about Noah's Ark? Was there a world-wide flood? We have evidence that says there was, and that says there wasn't. Who wrote *The Epic of Gilgamesh, Beowulf, The Arabian Nights* and all those other ancient, anonymous literary works? Why did Michelangelo take a sledgehammer to the *Pietá* that he had intended to stand over his grave? Why did King George III really stand at the premiere of Handel's 'Hallelujah Chorus?' Was it really that he was so moved by the music or that his backside was tired from sitting through the entire oratorio? Was there a city of Atlantis? Where was it? What happened to it? These, Lordship, are the questions that only time travel can answer—the questions that so captivate me that I needed to find a way to investigate them. That is why I explored the possibility of time travel."

His Lordship nods, "Mm hmm. Your passion testifies to your veracity. Very commendable. Far too many people would have wanted to learn the final scores of sports events to come, or the future of the stock market, or worse." When His Lordship closes, Henderson takes advantage of the silence to add a further thought in his own defense: "If I may, Lordship: If travel into the future is to be done any faster than the speed we are heading there right now, my creation won't take us. Forward travel from our present is quite different from travel back, and I researched time travel so that I would be able to answer questions, not create them."

"Very good, Jack. That certainly adds to my confidence. Still, as you are most assuredly aware, literature that deals with time travel almost always testifies to the many real dangers for a society that begins travelling to the past. The minutest mishap might create a chain of events that alters our present. A traveller may catch the malaria, for instance, that was meant to kill a person of that time. That person then lives and changes his of her own future to our potential detriment. There are theories that both support and deny this hypothesis, but the reasoning seems sound. We must proceed cautiously. Now, tell me, Jack, how far have you progressed in your research?"

A long, nervous silence ensues. Henderson feels drops of sweat form on his brow.

With a note of apprehension, His Lordship asks, "Jack, you *are* confining your research to your laboratory, are you not?"

No response.

Finally, with a hint of exasperation, "Jack, your research should be confined to the lab at this point. Are you or are you not conforming to that expectation?"

"No." Henderson says at last to the floor.

"Pardon me?!" His Lordship stands.

Henderson takes a deep breath and repeats, "No, Lordship, I have not confined my research to the lab." He hesitates. "I have already sent three men to different times in history—as observers only."

His Lordship turns on the elders with angry surprise, "Why was I not informed of this?" Suddenly an uproar among the Council consumes the silence that had prevailed. The elders gesture to others across the bench, asking if so-and-so wasn't supposed to be in charge of that. They raise their palm, denying any knowledge or place their hands on their breasts, disclaiming responsibility. Finally, His Lordship serenely rests his hands on the bench looking solemnly toward them to regain order. The elders quickly calm, and Henderson interjects, "Lordship, I can assure you that I have taken every precaution against mishap."

"Have you, Mr. Henderson? And just how can you be so certain?"

Henderson hesitates again. Without some precedent, there is no way he can prove that he's taken every precaution, but he knows that he has; he can feel it. He'd quadruple-checked his figures independently. He and the travellers had anticipated every conceivable contingency. He knows that's not enough for a discovery of this magnitude when it's still so new, but his gut tells him that he's right. He is just about to respond when His Lordship cuts him off. "Never mind, Jack, I withdraw the question." Briefly considering what further information he may need and with a sense of resignation His Lordship asks, "Tell me, then, what precautions you have taken."

After a moment to collect his thoughts, Henderson explains his careful approach: "The reason that I began my research in Chicago, Lordship, is that I knew that I would have a larger population of educated people to draw from in our nation's capital, than I would if I'd stayed in New York. I found three people who are experts in their fields; each is highly intelligent, well educated, and capable of completely independent work. Two of them, Daniel Kauffman and George Sipiros, entered career fields directly related to their distinct cultural pasts; the third, Brian Guo, is a brilliant astronomer. All three, because of their interest in this project, eagerly became fluent in the languages of the countries and times to which I sent them; that way they have a tool to help them remain unobtrusive if interaction were to become necessary; I didn't send anyone who might be interested, Lordship. I chose those who best suited my purpose, clothed them in costumes appropriate for the areas and eras they were to travel to, and sent each to his own cultural past: Dr. Kauffman to Israel in 1004 B.C. to study

188

the architecture of Solomon's temple; Dr. Sipiros to the island of Rhodes in 285 B.C. to study the Colossus; and Dr. Guo to China in ... uh, ... yes, 1054 A.D. to observe the supernova that created the Crab Nebula. I chose the travellers first, Lordship, then gave missions specific to their own cultures. I denied them all modern instruments; each went as someone from the time to which he was sent, and each was given a clearly-defined, twelve-hour mission with explicit instructions to interact with no one if at all possible. They know precisely what the portal looks like for their return trips, and I can recall each of them in history without concern about geographic or temporal distances."

His Lordship concedes, "You seem to have covered all the problem areas," then, leaning forward for emphasis, "but we will never know, will we?" His Lordship reclines again with a fore-finger across his mouth, and after a long moment, he closes his eyes and massages his brow: "How long have your men been gone?"

"With due respect, Lordship, the question is irrelevant. At any time here I can bring them back from any time there, if Your Lordship gets my meaning. I can wait ten years here and bring them back from there the moment they arrive. Or, right now, I can recall them from ten years after their arrival there. But if Your Lordship's question is 'when did I send them?' Well, I sent them only moments before Your Lordship's men came to bring me here, coincidentally. I was making the adjustments to recall them, but I was suddenly brought before Your Lordship, and that's one reason that the timing of my appearance here was so problematic."

"Then you can bring them back before they damage the past?"

"Lordship, these men and I did everything humanly possible to prepare for such travel and to avoid causing any damage to the past; in all honesty, though, if there is damage, we can't know about it until they return. But, may I remind Your Lordship that I can bring them back anytime I wan ..." he switches direction when he sees His Lordship's disapproving expression, "... anytime it is required of me."

His Lordship smiles, "It must feel nice to wield such power."

"Yes, Lordship," Henderson returns the smile, "it does."

The two hold each other's eyes for a long moment before Henderson finally drops his gaze to the floor. "Good," His Lordship asserts with a nod of his head. "Now, the elders and I are going to meet in chambers for a time, Jack; wait here until we return." Without a pause, the Council stands and files through the door behind the bench.

*　　*　　*

Strange how father-like he is, Henderson muses. The apprehension that he had known earlier has returned, and he slouches again like a boy waiting to see the principal. He is entirely unaware of how long the council has been in chambers, but he *is* aware of how utterly anxious he is. Twenty-five years. This entire project—all of his research, all of his experiments, all of his careful calculations and cautious dry runs, all of his extraordinary financial investments, his secrecy, his sacrifices, his dreams—everything hangs in the balance to be decided upon right this instant. *If it goes my way,* Henderson promises himself, *there is no foreseeable end to my celebration, but if it doesn't ...* Henderson brushes away the thought; it's too much to think about right now, but the thought proves relentless; it *will* be considered. *What shall I do? I suppose I have other projects to keep me busy—ideas stuffed in the back of my mind for future reference, but this ... this would be such a grand success! And if the Council endorses it, there'll be no end of my success hereafter. But if they don't ...*

Finally the Council enter and resume their places without the formality and rigamarole of their first appearance. Once seated, His Lordship begins. "Jack, I want to tell you a story: There was a king who ruled an ancient, illiterate society, Now, they were illiterate only because writing, for them, had yet to be invented." His Lordship leans forward, lacing his fingers together and resting his forearms on the bench. "One day, a citizen of this country travelled to another kingdom where he learned the skills of reading and writing and eventually brought them back to his country to present to his king. 'Here, my Lord,' this citizen said, bowing reverently, 'is what your servant has brought back from distant lands. If it pleases your majesty, he may command me and I, your humble subject, will teach these arts to all your majesty's people.' The king took his citizen's gift to ponder it for several days, then, when he had decided what benefit these skills might have, he had the citizen brought before him again. 'I will not have these crafts in my kingdom, for if my subjects resort to recording everything they need, their minds will weaken until they depend on records rather than on their wits.' The king made the citizen swear to keep writing a secret, for on the day another citizen was taught to read or wright, both he and that citizen would be banished." His Lordship pauses, then, "Tell me, Jack, what's your opinion of this king's edict?"

Henderson is unable to respond for a few moments, vexed by the nagging question, *Does this mean what I think it means?* He squeezes his eyes closed, forcing himself to think but reluctantly conceding that there may be some wisdom in the king's decision. *Dependence does weaken,* Henderson's mind tells him. *And the fact that the king was able to foresee his subjects' dependence on reading and writing shows insight, especially for an ancient king.* Henderson must

190

acknowledge the truth of these ideas, *but I don't dare respond like that! I'll be condemning my own work! What's wrong with the king's decision? Focus on that, Henderson. Focus on the problems it may cause!* With much struggle, Henderson's mind finally folds around an idea; he feels the muscles around his eyes relax and a self-assured smile form. He opens his eyes and says, "I do see some misguided wisdom in the king's decision, Lordship, but his wisdom would ultimately be wiped from the earth. In fact, so would his name, the knowledge of his country and his people; the very fact that he had lived would ultimately be forgotten because the king, himself, banned the only method of recording any of this information, preventing him from being remembered, Lordship, that is, unless it's through time travel." He bites his lower lip, not wanting to smile too broadly in this forum. His Lordship does smile, albeit mildly, and Henderson is amazed that, while His Lordship smirks at a weak joke, his eyes can simultaneously transmit a warning—a reminder not to push too far. *It's no wonder he's leading this country,* Henderson concludes.

"So, you find the king's decision to be unwise?"

"Yes, Lordship. After all, 'knowledge is power.'"

"Is it? No decision, perhaps, can be fully assessed except in hind sight. Do you agree?"

"I have no knowledge in that area, Lordship."

"Haven't you? Interesting. Now, concerning your time travel discovery, Jack, I want to commend you on both a fascinating achievement and a thorough job of dealing with potential problems in the matter; I see no real oversight," His Lordship meets Henderson's eyes, "but that doesn't mean there aren't any." Suddenly His Lordship appears fatigued, even sad. "Let me share another thought with you, Jack. Please listen carefully."

Henderson feels completely off balance. Whenever he thinks he knows where the discussion is leading, His Lordship seems to shift directions.

"The relation between wondering and knowing," His Lordship says, "is often the same as that between wanting and having. We feel that our wanting will be fulfilled by having whatever it is that we want, when in reality, wanting is often its own fulfilment. The same is true of wondering and knowing. People don't wonder about the colour of an elephant, do they, because they know that a elephant's colour is roughly grey. Am I right?"

"Yes, Lordship." Henderson responds, as dazed as he had been before, and not a little confused, and perhaps even annoyed with His Lordship's discourse.

"So when a person tells us that he's seen ... pink elephants, if you'll please pardon the cliché, the rest of us know there's a problem. Elephants aren't pink except to those who are unable, for whatever reason, to see clearly. We know the elephant's colour, but we don't know the colour of, say, the tyrannosaurus. He may very well have been pink; it's doubtful because there is no precedent for large, pink, presumably hairless animals, but it is possible. Are you with me?"

"Yes, Lordship."

"Some people, though, think that the tyrannosaurus may have had stripes, some say spots, some say that it was just a single 'lizard' colour, whatever that means, while the leading theory is that it was covered with brightly coloured feathers. The point is that not knowing the colour opens the door for people to suggest a colour. So, yes, knowledge is powerful, in as much as it either stifles or sparks imagination, but imagination is the real power because it gives us unlimited options. In fact, the answers that come through people's imaginations can be more amazing than facts, which often seem trivial by comparison." His Lordship pauses for just a moment. "Consider the mass's reactions to the first photos from the surface of the moon, Jack. They removed all of the speculation, all of the wonder from how people thought the surface might appear, and it became a rather dull, hilly terrain much like we see on the surface of earth? And no one can paint the fantastic, crystalline surface anymore because the facts now get in the way.

Finally anticipating His Lordship's direction, Henderson opens his mouth to protest. He wants to say, "What about education and learning, Lordship? They lead to knowledge, and if knowledge closes doors to imagination, shouldn't they be banned?" These things he wants to say, but His Lordship responds to Henderson's unspoken protest, "Some things don't need to be known, Jack, like the mysteries that are hidden in time. The fact that you and I are here discussing that idea is proof. Still, your questions can be answered through literature and art, through formal debates or friendly discussions, through discoveries and interpretations of new artifacts or the research of fresh, young minds. We base our arts and sciences on what we know, but where there are gaps in knowledge, we supply the missing information through our imaginations, and they give art and science real power; imagination, in fact, is the very thing that motivated you to create time travel. The questions that you want answered came into your mind through your imagination, Jack. Answer them through your imagination. Everything that you *need* is right before you. Put time travel out of your mind."

Again, His Lordship pauses. When He speaks again, his tone is decidedly more administrative than it had been. "I'm sorry, Jack, but you are to go home and immediately recall your people on assignment; recall them from the moment they step foot in the past. Further, you are to disassemble your lab, erase your disks and destroy all research and data pertaining to time travel. Burn whatever burns. It is not to be simply thrown away because it could be too easily retrieved. Have I made myself clear?"

Nearly in tears, Henderson nods.

"Let the record indicate, however, that Jack Henderson's creation was abandoned only due to potential dangers to national security. I want to make no declarations that might hinder his creativity.

"I'm sending some of my people with you, Jack ..." Three men enter the Audience Hall. His Lordship emphasizes to them his final instructions, "... as assistants only, is that clear?" The three men, and Henderson, too, nod. "Good. I want this done today. Nothing hanging over our heads." His Lordship continues, making eye contact with Henderson. "Jack, you're a brilliant, innovative engineer. In time, you will create something that I will approve. Don't lose heart."

"Yes, Lordship." The three men lead Henderson out. He's still dazed, but only for the present. The door to the audience hall closes decisively behind them.

* * *

Several hours later, Mike Reynolds, one of the three who accompanies Henderson to his lab, will return to His Lordship's office and knock quietly on the door. Upon hearing permission to enter, he'll open the door just enough to poke his head in, and he'll find His Lordship seated behind his desk reading through stacks of papers.

"Yes, what is it?" His Lordship's voice will indicate his intensity, but he won't sound unkind when he makes eye contact with Reynolds.

"An update on the Henderson affair, Lordship. All materials and data concerning his project have been destroyed as you ordered ..." He'll pause here, looking nervously to the floor.

"Yes, go on," His Lordship will encourage, sitting back in his chair.

"The three travellers have returned safely, Lordship."

"Good. What's the problem?"

"Bio-scans indicate that all three aged roughly five hours under Henderson's ... care, Lordship, but there's clearly nothing we are able to do to fix it."

"Five hours?"

"Yes, Lordship."

Smiling mildly, His Lordship will look quickly around his office as He pats his torso with his palms. "Well, everything seems to be in order; don't you agree?" He'll ask.

"Everything appears to be consistent with all that I took for granted prior to Mr. Henderson's hearing, yes, Lordship," Reynolds will concede.

"Thank you, Mr. Reynolds. I'll take care of it."

"Yes, Lordship." Reynolds will say and close the door.

Smiling, His Lordship will return to his reading.

THE END

NOTES ON QUOTES:

In the three "false starts" of this story there are quotes from the works below:

- "look'd up in perfect silence at the stars" from Walt Whitman's poem, "When I Heard the Learn'd Astronomer"
- "the perfection of beauty, the joy of the whole earth!" from Lamentations 2:15
- "brazen giant of Greek fame" from Emma Lazarus's sonnet, "The New Colossus"

Introduction to
"Come, Fade Away"

"Come, Fade Away" was supposed to have been a sequel to a Ray Bradbury story called "Here There Be Tigers," the title being a reference to pre-19th-century maps when the world was not yet fully explored. This story was about space exploration, and it was one of Bradbury's finest, although I never really thought of him as a great writer at all. Most of his stories are just not believable, but "Here There Be Tigers" was more believable and left the door wide open for a wonderful sequel that shall never be. Alas. My sequel was going to be called "Caressing the Tiger." The plot was all worked out, but I could not get permission from Bradbury's agent to write it. To be honest, I met Bradbury, and I have a tough time believing that he wouldn't grant such permission; I remain dubious that his agent even broached the subject with him, but it's not an important enough point to pursue.

"Come, Fade Away" is the closest I can come. I had to alter some of the story elements and change the names of my characters (legally "had to"), and once I made some fundamental changes, I was able to draw a little more from the Star Trek TOS episode, "Metamorphosis," for further inspiration, creating, what I think is a charming tale with humans on another world. Like my story, "Metamorphosis" is about love and sacrifice. If your familiar with that story at all, I think you'll see where I drew inspiration. For example, the name of my main character is Crane. In "Metamorphosis," a main character is Zefram Cochrane. All I did to make my character's name is remove the second, third and fourth letters of the last name. But from there, I thought about Stephen Crane, and in that light, I named my other characters—at least as far as surnames go—after other Sci-fi writers: Wells is named after H. G. Wells, and Stevenson is named after Robert Louis Stevenson.

To be honest, there is more than just a residue remaining of the original story. It is still clear that Bradbury's work inspired me, but being inspired by work and writing a sequel to it are vastly different things.

Come, Fade Away

There's no colour I can have on Earth
that won't finally fade.
—*Pippin*

He saw the ship sailing his sky in the night as he lay on his back in the grass. It appeared, at first, as nothing more than a faint, swiftly moving star, not unlike the innumerable satellites he used to watch at night as a kid. But even though those distant days shone more feebly in his memory than this ship did in his sky, he *knew* it to be a ship; there were no satellites orbiting *his* World. It grew steadily brighter as it moved, until it dropped below the horizon. His curiosity piqued, he waited for its appearance at the opposite skyline; in time, there it was, distinctly brighter—lower. He watched it traverse his sky twice more before he finally rolled onto his side; they would either touch down, or they would head out; either way, they posed no danger; they could pose no danger. He reached a hand out, smiling sleepily, and lightly stroked the grass, then, quite on its own, the ground beneath his head rose, forming a small knoll that allowed his neck and skull to rest in line with his spine, and he quickly fell asleep. The ship continued to orbit.

196

It wasn't until early the following evening that he was able to see it again as it slowed over his position, finally stopping above him to descend. The brilliance of its flames hurt his eyes, forcing him to shield them; *Better protect yourself* he decided. Suddenly, the grass and soil pulled away directly below the ship, exposing a 400 metre circle of black basalt directly below the ship; shortly thereafter, he felt the air heat as the ship descended. It was a simple rocket, not at all dissimilar from the one that had brought him to his World. It stood some eight stories tall with convex edges forming a needled peak. The titanium hull glistened in the sunlight now striking the ship from just above the horizon. The name of the ship displayed on its side was *C. N. S. Aeneas,* though it bore little relevance for him. Three fins at the base performed the service of landing gears, just like those on his own ship had. Between the fins, the residual energy of the main engine continued to heat the surrounding air, creating a shimmering effect crawling up the sides of the ship. He could see the outline of the hatch just above the mid-point of the fuselage; it would remain closed while the engine cooled. Strewn about the craft were viewports, windows through which he could see nothing, but he was well aware that whatever travellers were aboard were quite able to see him; they were, no doubt, watching him at that very moment. But it didn't occur to him to conceal himself; he was struck by the distinct similarity between this craft and what he remembered of his own. It was like looking back in time, to an age he'd almost forgotten. It struck in him no sense of nostalgia but of incredulity: surely, technology had progressed beyond such simple designs. But this ship was so much like his own, it was as if there had come a day when the earth stood still.

He sat to wait at the edge of the basalt circle, and the grass around that landing site slowly crept back over the rock, indicating a fully cooled engine. Then the hatch lowered toward him, revealing a stair that extended to the ground. He remembered that the descent from the craft to the ground seemed to him the most precarious part of any interstellar trip because the stairs felt so flimsy. Bad design. Three crewmen descended. They were dressed in pressure suits with boots attached and sidearms belted in place. They wore no gloves or helmets, although the suits were clearly designed to accommodate both; instead, settled smartly on each head was a navy-blue baseball cap with their ship's name adorning the front. On the ground, the crew stood arm-to-arm before the tallest of them stepped forward, toward his host, who took that as his cue to approach. Once or twice, the leader turned awkwardly to his companions, seemingly insecure of precisely how he should proceed, but otherwise, he kept still until the two stood

197

in reach of each other and shook hands. The visitor was the first to speak: "Captain E. J. Smithson, sir." He was a good six feet tall with dark features, including a stark, two-day beard. His brown eyes conveyed confidence, and his apparent age, about 40 years, gave his confidence credibility.

The host hesitated, barely comprehending these words that seemed familiar, however distantly. "Your name!" he asserted. "That ... that is your name, yes?" he asked haltingly, with a voice that sounded as if he had never heard another person speak at all.

"That's right, sir," Smithson responded with both confusion and encouragement. There was another pause. "And have you a name, sir?"

It had been so long since he had spoken with anyone that he had to remember, first, the purpose of a name before he could remember how the term applied to him. "Do I ...? Yes, I... I do. I, um ... I am ... *Care*, ..." he shook his head sharply, the strain of concentration showing in his expression. "*Crane*," he asserted. "Yes, that is it. I am Crane."

"Is that all, sir"

"Hmm?"

"Have you ... a first name, perhaps, or maybe ... a rank?"

"Oh, uh, hmm, I am not sure. Do I need one?"

Smithson smiled reassuringly, "I suppose not. It's a pleasure to meet you, Mr. Crane."

"Uh, thank you. You too."

"Allow me to introduce my staff." Gesturing toward the person closest to him, Smithson said, "This is Commander Wells, my adjutant."

Wells, a tall man in his late 30's, with virtually no hair showing beneath his cap, thrust out a hand so smartly that Crane leapt backward: "A pleasure, Mr. Crane," he barked. His clean-shaven appearance complimented his blue eyes that hinted at a certain enthusiasm in his chosen profession.

Taken aback by Wells's crisp, militaristic deportment, Crane shook the other's hand with little more than a diffident nod of his head, and Smithson continued: "And Lieutenant Stevenson ..."

When Crane's glance met with Lt. Stevenson's, he froze, feeling suddenly very exposed. The lieutenant, though, who was more cognisant of Crane's difficulty than the Commander, reached out a hand slowly and spoke gently: "Please, call me Amy."

Crane stammered and backed away, and Stevenson looked meekly to the ground, while the other two men smirked. "I'm sorry, Miss ... Ma'am, um ...

198

Lieutenant," Crane stammered. "I have been here with no other people for so long, I had no need for clothing. It didn't occur to me until ... well, when I saw that you were, you know ... I meant no offence."

"I understand completely, Mr. Crane," the lieutenant soothed. "There's no reason to apologize."

"Be that as it may, Lieutenant," Smithson interjected, "perhaps you'd be kind enough to return to the ship and toss down a spare uniform for Mr. Crane."

"Aye, sir," Stevenson responded and quickly turned and ascended the flimsy-sounding stairs.

"Thank you for your clothes, Captain," Crane offered. "I will return them when I am finish with them."

"That's fine, Mr. Crane. You may keep them." There was a pause, and Crane ran his hand through his hair. Smithson found it odd that this man, who couldn't be older than, say, 35, lived in complete solitude, yet his hair, which was uncombed—as seemed appropriate, given the circumstances—was also clean and regulation length, and he was clean shaven, too, despite the primitive conditions in which he apparently lived, but Smithson said nothing. It was a matter that would, hopefully, clear itself up in time.

"Please forgive my ... speech," Crane continued. "It is odd to talk with other people after so long."

"It seems to be coming back to you quickly enough. Just how long have you been here, Mr. Crane?"

"I do not know, but not as long as I thought."

"Why do you say that?"

"Your ship is same as the one that brought me here. I thought ... new ships by now."

Just then Stevenson called from the ship, "Heads up!" and tossed a jump-suit style uniform down, then retreated back inside, giving Crane time and privacy to don the garment while Smithson continued with his questions: "I'm sorry, Mr. Crane, you say you arrived in a ship like the *Aeneas*?"

"Yes. As far as I remember, yours and mine are the same."

"I'm afraid that's not possible."

"Why?"

"Because this is the first of her kind. There aren't *any* ships like her."

"That cannot be right."

"But it is, I assure you."

"I do not mean to . . . ar . . . arg . . .Ooh, what is the word?"

199

"Argue?"

"Yes, thank you. I do not mean to ar ... gue with you, Captain, but I came from Earth on a rocket like this one, and it was one of doz ... ens. Is that the right word?"

"Sounds right. What was her name?" Smithson encouraged, but stopped just shy of challenging him.

"Oh, the name, let me see ..." He paused and spun his hand vaguely around the side of his head. "It was named for a flying animal—one that was not supposed to fly."

Smithson's jaw dropped, "A flying *horse*, maybe?" He glanced at Wells, then back, "*Pegasus?*"

Crane snapped his fingers, "That is it! Yes! *Pegasus!*"

"That's not possible."

"Haven't we been through this?"

"No, you don't understand, Mr. Crane ..." He broke off looking toward Wells, who seemed just as startled as Smithson, "Mr. Wells, front and centre."

Wells stepped forward, and Smithson continued, "Get back up to the ship. I want you and Stevenson to find everything you can in the database on the *Pegasus* pertaining to her crew and missions. I want it printed and in my hands in ten minutes."

"Aye, sir." Wells turned sharply and climbed the stairs.

"Let's take a walk, Mr. Crane," Smithson suggested. "I have a theory. It seems impossible, but one thing we've learned about space travel is that you can always expect the impossible to be, not just possible, but probable. I can't afford to dismiss anything. But if I'm right, you've been here for a very long time. Longer than you might even be aware."

"Can you tell me?"

"Not just yet, if you'll pardon me. I would like to have more facts first. It would help, though, if you would tell me everything you can about your trip here."

"Are you going to—what's the word?—look at it beside other information?"

"Compare."

"Yes, that is right. 'Compare.' Thank you."

"That's the plan."

"I see. We were looking for Earth-like planets when we came across this tiny world. She caught our attention at first because it would normally have been categorized as a ... um, a mini-planet?" He spoke indicating a small sphere with both hands.

"A dwarf-planet," the Captain offered.

"Yes. She didn't share her orbit with any other celestial bodies. She seemed so lonely."

"She?" Smithson interrupted.

"Is there a problem?"

"I suppose not."

"So," Crane continued, "we entered orbit and realized we had found a tiny planet with an Earth-like atmosphere because her large ..." he gestured with his hands trying to describe a word he'd forgotten, "um ... compact ..."

"Dense," Smithson suggested.

"Dense ..." Crane repeated, still uncertain, and Smithson nodded, "her dense core is ... li-quid and slows her ... spin and ... increases ..." He looked to Smithson, who completed the thought for him: "increases her mass and magnetic field to help her keep her atmosphere." Crane nodded his gratitude. "There also was a ... variety?" He looked to Smithson for assurance once again, and Smithson nodded once again. "... a variety of fuels and some good mineral ... areas. And, since her orbit is a circle and there's no tilt to her axis, we knew that we'd find a mild, global climate the full year around. The thousands of lakes all over the surface—all fresh water—contained Earth-like fish, and the entire surface was green and lush, and we all just fell in love ..."

"Excuse me," Smithson interrupted, "the *entire* planet was covered with lakes and vegetation?"

"Yes, that is ... *that's* right," Crane managed to say.

"Huh. Please continue." As he did, Wells and Stevenson showed up with reports. Smithson regarded them quickly, then turned his attention back to Crane: "... It's a truly lovely world. I've never been sorry to have stayed."

"'Stayed?!' You *stayed* behind?!" Smithson was stunned.

"That's right, and I'd do it again."

"The others left you willingly?"

Crane shrugged, "They left in a bit of a hurry. I doubt they noticed my absence until it was too late."

"So, there was some danger. Interesting," Smithson noted with developing clarity. "The rest of the crew got away safely?"

"I assume so."

"I see. Can you remember any of their names?"

Crane's eyebrows shot up for an instant; it had been a long time, but he set a finger to his chin and turned away from the others to ponder. "I think our captain was ... Robinson? And there was Lieutenant Friday; he and I were friends; I think of him often. There were some twenty others, but that's all I remember off hand. If I think on it for a while, I might be able to recall more."

"Good," Smithson nodded. "Anything might be helpful." He paused for thought, then, with a sense of resignation, "It's getting late, everyone. Let's call it a night and pick it up again in the morning. Mr. Crane, you're welcome to spend the night on the *Aeneas*."

"Thank you, Captain, but I sleep quite comfortably—how did we used to say it?—'under the stars.' But you may also find such a sleep a pleasant change."

"Well," Smithson began, "I really prefer the comfort of my own bunk, but"—turning to his crew— "anyone who'd like to camp out is welcome to."

None among the crew was eager to sleep outside the safety of the ship, but Stevenson did make a request: "I would also prefer to sleep aboard ship, Captain, but I wouldn't mind a few more minutes of fresh air, with your permission."

Smithson agreed with an official nod: "I'll look over these reports in the meantime."

"One more thing, Captain," Crane interjected, "It's been a very long time since I've been able to ... play host. My World has a lot to offer for great food, if you're partial to camp-style cooking. No fancy china, but I can offer a tasty morning meal. Let me prepare breakfast for you and your staff."

The group looked to each other for a decision. "Please, everyone," Crane continued. "You must be getting tired of your supplies and—what's the word?—syn-the-sized cuisine." He smiled knowing he had said it correctly. "Allow me this honour."

"Very well, Mr. Crane," Smithson said with a tone that informed the others in no uncertain terms that they, too, were pleased to accept the invitation. "You may expect us for breakfast at first light."

"Excellent. I'll see you then. And Lieutenant—I'm sorry—Amy, perhaps you would care to tour the local sites while you enjoy the fresh air. I'd be happy to show you around."

"I'd be delighted, Mr. Crane," she said, and the pairs set out in opposite directions. Stevenson had changed into a uniform like the one Crane wore and left her ball cap in the rocket, letting her golden hair fall to her shoulders. It wasn't regulation, perhaps, but it was respectful, if also very attractive. At 30 years of age, she stood six inches shorter than Crane, who, now and then, would pause and point: There was the site where the *Pegasus* landed, and there Crane's favourite wooded area; there a stream teeming with delicious, Earth-like fish, and

202

there the volcano that, at their angle just then, seemed to be swallowing the setting sun. And even to Crane, everything seemed enhanced—the colours more vibrant, the contrasts more stark. It felt to him like everything was made to look and feel more amazing than ever. Stevenson became so comfortable after a time that she finally commented, "I feel very distanced calling you 'Mr. Crane.' Have you been able to recall a first name?"

"I'm honoured," Crane began, "but you have to remember, I was also in the Space Admin; we went by last names, as you do. At least, I haven't heard any of your shipmates call you 'Amy.'"

"That's a good point," Stevenson conceded, and Crane regarded her with a smile.

"But if it would make you feel more comfortable, I would be pleased to give it more thought."

"I'd like that," she admitted, then added, "Your communication skills are returning very quickly."

"Ah ha! You were expecting the likes of Ben Gunn, says I," he accused, imitating the character.

"The castaway from *Treasure Island*?" she asked. "Your memory is quite impressive, too. Much more so than you may realize." She reached for his arm, and he allowed her to take it.

"Yeah," Crane sighed, "Well, I've spent many a night hoping that I wouldn't become like him."

"And you don't sound like someone who's been alone for any length of time: no delusions, no significant speech deviations, and even your lethologica seems to be diminishing very quickly."

Crane furrowed his brow, "My what?"

"Oh, Sorry," Amy said. "'Lethologica.' It's the momentary inability to recall a word."

"I see," Crane nodded. "Well, I suppose talking's just like riding a trike."

Amy giggled, "You mean 'a bike!'"

"Fine," Crane conceded, sheepishly.

"I'm sorry. I don't mean to laugh," Amy confessed. "In fact, I'm beginning to admire you a great deal."

"Oh? How's that?"

"You've been alone here for … well, a long time if those reports are accurate …"

Crane interrupted, "How long, Amy?"

"How long would *you* estimate?"

"Oh, I don't know ... ten years, maybe." He looked to see Amy's reaction, but if she did react, she hid it well. "Is it longer than that?"

"Yes."

He took a moment to ponder the swiftness and brevity of her reply before responding: "I see."

"And yet, as I said, you don't seem to be suffering from any typical conditions associated with prolonged solitude. Rather than being bitter and surly, you seem truly optimistic. How is that possible?"

He hesitated: "Uh ... unlike our friend, Ben Gunn, I've not been alone, Amy, not for a minute."

"But you *are* alone. There's no one on this planet besides you. There's no reason for you to be *alive*, but the fact that you are leads me to wonder if you're, perhaps, *imagining* company?"

"That would make sense, but I assure you, it's not the case." He hesitated again. "Do I act—delusional—is that the right word?" Amy nodded. " ... delusional in any other way?"

"Not at all."

"Then let me help you to understand: This planet is alive in ways unlike any planet I've seen."

"What do you mean?"

He could feel his heart begin to race. He was about to share a secret with someone who would probably walk away, certain of his insanity and afraid for her life; he continued carefully: "I mean that it's alive, not in the way that Earth is: alive meaning that it's capable of *supporting* life. I mean that this planet is *alive*: a life unto itself; that it breathes, thinks and has a soul, Amy. That's what I mean." Another pause gave Crane the opportunity to observe Amy's reaction. When he saw that she apparently had none, he continued. "This planet itself is self aware, a sentient being. It—*she*—thinks, understands and feels ... and she loves me, Amy, as surely as any woman loves her man."

"And you love *her?*" There was still no surprise, no skepticism in her voice. Only the reassuring tone of genuine, personal interest.

"Indeed I do."

Amy stopped and looked into Crane's eyes. "Mr. Crane, I believe you."

"Why?!" The question dropped from his mouth before it had fully developed in his mind. Surely, even for a well-travelled astronaut, the idea of a sentient planet would raise doubts as to his sanity.

204

She smiled and the two resumed their walk. "It's simple: I can hear the truth of it in your voice, for one. And for two, almost everything you've said is substantiated by our reports and even answers a lot of questions we've been asking about you. But I really shouldn't talk about the reports until the Captain has had a chance to discuss them with you."

"I understand."

"Thank you. Can you tell me any more?"

Crane stopped walking again and looked off to the horizon before he spoke:"Amy, you need to understand: This planet and I ... we're a couple in a way that is very deep and personal; as surely as any two people can be married, this planet and I are married. If I told you what a joy being with her is, and if other people were to hear of it, I'm frankly afraid that ..."

She finished his thought: "That others might try to take what you have?"

Crane sighed and nodded. "Yes, I fear that."

"I understand *that*," Amy assured him, and she led him to walk again. "Let me ..." she paused, clicked her tongue and dipped her chin to the side for the irony of what she was about to say: " ... 'encourage' you, I guess, by promising that no others will be coming here. There is no danger of some interloper interfering with your relationship with your World."

"Ha," Crane laughed mildly, "how can you promise that?"

"I can't tell you that now, but please, I believed you. Won't you believe me?" As she spoke, she rested her free hand on his upper arm, and he did believe her, so he continued: "After I was left here, I saw *real* miracles: cooked food provided for me; rain or a lake whenever I got thirsty; special warmth, especially at night, and ... I can *fly* here, Amy. I just think about it, step into the air and let the wind take me 'up, up and away,' literally." This time he did spy the unmistakable signs of skepticism in Amy's eye. "Oh. You don't believe me now?"

"I didn't say that."

"No. You didn't. Even so ..." He took both her hands in his, stepped to the side and lifted straight off the ground, feet first. Amy screamed, but more out of a childlike glee than fear. Finally, her arms were lifted high over her head, held by Crane's hands, as he floated with his feet pointing straight up. "Don't let go," he teased, "or I'll float up forever."

"No you won't," she chided.

"No I won't," he admitted as he came back to the ground. "I spent my first few days flying like a kid running around his yard with a bath-towel around his neck for a pretend cape." He mused for a moment. "I'd forgotten how amazing it was. I do it all the time now, but, wow! it was so strange and marvellous at first. After a time, I had no more need of miracles, and the way my World and I interact began to change. We were able to simply enjoy each other's company. I've never known such love."

"So, what's she like? What does she do?" Amy asked.

"Well," he began, "she's creative. Very creative. I mean, I'm not a biologist or a botanist or anything, but I've seen hundreds of different types of grass that she's made. And she can either create animals or even show herself to me as an animal. She made herself appear as a whale, like an orca, once. It was beautiful—elegant and not a little intimidating. She's made herself into flocks of birds or schools of fish." He smiled bashfully, "So you can see why I'm something of the jealous boyfriend."

"I certainly can," Amy said and there was a time of silence before she spoke again. "There's something else I'd like to ask, if you don't mind."

"I don't mind," Crane answered.

"I overheard you telling the Captain that you stayed on this planet purposely. May I ask ..."

"Why?" He looked to Amy. She nodded and tucked a lock of hair bashfully behind her ear, and Crane smiled. It was the first time he had seen a gesture from her that was entirely spontaneous, and he was charmed. "The rest of the crew would have been welcome to stay, but I was the only one who saw her beauty. The others were afraid of a planet that was clearly a living being. They felt that she could squash them at any time." He paused to consider that idea. "I suppose she is able, but she's not capable; it's not in her character. She was clearly angry when the others left. She could just as easily have held the rocket to the ground or destroyed it altogether, but that's not like her. The others got on the ship as quickly as they could, but in the confusion, I hid."

Amy watched him as he spoke. If it were possible for a man to glow with love, Mr. Crane, she decided, would have radiated like a type 'O' star. "I would like to hear more about that, but ..." she turned away, hiding a yawn. "Oh, I am sorry. I think it's time for me to turn in. Would you please walk me back to the ship?"

"Of course." He smiled at her teasingly. "Or would you rather fly?"

"What? Will she let me?"

"I don't see why not."

"I'm scared. What do I do?"

"Just ask her in your mind, then step into the wind. She'll do the rest. It's easy. Will you trust me?"

"Yes, I will, but I need to look at this as a scientist, not as a tourist or something."

"Oh, you're a scientist! What kind of scientist are you?"

"I'm the psychologist."

"Psychologist?! You mean that all of this was ..."

"No. No I don't mean that. I'm sorry. I can see how you might think that, but our conversation was personal, not professional. Really."

Crane smiled, "Had you been lying, my World would have told me. She knows these things."

"Um, not that I'm going back on what I just said, but is our conversation a secret? I think that the Captain is going to need to know what you told me."

"I haven't told you anything that I wouldn't tell him. You just helped me remember. Shall we fly?"

"Okay," she agreed nervously.

The planet carried the two back to the ship, and they seemed, for a moment, like some wiser version of Peter Pan and Wendy flying from the nursery. Amy screamed at first; Crane even showed off a bit ... to take her mind off her fears, of course. He flew in loops about her and even reclined on his back, resting his head on his hands in mid air. And together, they flew so high that, had there been light from above, they would both have lost their shadows to the height. They touched down at the foot of the ship's stair. Crane wished her a good night and walked away unable to stop smiling.

*   *   *

Morning shone bright and clear and warm and a pleasure to the senses. Crane met the staff at the ship; they wore the same jump-suit style uniform that he had given him to wear. They politely declined his offer to fly with him, so he led them on foot to the wooded area that he had pointed out to Amy, having already set the meal beside a charming waterfall that poured into a pool that overflowed to a stream. The three crew members were pleasantly surprised by Crane's preparations. A small fire on the bank cooked the fish that each picked from those that collected in the pool. Nearby stood a lush green-belt from which spread sweet-smelling air carried on a mild breeze that blew the smoke down stream; it never changed directions, so everyone sat comfortably the entire time.

In addition to fish, the meal consisted of a variety of berries and citrus fruit. There was a heated beverage that carried all the flavour, aroma and ... well, kick of coffee. There was even a coconut-like fruit whose milk, strained from the meat through its own fibrous leaves, was rich and sweet and as creamy as any grocery-store variety coffee cream. The men, of course, preferred their "coffee" black, but Amy was delighted with the milk and had extra servings of it just for the scientific pleasure of sampling something completely natural that seemed so deliciously decadent. Crane's utensils were made from something like bamboo, his plates from a fungus that grew on the trunks of trees, and his cups from gourds. All the comforts of *Gilligan's Island.*

Afterwards, when the dishes had been collected and faces and hands were washed, and after a few minutes of pleasant conversation, Smithson made things official again: "Well, Mr. Crane," he opened, "I've studied the reports on the *Pegasus,* compared them with what Lt. Stevenson told me from your conversation last night, and the conclusion, I'm afraid, is … disturbing."

"Alright," Crane breathed heavily, "let's have it."

"Well, for starters, your first name is Alan; you were 34 when you were left here," he paused and regarded Crane intently for a moment, "and you hold the rank of lieutenant commander."

"Your records are very thorough, it seems," Crane said, then turned to Amy and mouthed the words, "My name is Alan."

Amy smiled modestly and mouthed, "Thank you."

"Indeed," Smithson continued. "Everything you told me about your ship and crew is pretty much confirmed: Your captain's name was 'Robins,' not 'Robinson'—an understandable error. And according to his report," Smithson continued, "this planet is dangerous. He said that as they departed there were all manner of geographic and atmospheric disturbances. You were presumed dead, and this planet was listed as unsafe and off limits."

"But here you are," Crane said.

"And it's time for you to understand why." He folded his hands and regarded the ground between his feet in preparation: "Our mission is a simple one, Mr. Crane: reconnaissance. To go out as far as possible, given the fuel and supplies, reconnoitre some new worlds and return with our findings, in order, quite simply, to prove that we can—to prove that deep-space travel is possible."

"But your records …" Alan began, but Smithson cut him off: "It will all become clear. Give me some time. For now, it's important for you to know that most people back home thought that we couldn't do it, that we'd get into space and die due to the failure of some piece of our instrumentality. People invented some impressively specific predictions, none of which, obviously, came true, at least, not yet. The only people who thought we'd succeed were those who helped

208

build the *Aeneas* and her supporting equipment and structures. I met no one who wasn't associated with the Space Admin who thought we'd survive the launch." He raised his eyebrows for an instant, then added, "Mind you, we've had some close calls; human invention is fragile to say the least, but something's always gotten us through." He shook his head in a moment of silence as he briefly contemplated some of those close calls. "For the rest, Commander Wells will fill you in." His eyes turned from Alan, "Wells?"

"Yes, sir," Wells opened. "Mr. Crane, the *Pegasus* returned to Earth the very *day* that marked the beginning of social anomie, world wide. Earth was hit my by a Mega Coronal Mass Ejection from the sun. It hit us like a mega-tsunami, making the one in 2013 look like a Christmas light show, and not only was the entire, global electrical power grid knocked out, but it radically changed something in Earth's magnetosphere so that, not only could we not repair the damage, but we lost all ability to synthesize conventional electricity ... ostensibly, forever. Our best scientists are still trying to figure that out. The death toll was well over three-and-a-half billion the first year. Instructions how to construct, repair and maintain our machines had been printed, but it was useless without power. So the information was stored, and Earth fell into a global dark ages.

"Without electricity, the world suddenly became very big; family members who had been merely an ocean apart one day, found themselves half a world apart the next. We had to relearn how to survive like the Cro-Magnon. Life spans shortened dramatically, and disease and hunger were rampant. Humanity still moved forward in some healthy ways, but there was, and still is, a great deal of bitterness. I offer their estimation of our potential success in our mission as evidence. After a long time people finally found ways to store and use viable electricity through biological means—eventually using genetically engineered, biological components cultivated for that very purpose, and we started to relearn what we'd lost, but without such prodigious dependence on our own ingenuity. Does that make sense to you, Mr. Crane?"

"Yes it does. I learned the same thing here. This planet has cared for me in the same way the apes cared for Tarzan. If I'd been left to live by my own devices, like some celestial Robinson Crusoe, I'd have died long ago, but my World is a life unto herself with all the power of any other planet: power to destroy with great storms or quakes and power to produce and sustain life. It might be a healthy thing, after all, to outgrow our need for the things we make for ourselves."

"That's right," Wells asserted, "and one benefit of that truth is that our ship was designed by your contemporaries but built by ours; aside from the electronics, which is based on a different premise from what you would be familiar with, she's the same ship, and that's why she looks so much like the one you remember."

Alan sat quiet for a few moments; it's not every day you hear the man siting next to you tell you that you're from a time set far apart from his own. "Just how much time are we talking about, Mr. Wells? Decades? It sounds like you're talking about generations."

"Mr. Crane," Wells hesitated, glancing over to Smithson, "the *Pegasus* returned to Earth over seven centuries ago—a day commemorated as 'Pegatied.' People associated the return of the *Pegasus* and her crew with all the problems that started after their return, even though the events are entirely unrelated. But even now, a person who is suspected of being an unwitting cause of problems for others is called 'Pegatoid.'"

"Seven centuries?" Alan whispered.

"That's right," Wells affirmed, and Smithson added, "and you haven't aged a day, Crane. You look the same now as you do in the photos in those reports."

"That's probably why your speech came back to you so quickly," Amy offered. "Logically, you should have entirely forgotten how to speak after, oh, ten years or so, but since you've been saved from aging, you may have also been saved from forgetting—at least, forgetting entirely."

Alan nodded. "That's why my hair stopped growing, and I never need to shave. My World keeps me alive, keeps me young, even keeps me groomed, and helps me retain much of my communication skills."

"Presumably," Smithson responded, nodding.

After a moment, the idea of, "seven centuries," seemed to suddenly sink in, and Alan became agitated and saturnine. "I don't understand," he confessed. "I never thought that I'd return to Earth, and I have been perfectly content. I was never bothered until now by how long I'd been away, but suddenly it's like I've been hit by a ... I don't know." He stood and stared at nothing in particular for a moment, then, "I need some time, everyone. Please excuse me." And he disappeared into the woods.

Smithson stood and called after him, "But we have more to discuss, Crane."

"Give him a moment, Captain," Amy urged. "I'll follow him to make sure he gets back ok."

The men sat quiet and apparently unconcerned, but Amy was all too aware of the weighty thoughts Alan must have been carrying. She tried to follow his path, but he had already disappeared, and before she had walked thirty metres, she realized that she'd taken a wrong turn through the undergrowth, and trying to double back only got her entirely lost. When she gave up on finding her bearings, she sat on a fallen tree in hopes of being found. Then she heard a faint rustle of leaves behind her. Assuming it was Alan or one of her crew-mates, she turned to see a young woman approaching her; she met Amy's eyes as she walked, and she smiled. She was naked, and her beauty could not be denied. Amy needed no introduction; she knew that this woman was Alan's World, and she understood why. She appeared, at first, to be in her late twenties. Initially, her hair was a lovely red, full and radiant and hanging to a point below knee level. Her skin was a healthy Caucasian hue. Her eyes were of a blue so intense as to be almost silver. But as she approached, she aged a year or more with each step. By the time she had made it to within arm's reach of Amy, she had become feeble with age, unable to finish the walk without Amy's assistance, and the two sat together. The woman's hair had grayed and thinned; her eyes had darkened; her skin drooped and sagged; her smile had narrowed, and her posture had succumbed to the weight of time. The two women spoke not a word, but they were able to make each other understand, and among the more important thoughts that Amy perceived was, "Take care of him." Amy agreed—perhaps too willingly, but there was no condemnation.

Alan, for his part, had departed to seek the comfort of the one who had comforted him for nearly a millennium, but she was not to be found. He was confused by her absence at first then finally annoyed. In something of a brooding temper, he returned to where Smithson and Wells sat and took a seat across from them. Amy was finally guided back to the others, and she took her seat beside Alan who smiled at her as she did; his sulking quickly cleared, and he addressed the others: "I apologize for my sudden departure. Seven centuries! Whoo! It doesn't seem that long. You'd be surprised how difficult it is to measure any substantial amount of time on a planet with no moon and no seasons."

"I don't blame you for being disturbed, Mr. Crane," Wells offered. "It may seem kind to be kept alive so long, but what have you been able to accomplish? Everything's provided for you; you have no needs, nothing to work for. I'd have gone nuts."

"I've had my share of challenges, Mr. Wells."

"What challenges could you possibly have had? Deciding whether or not to cover up at night?"

"You underestimate my World." He leaned toward Wells, and, in the voice of Long John Silver whispered, "Here there be monsters, Mr. Wells." Just then, from the woods came the growl of a creature whose wind pipe resonated like the lowest string of a concert grand piano. Wells stood and drew his pistol. There was another growl, and Smithson followed Wells's example.

211

" *That* growl came from up there," Wells said, indicating up river. "The first one came from the opposite direction!" Then from the woods they heard a thunderous roar from an enormous throat. A loud snap of a branch confirmed the presence of something huge. "We're surrounded!" Wells declared.

There was another roar, and the men trained their pistols across the stream. "It's only my World proving my point, gentlemen," Alan assured. "Holster your weapons and you may get a glimpse of it."

"But they'll attack!" Wells argued.

"There's only one, and no it won't," Alan asserted. "Trust me."

"There has to be more than one. No creature that large could move from place to place so quickly."

"Trust me, Mr. Wells," Alan said again.

Smithson cautiously complied; Wells was slower, but he did respond. The moment the strap of his holster snapped across his pistol, the beast stepped out from behind some bushes across the stream and regarded the humans impassively. It was a saber-toothed tiger right out of the Pleistocene age, fully twelve feet long from tip to tail, and a tiny tail it was—proportionate to a bobcat's. It's hind legs were shorter than its front ones, but what they lacked in size, they made up for in muscle. Its mane was long and dark and heavily matted, beginning between its ears and continuing down its back and the upper portion of its shoulders, tapering to a point just ahead of its hips. The shorter hair on its lower shoulders, ribs and hips was reddish with darker spots; its tusks were the size of Bowie knives. It stood in place for a few seconds, then, having no appetite for human flesh just then, it licked his chops, blinked once or twice, and turned in to the brush.

"That was ... exhilarating!" Wells blurted.

"It's a peaceful place," Alan said flatly, nodding his head, "but never dull."

"And it's time for you to leave," Smithson announced.

Alan looked to him with surprise, "Leave?!"

Amy interjected at this point. "Mr. Crane ... Alan ... you must listen to him."

Smithson continued while Alan was too stunned to argue: "You have to understand, Mr. Crane, our instruments are able to detect human life from space, but such subtleties are nearly impossible to measure accurately beyond a mid-range orbit, say, 40,000 kilometres. Even so, we detected your *human* bio signs over four billion kilometres away—almost 30 AU's—as though your World were screaming for us to come. Do you know of any reason the planet would do that, Mr. Crane?"

"No, I don't."

"We have a theory, but it will not be easy for you to hear—none of this will be: We were on our way back to Earth when we detected your presence and got our first view of your World. We noted that its size compares roughly to Earth's moon, wouldn't you say, Wells?"

Wells nodded, adding, "But smaller."

"Right," Smithson agreed. "The one thing we noted was that its surface was entirely *incapable* of supporting life; quite a paradox considering we knew you were here. But on the opposite side of the planet from our approach, we found, quite literally, this circle of green centred on the equator."

"Captain, I have flown over this entire planet, and I have quite probably walked it in 700 years," Alan argued. "I assure you, it has been green the entire time—the whole body has been green."

"I certainly believe you, Mr. Crane, but ..." Smithson hesitated, so Amy took up the reins, "Alan, we measured the circle of green from orbit. It was a little over 900 kilometres in diameter at first—about the size of New Mexico; too large to see the borders from the centre where we are, but hardly a major portion of the surface even of this tiny planet. We measured it on every orbit; it's receding, Alan, and not slowly. We calculated that in about two of this planet's days, it won't be able to support life at all."

Alan smiled, "You're misunderstanding, I think. She probably is just trying to encourage you to not stick around too long. As soon as you leave, she'll be right as a fiddle." He smiled, knowing that he had successfully mixed two metaphors and confused his listeners.

"Then why did she call us here?" Wells broke in, ignoring the humour "and why did she allow us to land in the first place, since she apparently threw quite a tantrum when the rest of your crew left—warning people to stay away? Captain Robins was convinced that no human should ever land here again."

"Maybe she thought I was lonely!" Alan insisted. "Maybe she's testing my faithfulness!" He blanched and glanced to Amy who turned her gaze quickly to the ground. "I don't know," he muttered.

"You know neither of those is true, Alan," Amy said after a pause. "There's more that you need to hear. And, Captain," Smithson raised his brows, "this is also an official report." Smithson nodded. "Alan, I met the planet in her woman form when I was in the forest just now. We ... talked. She loves you a great deal. More, I think, than I can explain. Definitely more than I have ever known, or, know how ... to love, that is. She and I understand each other now, too." She paused,

213

searching for words, anticipating his hurt, wanting desperately to spare him that hurt and realizing the impossibility of doing so. "She's dying, Alan."

"You must be mistaken. There's no way a planet can die!"

"She's alive, Alan, just like we are, and she's ancient. Imagine the age of a planet that has lived a full life span. One of the conditions of being alive is that, one day, we must die."

"You're overgeneralizing."

"I don't think so," Amy asserted. "Alan, I have the truth of this from her. If you won't believe me, believe her."

Alan pondered that idea for several moments, then shook his head, "No. She would have told me."

"Why?" Amy pointed out. "Would you be able to help her? Would you be able to prolong her life? Is there any reason that *both* of you needed to suffer over something so serious? Instead, she kept it from you and used her ebbing strength to maintain this living area while searching the heavens for someone to rescue you. It's perfectly logical, Alan."

"And you just happened to be passing by at the right moment," Alan said with acerbic sarcasm.

"Apparently," Amy said, hurt by Alan's tone.

At that, without another word, Alan stood and took flight away from the group. The group stood and considered following him, but finally thought better of it. Alan needed to both learn the truth and accept the truth, and that would require time. Ultimately, one by one, they sat to wait.

Alan flew faster than he'd ever flown. After several minutes, the air began to thin, so he descended. Eventually, he noticed the colour of the sky ahead darkening as though it were approaching dusk when it was not yet noon. Finally, near the horizon ahead, he saw stars against a black sky even though the sky directly above him was blue. The temperature began to drop rapidly, but he headed forward until the tips of his fingers began to hurt. He finally landed twenty paces from where the green suddenly stopped. There was, perhaps, twenty feet of dead grass and then ... nothing. It wasn't a river or an outcropping of rock or the tree line of a mountain—the grass simply stopped—and beyond that, another world: dark, cold ... dead. He flew again, following the perimeter of the grass, and he noticed by the motion of the sun that he was, in fact, travelling in a large circle; after a long time, before he had fully circumnavigated the living area but well after his arms began to ache and his breath grew hard to catch—and after he had come to see Amy's words as truth—he headed back to the group. They stood to greet him, and all Alan did as he approached Smithson was point a finger in his face and declare, "I'm not leaving her." He marched another ten paces, folded his arms and stopped with his back to the others.

Smithson walked to him, "Crane, I'm not going to pretend to understand the complexities of all that you're feeling. This is a seven-century relationship, and I can't compare any relationship of mine with yours, but if you stay here, you'll die too."

"I really don't think that my death is a whole lot to ask after seven centuries, do you?"

"Do you think that's what she's asking, Crane?"

He scoffed, "She doesn't have to."

"We can't leave you behind. You know that."

"I'm afraid that you haven't any choice, Captain."

Smithson tried a different approach, speaking as a commanding officer rather than just a fellow human being: "Commander, you may spend the night, but tomorrow morning I expect you to board ship with the rest of us. That's an order."

"Oh, please," Alan said dryly.

"Oh, I understand," Smithson cajoled. "You think she'll protect you if there's a conflict between us." He shook his head, "But she won't. She called us here because she knows she's dying, and she wants you to be safe. For your sake, she'll even turn against you."

Alan turned on Smithson, standing almost nose to nose with him: "I ... will not ... leave."

Smithson was not in the least deterred, "Commander Crane, for you to insist on remaining in a hazardous situation in direct violation of orders is evidence of suicidal tendencies. You've been here a long time; it's understandable for you to be suicidal, but suicide is not an option, not on my watch. If you do not comply, then come morning, I'll have no choice but to have you tied and strapped in the rocket; you can voice any grievances against me to the Space Admin upon your return to Earth, but you will be on that ship when we take off. Do I make myself clear?"

Alan didn't alter his posture one iota: "Perfectly... but I'm not getting on the ship."

"Don't be a fool, Crane."

Alan let the tension drain from his body. He sat on a rock and rested his elbows on his knees. "Captain, is the book *Charlotte's Web* still available on Earth? Did you ever read it as a kid?"

Confused by the sudden change in topic, Smithson shook his head as much to try to find his bearings in the conversation as to indicate a 'no:' "I watched an old animated version. Why?"

"Ah, the movie. As I recall—remember it's been 700 years—it's good, but it differs from the book in a lot of ways; one of the most significant ways is in Charlotte's demise. In the book, she didn't die with Wilbur right next to her; had that been the case, I doubt it would have made such an impact on me. In the book, she tells Wilbur that she's dying, then Wilbur is crated and loaded, the family returns to the farm, and Charlotte stays behind at the fair grounds." Once again Alan looked Smithson in the eyes. "Three days, Captain. It took her three days to die, and she was alone all that time. That thought horrified me. I remember having nightmares about it—waiting three days to die … all alone. How awful! No, Captain. I will not make my World die like that."

Smithson backed down just a bit, nodding his head and letting out a large breath: "Fair enough. It's not a pressing issue yet. Whether you stay or not, the best thing that you can do right now is spend the rest of the day with this planet-person of yours. We'll talk again tomorrow." He began walking away.

"I won't change my mind!" Alan called after him.

Smithson turned back to Alan and raised his hands, "No pressure," he said amicably, then turned again and walked out of Alan's sight. Wells followed, but Amy stayed with Alan; she even took his hand, and he let her, even tightening his grip, and he asked, "Do *you* think I'm wrong, Amy?"

She considered his question. "No, I don't think you're wrong, but I do think that you're being guided too much by your heart, and not enough by your head."

"Is that such a bad thing, I wonder."

"I think it might be best," Amy suggested, "if I leave you for now and let you spend some valuable time with your World, but there is one more thing that you need to consider."

"What's that?"

"She's very weak, and she's using a great deal of her last bit of energy to keep this area alive for us. Staying with her is, in a way, making her last hours very draining and painful. And she may not pass away so quickly or painfully if you depart with us. Go to her now. I'll see you tomorrow."

*　　*　　*

The next morning, Amy woke early and departed quickly. She found Alan with his World, and she smiled, albeit wanly. Alan's World appeared young again. They knelt together on the grass in a large glade with low, rolling hills gently caressed by the morning sun, in an embrace from which, to Alan's surprise, she broke away, suddenly and joylessly. She and Amy made eye contact, and Alan's World began pushing him away. His expression was one of confusion, even disbelief, but when he tried to embrace her again, she refused and began to age again—rapidly; still, he refused to leave her side. Finally, there was a roar amid the trees. The tiger had returned, perhaps hungry, perhaps simply vicious, but there was a distinct malevolence carried from it on the wind, and instinctively, Amy sensed that she, in particular, was in very real danger. There was another roar from among the trees much closer to her, but the animal was still hidden. Amy moved toward Alan, toward the centre of the clearing, just to put some distance between her and the trees. It roared again, from an entirely different direction, and Amy's heartbeat and respiration rocketed. The cat was stalking her, she realized, toying with her, taunting her, and breathing in the musky aroma of her terror. Amy knew this. She could feel its eyes watching, sense its craving for her flesh. When it roared again, she looked to Alan, and he met her gaze, then he turned again to his World, and Amy saw in his posture the question, "Why are you doing this?" His World didn't respond, but turned her eyes down and away from him. Finally, while Alan's heart remained hesitant, his body responded dutifully. He rose and ran to Amy at the same instant the giant cat sprang from the more distant trees, having also decided to run to Amy. It was a contest, then, to see who would get the girl—a contest of brain against brawn, heart against hunger, intellect against instinct. Alan's World, now an ancient wisp of a woman, remained kneeling, an observer of sorts, a puppeteer of sorts.

Alan reached Amy first. He grabbed her hand, yelling, "Fly!" She did; just as the tiger leapt, the two were airborne. The cat ran under them with great determination and speed; it followed them as though hoping it would have them both. The two flew over the trees. The tiger followed them *through* the trees. They flew the length of the river; the tiger followed them *down* the river, and they finally started to circle overhead like a pair of eagles.

"We can't stay up here for ever!" Amy said.

"Why not?" Alan asked. "I've stayed aloft for hours at a time. It can't get us up here." Suddenly the pair began to fall as though a door had opened beneath them; they screamed in fright, falling some 25 feet before beginning to float again just out of reach of the tiger who leapt at them, snapped at them and clawed at

217

them. They hurried to regain their altitude; the tiger sat beneath them and began bathing nonchalantly, like any household cat that had trapped a mouse in a hole would sit and wait with a frolic patience for the mouse to attempt an escape.

"We should go to the ship!" Amy declared, her eyes wide and her voice tense.

"I'm not getting on that ship," Alan asserted. "As long as we're airborne we're safe."

"But we're only airborne as long as the planet allows it. We need to get to the ship to be safe."

Alan tried to reassure her: "My World won't let anything happen to me. I know it. And she won't let anything happen to anyone I care about. She wouldn't do that to me. We're safe up here. Trust me."

The tiger, apparently having heard and understood, looked off toward the rocket, then back to Alan and Amy, then back toward the ship. It licked its chops and took off in a mad dash toward the rocket.

"Alan! It's heading for the ship!" Amy cried. "We have to go to warn the others!"

"Amy," Alan said somewhat patronizingly, "they'll be safe. The tiger can't get in the ship. As long as we stay aloft ..."

"And how long will that be, Alan? Months? Years? It doesn't make any difference. The ship's hatch is open. The tiger *can* get inside. We have to go to warn them!"

Alan hesitated. He saw Amy's logic, but his heart refused to let him go near the rocket, seeing it as something of a trap. Amy waited only a moment before she decided to leave Alan and go alone to help her shipmates. But as she turned to fly away from him, she began to fall. Alan sped downward to help her, and as soon as he caught up with her, she began to float again. It was then that Alan understood. He closed his eyes tightly for the briefest of moments, took in a deep breath, then acceded: "Ok," he said. "Let's go help them." Amy smiled. She would have hugged him, but there wasn't time. The two flew off together toward the ship.

The staircase still rested on the ground and the hatch stood open, just as Amy had predicted. As they approached, the tiger began its ascent with the conniving, stalking stride of a fierce predator. Amy and Alan flew their fastest toward the ship and directly through the open hatch, tumbling on to the deck. Amy rose as quickly as she could and headed for the open doorway. Looking down, she met the cat's eyes. They both froze for an instant, regarding the other,

218

then the cat began to leap up the steps. Frantically, Amy punched a knob by the hatch, and the stairs began to retract, telescoping upwards. The tiger proved too heavy for them, and they complained loudly after being pulled from the leverage of the ground. The tiger's weight became too much; the lower half of the stairs sagged just above the tiger, who tried desperately to maintain its position, frantically grabbing for a more secure hold like Sylvester or Jerry spinning their legs in mid air before falling from view. The stairs bobbed up and down in response, and finally the cat lost its footing and fell to the ground with a loud thud and a groaning growl of pain. The stairs retracted all the way, and Amy closed the hatch. It locked in place; they heard the hiss of the airtight seal. She leaned against the bulkhead breathing heavily, "They're more sturdy than you'd think."

"Good design," Alan agreed resting his back against the wall with relief.

Just then Smithson entered where Amy and Alan were still catching their breaths. "Welcome aboard, Mr. Crane," he said. "We're preparing for departure. I'm glad you came to your senses."

"I didn't," Alan remarked; "I was Shanghaied." He and Amy walked to the viewport. Alan's World stood below the ship. The tiger walked to her, circled her, then sat beside her and looked up with her. She was young again, for the last time, for it took a great deal of energy to maintain a youthful appearance, but that is how she wanted Alan to remember her.

From their height, halfway up the length of the rocket, Amy and Alan noticed the edge of the grass in the distance and the black, dead rock beyond. It was near the horizon, but too close to feel comfortable any longer outside the airtight safety of the ship. Smithson stood behind the two of them: "I had Commander Wells look into our fuel and supplies, Mr. Crane. We have enough to orbit for a few days and maintain a margin of safety. She won't be alone."

"Thank you, Captain," Alan said. Then there was a monstrous thud and a hiss as the fuel pumps engaged and the engines began to warm for ignition. In response, the grass below the rocket pulled away in a circle, revealing the basalt that lay beneath, just as it had when the rocket touched down.

"I'm sorry," Smithson said, "but I need you both to get suited up and belted in for take off. Immediately."

"Aye, Captain," they said. Alan took one last look out the window. He knew that she couldn't see him, but he waved anyway. Then she, too, reached up her hand and waved; even though she couldn't see him, she knew he was there. Alan went obediently to suit up and find his seat. Wells helped strap him in before strapping himself into his own seat at the helm. Finally, the engines made a great rumble as they ignited, and the entire ship shook as it began its ascent.

In orbit, some hours later, Alan stood looking out the viewport. As Amy approached, he didn't turn to her, but he knew she was there. "It's a funny thing," he said, "but in 700 years, I never understood that I had been needed. I knew she cared for me, but I hadn't a clue until moments ago that the care I gave her is something that she would have otherwise missed."

"I wonder if that was part of her plan, Alan," Amy postulated.

"What do you mean?"

"I mean, I wonder if she didn't know she was dying seven centuries ago and called the *Pegasus* to her hoping for company. If a planet lives for billions of years, then the last millennium for her might be like the last minutes for us, and she just wanted somebody in the room with her to hold her hand."

"Hmm," Alan said thoughtfully. "She never said anything about that. All I know is that I was needed, that I met that need, and I wasn't even aware of it."

"Are you afraid of feeling unneeded back home?"

"I hadn't given it much thought."

"Well," Amy declared, folding her arms, "just in case the question ever does arise, let me fill you in: You'll be going to a world 700 years ahead of you, but it will be virtually identical to what you remember because when we came out of our 550-year dark age, we did what we could to restore the best of what we'd had; you won't be a man outside of time. Not only that, but back home, people stew in bitterness and anger. You may have been needed here, but now we need you at home. We need your optimism and your ability to trust the things that might pose a threat; you didn't fear your World when the rest of your crew did, and you didn't fear us even though you had feared possible intruders before us. That's what people need. Besides, think about how it will impact humanity to meet a member of the *Pegasus* crew when things are going well. You might end up changing the meaning of 'Pegatoid,'" she smiled.

"That's good to know. Here I am meeting my World's last need, and now, because of my World, I go to meet the needs of another world. Everything seems to have been well orchestrated, like someone had it all planned out, doesn't it?" There was a long silence between them, but it was peaceful. Then Alan shook his head and brushed a tear from beneath his eye. "It never occurred to me that she'd die. It still doesn't make sense that a planet can die like any other traveller. You want it to go on for ever, so you decide that it will. Reality has a rude way of shaking us up, doesn't it?"

"Yes," Amy agreed, "but the after effects are often pleasant." She rested her head on his shoulder, and he held her.

The *Aeneas* orbited for three days as measured by the planet's rotation, just short of 90 hours according to the ship's clocks. During that time the circle of green on the planet's surface shrank from sight and finally from the detection of the ship's instruments. And then, as if she'd summoned every tittle of her last bit of strength, the entire planet once again ignited in green. For an entire orbit about the planet, there was not the smallest spot that was not in some way alive. Lakes teemed with fish; tree lines stood out clear, the skies were filled with birds, even the snowy mountain peaks supported vast arrays of living creatures, and there was a sense of great joy emanating from her. Then, as quickly as all that life appeared, it vanished. Gone like the light from a tired bulb that dies the instant a current is sent through it, and the *Aeneas*'s crew suddenly found themselves orbiting a black, barren ball—no life, no mineral deposits, no sources of fuel—just rock, and the ship sailed in reverent silence.

Smithson, having caught the eye of Wells, nodded. Wells, understanding the command, nodded in response. He turned to his panels and consoles, spun some dials, flipped some switches, bleeped some buttons, and that which had once been a glorious, green jewel in the heavens, faded from sight.

THE END